LOST
LAKE

LOST LAKE

SARAH
ADDISON
ALLEN

St. Martin's Press
New York

LOST LAKE. Copyright © 2014 by Sarah Addison Allen. All rights reserved. Printed in the United States of America. For information, address St. Martin's Press, 175 Fifth Avenue, New York, NY 10010.

www.stmartins.com

Postcard design by Helene Saucedo

Library of Congress Cataloging-in-Publication Data

Allen, Sarah Addison.
  Lost Lake / Sarah Addison Allen.
      p. cm.
  ISBN 978-1-250-01980-6 (hardcover)
  ISBN 978-1-250-01981-3 (e-book)
  1. Widows—Fiction. 2. Mothers and daughters—Fiction. 3. Summer resorts—Fiction. 4. First loves—Fiction. 5. Georgia—Fiction. 6. Domestic fiction. I. Title.
  PS3601.L4356L67 2014
  813'.6—dc23

                                                              2013030138

St. Martin's Press books may be purchased for educational, business, or promotional use. For information on bulk purchases, please contact Macmillan Corporate and Premium Sales Department at 1-800-221-7945, extension 5442, or write specialmarkets@macmillan.com.

First Edition: February 2014

10 9 8 7 6 5 4 3 2 1

For the lost ones

Paris, France
Autumn 1962

*T*he wet night air bounced against the electric streetlamps, giving off tiny sparks like flint. Almost tripping again, Eby Pim laughed and looped her arm through George's. The uneven sidewalk was buckled by old roots of lime trees long since gone. George's large flat feet made him sure of his step, but she was in heels and her gait was unsteady, the tick-tick-pause-and-sway making her feel quite drunk or like she was dancing to music that was out of tune.

George leaned in and whispered that he loved her, that she looked beautiful tonight. Eby smiled and buried her face in his shoulder. They had such an easy sense of themselves here. And the longer they spent away, the longer they wanted to stay away. They wrote short notes on postcards to their families, and George regularly sent home crates of extravagant furniture and antiques, but to each other they never spoke of going back.

Paris was the perfect place to disappear, with its dark, sinewy streets. The first week of their honeymoon, they got lost here in the fog for hours, ending up in strange intersections and alleyways, tripping over feral city cats, who would sometimes lead them to warm cafés and restaurants if the cats were feeling generous and full of tasty sewer rats. More often than not, George and Eby wouldn't get back to their hotel until daylight, then they would sleep in each other's arms until the afternoon. George paid the owner's young son to bring coffee and pastries made with cheese and spinach to their room at dusk. They would enjoy the food in bed, curled in wrinkled sheets, watching the sun set and discussing what direction to head in when darkness fell and made everything a game of hide-and-seek again.

Tonight they walked aimlessly, trying to get lost. But they failed. For four months now they had been traversing these streets. Even in the dark, they were beginning to recognize some neighborhoods by a vague scent of char from the war. And there were various points along the river they knew just by the tone of the water. Over dinner, a meal that had consisted wholly of mushrooms simply because they felt like it, they still couldn't bring themselves to talk of home yet. Instead, George brought up the young couple they'd met the other day, the ones from Amsterdam.

"Amsterdam sounds nice, doesn't it?" he asked Eby.

She smiled, knowing where this was going. "Yes, very nice."

"Maybe we should visit."

"We might get lost," Eby said.

"That's the idea," George said, reaching across the table and taking her hand and kissing it.

And so Eby's family would have to wait a while longer, even though letters from home were becoming increasingly more forceful and concerned. *It's not seemly,* her mother wrote, *to stay on a honeymoon this long. You were only supposed to be gone two weeks! Your sister and I are getting tired of making excuses for you. Come home to Atlanta. Take your place.*

On their way back to the hotel, they approached a restaurant they knew by the smell of fried sausage thick in the air. The bell over the restaurant door rang, and yellow light from inside melted into the fog like butter. They stopped when they heard voices. A man and a woman walked out of the restaurant laughing, whispering. Their voices faded into the seductive night, where couples often pressed themselves into dark doorways, unseen. They could be so silent you didn't even know you were walking by two people making love until you passed though the red-lit steam of their desire. There had been times when Eby and George had been overcome. Their first night in Paris, Eby had felt reluctant when George had taken her by the hand and led her under a footbridge, pressing her against the damp stones, kissing her while lifting fists full of her skirt. But then she'd realized how free she was here, and she'd begun to think, *This is me. This is the real me. C'est moi,* she'd whispered over and over.

And this truly was her. This was her decision, her happiness. Marrying George wasn't something she did to help her family. Money flowed through her family's fingers like springwater. They couldn't seem to keep hold of it. And generations of Morris women had sincerely tried to fall in love with rich men. Eby's sister, Marilee, had been their one true hope. Rich men liked beautiful wives, and Marilee was sure to snatch one with her blond hair, which shone like rabbit fire, and her fierce green eyes. But the moment Marilee set eyes on the boy who filled their family's car tank with gas, she was gone. To everyone's surprise, it had been Eby, tall and strange with crooked features— whose one true accomplishment was that she was the first child to read every single book in the school library—who ended up marrying rich. Morris relatives in five surrounding states had attended the wedding, their hands out for money, like this was their triumph. What they didn't seem to understand was that Eby didn't do it for them. She'd been in love with George since they were children. But not a single soul believed her.

George was talking of Amsterdam again as they approached what the Parisians called the Bridge of the Untrue, rumored that young lovers weren't able to cross if their love wasn't real. It was the last bridge they crossed before their hotel came into view. Eby almost pulled back as they drew near. She didn't want to return to their hotel so soon. But that made her smile to herself. When did after midnight become soon? What she was really avoiding was the post that would inevitably be waiting for them: more concerned letters from her mother, more requests for loans from relatives, more invitations from her new peers to join clubs and parties when they returned, more snarly notes from her sister, Marilee, for whom all of this was supposed to happen, and because it hadn't, she seethed like water the second before it rolls to a boil. There might even be a phone message, which the owner of the hotel thought was rude. Eby's mother didn't understand. She was a typical southern American woman whose social lifeline was the telephone wire, to be used as often as possible.

It would take time in Amsterdam for their old lives to catch up to them again. They would have a few weeks to themselves there, at least. That was good.

Eby and George stepped onto the bridge. Ancient lemon-ball lamps appeared one at a time in the fog, growing gradually brighter as they approached, then dimming out as they passed, as if invisible hands were flicking them on and off.

It was in the darkness between the lights, at the center of the bridge, where it arched like a cat's back, that the fog seemed to shift and take form. A pale arm came into view, then a gray nightgown, the hem of which was flapping in the breeze from the churning water below. They were only feet away when Eby realized it was not a ghost but a young woman, a teenager, standing on the bridge railing, her bare toes curled around the cold narrow stone like claws.

Eby froze, pulling George to a stop.

"What's wrong?" George asked, then he followed Eby's gaze up. "My God."

For several moments they didn't move, for fear any disturbance in the air would push the swaying girl over the edge.

Eby had heard rumors of the brokenhearted committing suicide on the Bridge of the Untrue, but, like all rumors, they were myths until proven. Her heart suddenly felt heavy. There was so much happiness in the world. It was everywhere. It was free. Eby never understood why some people, people like her family, simply refused to take it.

The girl was beautiful, her skin like fresh cream and her long hair so dark it seemed to suck the color out of everything it surrounded. She was small. French women all seemed to be small-boned bird creatures, delicate in a way Eby could never be.

The girl didn't turn. Eby wondered if she even knew they were there. Eby slowly reached out a trembling hand. At her farthest stretch, she was still inches from the girl. Wasn't happiness like electricity? Weren't we all just conduits? If Eby could just touch her, maybe the girl could feel it.

"*S'il vous plaît,*" Eby said softly, wishing she knew something else to say. She'd studied French in finishing school in Atlanta with her sister, Marilee. Her mother had mortgaged the house in order for Marilee to attend Goddell's School for Fine Young Women, hoping it would later put her in the path of rich men. Eby was sent on the small chance that one of the male teachers would take a liking to her and her studious ways, and at least she'd marry a man who wore a tie. Madam Goddell would have been horrified by how little French Eby remembered, though it was more than Marilee had. Eby at least knew how to ask for the time and a glass of wine. Marilee had filched Madam's dictionary one day and learned all she wanted to learn when she figured out how to say "Kiss me, you fool."

"*S'il vous plaît,*" Eby said again. "Please."

The girl slowly turned her head, her eyes falling on Eby. They were dark eyes, like her hair, beautiful and soulful, and tears dripped from them, staining the front of her nightgown. She had to be freezing on this autumn night, with the scent of wood smoke settling low in the air. The girl's mouth moved, forming words, but no sound came out. She impatiently waved at Eby and George to move on.

"*S'il vous plaît,*" Eby said.

"*Joie de vivre!*" George suddenly said loudly, the only French he knew, which he'd learned in a bar their first night here. It was just like him to say that at a time like this. He was a hearty, gregarious man. He was rich, but newly rich, and so very sincere about it. He lacked the natural languidity that came with old money, the kind that made others feel like they were only walking through the dreams of the wealthy, barely there at all. People couldn't help but like George. His laugh was like a barrel of whiskey. His cheeks were almost as red as his hair. Just looking at him, you could see that his capacity to love was as wide as the world. He wasn't going to stand a chance against Eby's family when the couple returned.

The girl's eyes flicked to George, nimbly assessing him, and she smiled, just slightly. Her eyes then went to Eby's outstretched hand, to the wedding ring there.

She nodded at them, an unspoken acknowledgment, and Eby felt a rush of relief.

But then the girl calmly turned back to the water.

And jumped.

PART 1

1

Atlanta, Georgia
Present day

*W*ake up, Kate!"

And, exactly one year to the day that she fell asleep, Kate finally did.

She opened her eyes slowly and saw that a pale lavender moth had come to a rest on the back of her hand. She watched it from her pillow, wondering if it was real. It reminded her of her husband Matt's favorite T-shirt, which she'd hidden in a bag of sewing, unable to throw it away. It had a large faded moth on the front, the logo of a cover band out of Athens called the Mothballs.

That T-shirt, that moth, always brought back a strange memory of when she was a child. She used to draw tattoos of butterflies on her arms with Magic Markers. She would give them names, talk to them, carefully fill in their colors when they started to fade. When the time came that they wanted to be set free, she would blow on them and they would come to life, peeling away from her skin and flying away.

She'd always been a little different as a child, that strange girl who kept her imaginary friends well past the age of most children, the child people called a *free spirit* in a way meant to console her parents, as if, like a lisp, she would hopefully outgrow it. Her parents hadn't minded, though. As long as they'd had each other, they'd let Kate be as free as she wanted.

Kate thought about blowing on the lavender moth, to see what would happen, but before she could, her mother-in-law walked into her bedroom with a cup of coffee and a brisk, "Good morning!" When Kate looked again, the moth was gone. She sat up as Cricket threw open the curtains and said, "It's the big day. The movers are coming."

Kate felt vaguely panicked, like she was shaking off a nightmare she couldn't fully remember. "Movers?"

Cricket snapped her fingers in front of Kate's face as she handed Kate the cup of coffee. "Yes, movers. You're moving into my house today. Did you take something to help you sleep last night?"

She hadn't dreamed this. It was real. She looked to the left side of the mattress. Matt wasn't there. She could have sworn she'd heard his voice, heard *someone's* voice. "No. I don't take anything. You know that."

"You're cranky this morning," Cricket said. "It's a good thing I got here early. I got Devin up and dressed and fixed her breakfast."

"Devin's up? This is the first day of summer vacation," Kate said. "She's never up this early on vacation."

"I think it's best to keep her on a schedule. It makes going back to school in the fall so much easier, don't you think? She's in the attic. You'll keep an eye on her, won't you?"

Kate could feel a strange heat along the back of her neck, something she hadn't felt in a while. It was almost exotic, like tasting turmeric or saffron after a year of eating pudding. There was a bite to it.

She was *annoyed*.

She was finally awake and annoyed. Of course she would keep an eye on Devin. For the past year she'd made Devin dinner and attended school plays and chaperoned field trips and taken her to the eye doctor. She'd been sleepwalking, but still, she'd done it. Cricket had no reason to distrust Kate's ability to mother her own child.

Except for that one time.

There would always be that one time.

"It's such a mess up there," Cricket said, clicking around the bedroom in her Louboutin shoes, her smart black suit, and big immovable southern hair. She checked the closet for leftover clothes, to make sure Kate had packed everything. "I thought I told you to go through the things in the attic and put what you wanted in the living room. Otherwise, it's just going to be left behind for the new owners to deal with. It's probably for the best not to let Devin take all those old clothes with her. We'll never get her out of them in the fall. I found her school uniform in the trash can this morning!"

Kate put the cup of coffee on the floor beside the bed. Every day for a year Cricket had come by to take Devin to her new school, and she always made coffee while she was here, horrible, tar-black coffee that Kate hated. Kate didn't want to drink it anymore. It was such a small thing, to put the cup aside and not drink it, but as she watched Cricket's eyes take in the movement, Kate felt a small thrill from this first real act of rebellion since she'd gone to sleep a year ago. "I've always told her she could wear whatever she wanted in the summer."

"We both know that's not a good idea, especially now that she's moving into my neighborhood."

"Matt agreed with me," Kate said, his name unfamiliar on her tongue now, and it felt like saying something unspeakable, a curse.

Cricket turned away at the mention of her son's name. She didn't like to talk of him. Ever. She was holding him inside, captive within her rib cage, not willing to share her grief with anyone else. Not even with Kate, who wanted so badly to find pieces of affection for Matt in his mother, to be consoled in some way. "You've let her get away with too much over the years. You're getting up now, aren't you? Because the movers will be here at noon. I can probably leave work around three. You know I'd be here to help if it weren't for that big closing today. I'll see you at my house later this afternoon. Everything should go smoothly. I left a list. You're getting up now, aren't you?" she asked again.

Kate slowly stood, as if testing her balance. It felt strange. Her muscles felt weak.

Cricket turned in the doorway and stared at Kate. Kate had no idea what she was thinking. She never did. She was as unreadable as a lost language. "Are you excited about coming to work in my office? We'll get your hair trimmed tomorrow. Would you like that?"

Kate put her hand to her hair and felt a year's worth of choppy growth framing her face.

It had been exactly one year since Kate had picked up those scissors in the bathroom, after locking herself in after Matt's funeral. She'd stared at them, the stainless steel winking in the noon light, and she'd thought things she'd never known she was capable of thinking—dark, unforgivable things. But when she'd lifted the scissors, she instead took her grief and frustration out on her long brown hair. With every snip of the scissors, clumps of her hair had fallen, and she'd watched them turn into tiny birds that cawed and flew around her, swarming in a heavy circle.

Matt had loved her hair, and she'd worn it long just for him. Kate had lived for the times when, as she was doing the books at the shop, Matt would casually walk by and slide the pencil holding up her hair, just to watch it cascade down her back. When they'd made love, he'd liked her on top, with her hair falling down around him, sticking to his skin.

Hours later, Cricket had found her on the bathroom floor. Cricket had gone to her knees in surprise, and Kate had cried, holding on to Cricket so tightly she was sure she'd left bruises. Cricket had helped Kate clean up the places where she'd nicked her scalp, and trimmed what she could so Kate wouldn't scare Devin. Cricket had made light of it for Devin, telling her that Kate just needed a hairstyle that was easier to take care of.

That had been the last day she'd been awake.

Until now.

Cricket was waiting for her to answer.

"Yes," Kate said. "Thank you, Cricket. For everything."

"I'll see you soon," she said, then turned to go. "I have big plans to tell you about."

Kate listened to the sound of Cricket's heels as she walked down the hallway.

The opening and closing of the front door.

The sound of Cricket's car pulling out of the driveway.

Kate then hurried out of her room, trying to blink away the sleep and disorientation. *My God,* she thought, *this is really happening.* She went to the closet down the hall, where the folding stairs had already been pulled from the ceiling.

She climbed the ladder and emerged into the light from the single window in the attic. Dust motes floated around her like ash. Her eight-year-old daughter was humming as she plowed through the detritus of a large black trunk whose hinges were red with rust and the faded word MARILEE was stamped in gold on the lid.

Devin had grown in the year Kate had been asleep, grown in ways Kate was just now seeing. Her face was fuller, her legs were longer. Kate wanted to run to her and hold her, but Devin would think she was crazy. Devin had seen Kate just last night, when Kate had tucked her into bed. It hadn't been a year for her. Devin didn't know Kate had been asleep all this time.

So Kate just stood there and drank in the sight of her. Devin was the most gorgeous, unique creature Kate had ever known. She'd come out of the womb an individual, refusing to be defined by anyone. She didn't even look like anyone on either side of their families. Matt's family was so proud of their dark hair, a blue-black that had been the envy of generations, the way it caught the sun like a spiderweb. From Kate's own side of the family, there was a gene that made their eyes so green that they could trick people into thinking that even the most unattractive Morris woman was pretty. And yet here was Devin, with fine cotton-yellow hair and light blue eyes, the left of which was a lazy eye. She'd had to wear an eye patch when she was three. And she'd loved it. She loved her knotted yellow hair. She loved wearing stripes with polka dots, and tutus, and pink and green socks with orange patent-leather shoes. Devin could care less what other people thought about her.

And that drove Cricket crazy.

How had Kate let this happen? How had she gotten to the point where she was slowly turning over control to the one person who wanted to change her daughter from the glorious thing she was? The very thing Kate used to be, that she used to be so *proud* of being? Kate swallowed before she felt she had the voice to say, "Hey, kiddo. What are you doing?"

Devin looked over her shoulder with a smile. "Mom! Look. This one is my favorite," Devin said, pulling out a faded pink dress with a red plaid sash. The crinoline petticoat underneath was so old and stiff it made snapping sounds, like beads or fire embers. She dropped the dress over her head, over her clothes. It brushed the floor. "When I'm old enough for it to fit me, I'm going to wear it with purple shoes," she said.

"A bold choice," Kate said as Devin dove back into the trunk. The attic in Kate's mother's house had always fascinated Devin with its promise of hidden treasures. When Kate's mother had been alive, she had let Devin eat Baby Ruth candy bars and drink grape soda and play in this old trunk full of dresses that generations of Morris women had worn to try entice rich men to marry them. Most of the clothes had belonged to Kate's grandmother Marilee, a renowned beauty who, like all the rest, had fallen in love with a poor man instead.

"Who is Eby Pim?" Devin suddenly asked.

"Eby?" Kate walked over Devin, measuring her steps, trying not to seem too eager. Devin had climbed inside the large trunk. The only part of her visible was the vintage green cap she was now wearing. It had a long dramatic feather pinned to it, and as she moved her head, the feather wrote invisible letters in the air. Kate sat on the floor beside the trunk, as close as she could. "Eby was Grandmother Marilee's sister. My great-aunt. Your great-great-aunt. I only met her once, but I thought she was wonderful. Different. A little scandalous."

"What did she do?"

"Eby married a man with money, and her family expected her to share all that money with them," Kate said. "But when they came back from their honeymoon, Eby and her husband suddenly decided to give all their money away. They sold their home in Atlanta and bought some swamp property down south. No one saw them for years and years. I was twelve the only time I met her. My mom and dad and I went to visit Eby after her husband died. There was a magical lake there where they'd made a living renting out cabins. I think that was probably the last best summer I ever had."

"Can we go there?"

Her voice was small as it came from the trunk. It made Kate close her eyes with emotion. "I don't know if it's still there. It was a long time ago. What made you ask about her?" Kate asked. "Is there something of hers in there?"

Devin's hand appeared from the trunk, holding an old postcard. "Just this postcard. It's addressed to you."

Kate took it. On one side were the vintage bubble words

LOST LAKE, each letter large enough for a lake image to fit inside it.

Kate turned the card over. It was postmarked fifteen years ago, the last time Kate had seen Eby.

Kate, I know you enjoyed yourself here and didn't want to leave. You're welcome to come back anytime you'd like. I just wanted you to know. Love, Eby Pim

It was the first time Kate had ever seen this. Her mother had never given it to her. She knew her mother and Eby had had a falling out that summer, but Kate never knew Eby had tried to contact her.

Devin got out of the trunk and started putting the dresses back in it. Some were so old that light shone through them, like ghost clothes. "Can we take this trunk when we move in with Grandma Cricket?" Devin asked, taking off the hat and dress she was wearing and putting them inside, then slowly closing and latching the lid.

Kate could tell that Cricket had already told Devin no. And that should have been that. Her mother-in-law was going to a great deal of trouble and expense to move Kate and Devin into her home in Buckhead. A year ago, after Matt had been hit and killed while cycling home from work, Cricket had swooped in and had suddenly become a part of their lives in a way she'd never been when Matt was alive. And, in her sleep, Kate had made it so easy for her. She was no match for Cricket's money, even now, with the sale of this house and Matt's bike shop in Kate's bank account—sales overseen by Cricket, who had so smoothly negotiated the deals, it was like she'd put the buyers under a spell. In the back of Kate's mind rested a very real and persistent fear that Cricket could take Devin, if she really wanted to. She would always have that incident with the scissors as leverage. Kate should consider herself lucky that Cricket was taking her along with Devin, that Cricket was giving her a job answering phones in her real estate office. She should be grateful Cricket was giving them the entire third floor of her house, where Cricket could walk in and check on them anytime she liked, instead of coming all the way here every day to do it.

"Of course we can take the trunk," Kate said, tucking the postcard into the chest pocket of her wrinkled nightshirt. "We can take anything you want. Help me get it downstairs."

It wasn't heavy. But when it slid down the folding stairs, it nicked the floor a little.

They pulled the trunk into the living room, which was piled with boxes, suitcases, and some of their better furniture.

Kate saw Cricket's list taped to the upright box with Kate's clothes hung inside. Kate didn't even glance at the note as they scooted the trunk to the middle of the room. Even if she'd still been asleep, she could have done this without consulting Cricket's list. It was moving, not rocket science.

She didn't know that it read:

1. The movers will be here at noon. Do not ride with them. Do not let Devin ride with them.

2. Wait exactly thirty minutes. Then drive to my house. Don't wear anything fancy or put on makeup. It might help to look a little sad. I want Devin to wear exactly what she has on.

3. This is very important. There will be a film crew waiting at
   my house. They want to record your first day as you move
   in. Just act natural. They didn't want me to tell you so it
   would look authentic, but I was afraid you might go off and
   do something and not stick to the schedule if you didn't
   know. This is very important! I'll explain everything when
   I get there.

Cricket Pheris micro-managed everything. As locally famous as she was, not many people knew that about her. She'd
built her career on her supposed ability to go with the flow, to
weather any storm. The truth was, Cricket didn't weather
anything. She *controlled* storms. And it had given her a reputation as a quiet kingmaker. She was the perfect combination of
good taste and political ambition, but whenever she was approached to run for office, she always graciously demurred,
happy behind the scenes. She'd been known to increase the
numbers for any given candidate just by putting his or her
campaign poster on the same lawn as her real estate sign. And
all because, fifteen years ago, after Cricket's husband died,
she'd single-handedly turned her real estate agency into the
biggest in the state with a series of extremely successful commercials that had even garnered national attention. The commercials had chronicled the selling of the house where Cricket
and her husband and her son, Matt, had all once lived together, and the search for a new house for just Cricket and
Matt. *We know about moving on.* That had been the phrase that
had ended each commercial. Cricket had come across as lik-
able and competent, but also sensitive and grieving. But it had
been Matt who'd stolen the show. He'd been a beautiful child

with a remarkable face that had been made for television—peachy skin and big sad brown eyes. There had been something about him that had made everyone who'd watched him root for him. Everyone had wanted him to find his home.

Matt had later told Kate that he had hated those commercials. Cricket had scripted them entirely. They had made them look close, but Cricket had worked fifteen-hour days, and Matt had essentially grown up without her.

When Kate had first met Matt, they'd both been freshman at Emory. She'd been close to flunking out. She hadn't made friends easily, and she'd spent most of her class time staring out windows, imagining herself in some far-off place. She'd gotten so good at it that she could actually turn soft to the touch and wispy like a cloud as she sat there, and all it would have taken to send her away was one good gust of air.

She hadn't known it at the time, but Matt had watched her daydream in class. It had been the first thing he'd noticed about her, the first thing that had attracted him to her. She'd wanted to disappear almost as much as he had. She'd known who he was, of course. But she'd never dreamed she would ever catch his attention. She'd grown up watching those commercials. She, like everyone else in the greater Atlanta area, had wanted this sweet, beautiful kid to find where he belonged.

Kate and Matt had been only nineteen when Kate had gotten pregnant, and Cricket had been so upset with her son for dropping out of college and marrying Kate, whom she believed came from a family of notorious gold diggers, that she'd refused to speak to him and withdrew all of her financial support. Cricket had had big plans for Matt. If she always backed a winner, imagine what she could have done if her own son had gotten into politics. That *face*. He had that perfect face.

But Matt had had no interest in running for public office. He'd been shy and uncomfortable around people. After they married, Kate and Matt had moved in with Kate's mother, into this house, because Kate's mother had been convinced that Cricket would forgive Matt in time, and then all that money would be Matt and Kate's to share with her. Cricket had been wrong about a lot of things, but Kate's mother's obsession with money had not been one of them.

Kate's mother had died of a sudden stroke two years later, never having seen her dreams of wealth for her daughter realized. That was when Cricket started making halfhearted attempts at reconciliation, but it was too late. Matt had cut ties with her and didn't want them mended.

Kate and Matt had spent seven years here together in this small house, raising Devin, starting a bicycle shop called Pheris Wheels with the small trust from his father. This was the life Matt had chosen, the one that had brought him as close to content as he'd ever been, doing what he'd wanted in an anonymous existence that he considered bohemian. Plain old middle class to the rest of the world. But as Kate looked around at their belongings, there was nothing of Matt's here. The furniture had all been her mother's. He'd moved into her world, part and parcel, but added nothing of himself.

Kate sat on the trunk, and Devin pulled herself up and sat close to her.

"It's going to be all right," Kate said. "You know that, don't you?"

Devin nodded as she took off her black glasses, the ones

Cricket liked, and cleaned them on the J.Crew T-shirt Cricket had picked out for her to wear.

"I'll talk to Cricket about your clothes. Your dad and I always said you could wear what you wanted on summer vacation. Cricket is just going to have to deal with it."

"What about school?" Devin asked. This was a familiar argument. Devin hated her school uniform. The idea of being in uniform at all offended her. But in the year she'd been asleep, Kate had agreed to let Cricket enroll Devin in the same private school Matt had attended.

"The school requires a uniform, you know that."

"Can't I go back to my old school?"

Kate hesitated. "I'll talk to Cricket. But it's a good school. And your dad went there." Kate put her arm around Devin, and the movement drew her attention to the postcard in her chest pocket.

Kate took out the postcard, and she and Devin both stared at it as if new words might form on it, telling their fortune. Kate's mother had kept this from her for reasons Kate might never know. When she looked at the card, she experienced that same small sensation of rebellion she'd felt when she'd put aside Cricket's coffee earlier. Her mother hadn't wanted her to be in touch with Eby. Her mother hadn't wanted her to go back to Lost Lake.

That in itself was reason enough to go.

Escape.

The word came to her mind before she could stop it.

"You know," Kate said, "Lost Lake is only three or four hours away. At least, it was."

Devin looked up at her slowly, suspiciously, like there was trickery afoot. It almost made Kate laugh.

"It might be shut down. Eby might not be there. But we could go see. Just you and me." Kate nudged her. "What do you say? We don't have to be here when all this stuff is moved."

"Like a vacation?"

"I don't know what it will be," Kate said honestly. "If there's nothing there, well, we'll just turn around and come back to our new place. But if it's still there, maybe we can stay for the night. Maybe two. We won't know until we get there."

"Do we have to ask Grandma Cricket?"

"No. This is between you and me. Go change out of those clothes and into what you want to wear. We'll throw some things into the car and head out."

Devin tore off down the hall, but then stopped and ran back and hugged Kate.

"I've missed you," she said, then ran away again, leaving Kate standing there, shocked.

Kate didn't think anyone knew.

But Devin did.

She knew Kate had been asleep all this time.

2

Lost Lake
Suley, Georgia
One day earlier

*E*very year since her husband George died, the fat man with tight skin and fake hair showed up on the first day of summer and offered to buy Lost Lake from Eby. He would hoist himself from behind the wheel of his Mercedes, something that seemed to take more and more effort with the passage of time, then he would stare at the lake, his greedy thoughts mentally cutting down trees and building luxurious lakefront houses. Eby would watch as his fingers twitched and his knees shook, and there were times when she could actually feel the earth start to tremble, as if the sheer power of his will was going to develop the property right in front of her eyes.

When he was through staring, Eby always invited him inside and offered him iced mint tea and butter cookies, the ones Lisette made that looked like big shirt buttons. Something special to ease his disappointment, because Eby always said no. He wasn't used to people saying no, and Eby felt sorry for him, the way she'd always felt sorry for those who had everything and it still wasn't enough.

This year, though, Eby didn't offer him any refreshments.

When he drove away later that morning, Eby put her hand to her chest, where there was a sensation of tiny wings fluttering just under her skin. She finally did it. She finally agreed to sell the property to him. She'd never felt quite this way before. She was usually so sure of things. Now she felt . . . anxious. When his car disappeared through the trees, her eyes went to the picture-postcard swamp of a lake in front of her, flanked by cypress trees and loblolly pines, the area so quiet and so removed she could hear the water softly knocking against the aging dock.

This old cabin resort she and her husband George had bought after their honeymoon was slowly going downhill. Money was tight, and there was always a cabin in need of repair. Most distressingly, for the first time since buying the place, there hadn't been a single guest over the winter. They'd always had reservations in the winter. Being so close to the Florida border, snowbirds used to flock here from the north, woolen caps still on their heads, road salt still stuck to their tires. But the regular guests had aged along with everything else. Many of them were gone now. Some couldn't drive anymore. Some had simply grown fond of their comfortable chairs by warm windows and didn't want to leave home.

This was the right decision. It had to be.

A small beautiful woman in her sixties came to stand beside Eby in the doorway of the main house—a two-story clapboard structure with a roof that leaked, hallways that led nowhere, and stairways that narrowed into tight squeezes as you reached the top, like in a child's playhouse. The old house and the rental cabins had come with the lake, and one of the main reasons Eby and George had bought the place was because there had been so much to do. It had been a fitting metaphor at the time—repairing, rebuilding, reinventing.

Eby could feel Lisette's anger like a burst of heat. The force of it made the fine silver hair around Eby's face move, as if by wind. Eby sighed. Lisette had to have known this was going to happen sooner or later, but Eby could tell she was going to be difficult about it anyway.

Lisette opened the small notebook she had on a length of butcher's twine around her neck. She wrote something, then showed it to Eby: *You should have consulted me about this! How long have you been planning to sell? Why did you not confide in me?*

"You can't be that surprised, Lisette. Not after the winter we had. And I've been thinking of traveling again. You know that," Eby said. She had been dreaming of Europe lately, of Paris and its dark streets. In her dreams, she had lost George but was following a large orange one-eyed cat to him. He was waiting around the next corner for her. Always just around the next corner. "How about we go back to Paris? Wouldn't that be nice?" Eby asked, trying to make her decision sound like an adventure. "Your mother is almost ninety. You should see her again. Mend that fence."

Lisette was, and always had been, as combustible as an unlit match. Eby usually knew how to work around her tirades, to soothe her before she had time to get riled up. But mentioning Lisette's mother, Eby realized belatedly, had been a bad idea.

I do not want to travel. And I do NOT want to go back to Paris. Lisette underlined the word *NOT* twice. *I want to stay. Does that not matter?*

"Of course it matters," Eby said calmly. She felt that flutter under her skin again and wanted to touch it, but she didn't dare, not in front of Lisette. "Maybe the new development will have a club house with a restaurant. Maybe you can be in charge of the kitchen there. Or maybe you can buy a house on the lake, when they're built."

Lisette stared at her for a few long moments before writing, *You will not be here?*

"No."

But you do not want to leave the lake any more than I do! This is our home!

Eby stepped back and closed the front door before any more cold, air-conditioned air could escape. The electric bill was high enough already. The door frame was swollen, and she had to push the door shut with her shoulder. "Of course I don't want to leave. But I can't just watch this place disappear, like almost everyone who used to come here has disappeared. It's falling apart, and I can't save it. It's best to leave now, before we lose everything and we're forced out. It's best to go when there's a *choice*."

Your choice. Not mine, Lisette wrote. After she showed Eby, she angrily ripped the notes out of the pad and put the small pieces of paper in her pocket. Later she would undoubtedly burn them on the stove or tear them up and toss them into the lake. Written words were considered dangerous things by Lisette.

Lisette was born without the ability to speak, but she'd

been brazen with written words as a child, substituting a sharp tongue for a poison pen. She blamed herself for the suicide of a paramour when she was just sixteen, after she had slipped him a note during a romantic dinner, telling him she was too good for him and would never love him. The next day she'd learned he'd hung himself in his parents' apartment. Shocked by her own power, which hitherto had only been to hurt feelings, not end lives, Lisette's guilt had sent her to the Bridge of the Untrue in Paris that fateful night fifty years ago, where she had intended to kill herself. She'd thought it was the only way to snuff out this monstrous power she had. For stubborn souls like Lisette, death was easier than the courage it took to actually change your life.

When Eby had seen Lisette jump from the bridge, some great force had pushed Eby into action. She could remember racing to the end of the bridge and sliding down the bank into the cold water, yelling for Lisette to say something, anything that would let Eby know where she was in the fog. The current had swept them up in the darkness, and there had been a sickening sensation of floating in gelatin as Eby scrambled for some purchase, her hand miraculously finding Lisette's long hair, like a tangle of cold seaweed. She'd grabbed it and pulled her head above water, where Lisette had sputtered and clawed at Eby, obviously not knowing what was happening. Eby had held her and wouldn't let her go, but they had both been helpless to the current. Eby remembered thinking all they had to do was hold on to each other. Everything would be okay if they just held on to each other.

Sure enough, out of nowhere, two large arms had grabbed them and pulled, pulled so hard there was actually a sucking sound. The water hadn't wanted to let them go and had resisted. But George had won. He'd pulled them to the bank and stood over them, dripping, incredulous.

People on the street that night in Paris had heard the commotion and had come to their aid, leading George, Eby, and Lisette to the restaurant they had passed earlier, where they'd been given threadbare blankets and glasses of port. They had known Lisette there—she was the owner's daughter—and this kind of behavior apparently had not been unusual. In fact, no one had seemed particularly concerned. Some customers hadn't even looked up from their late meals.

Eby had been too exhausted to argue with George when he'd insisted they go back to their hotel, promising they would check in on the girl the next day. It turned out, there had been no need. Lisette had followed them and slept on the hotel's front steps that night. She'd followed them everywhere after that, as quiet and thin as a shadow, getting a room at their hotel, even later following them to Amsterdam, then finally back to America.

Lisette had turned out to be the best friend Eby had ever had, that thing she'd never known she'd needed, when all she thought she'd needed was George. They had saved each other so many times over the years now that they'd eventually lost count.

Eby turned. "I need to cancel the summer reservations. All three of them."

Lisette followed Eby to the check-in desk in the foyer, furiously scribbling something on her notepad as she walked. Eby sat behind the desk, and Lisette tore out the note and slapped it on the desk surface. Eby picked it up and read it.

I am not going. I will chain myself to a tree. They will not make me leave. You go. Do what you want. Leave me here to get flattened by a bulldozer. Leave me here to die.

Eby pushed the note back to Lisette. "Flattened by a bull-dozer? How unromantic. You'll have to come up with something better than that. You jumped off a bridge in the middle of Paris. It's going to be hard to top that one."

Lisette snatched the note and stomped to the kitchen.

"Everything is going to be okay," Eby called to her. She heard the smack of Lisette's palm against the swinging door. "I promise."

Eby worried about Lisette. Too much, probably. But Lisette had no one else to worry about her. The one true difference between them was that Eby had her memory of George, a memory that would always remind her that she was worthy of love. But Lisette only had the memory of a sixteen-year-old boy who committed suicide because of her. Lisette had pushed everyone in her life away except Eby. She had no one else real in her life, past or present, who had steadfastly loved her no matter what, and that was why the thought of losing this place scared her so. The memory of everyone who had ever loved Lisette was here.

That's when it suddenly occurred to Eby.

Jack.

Aha.

Eby picked up the phone with hope.

She knew what she was doing. She was focusing on Lisette instead of dwelling on this tremendous, life-altering decision she'd just made. But she was okay with that. She was good at being needed. It had been years since she'd felt really useful.

And if she just kept busy enough, maybe she could ignore the strange, anxious fluttering under her skin and the tingling in her fingers from where she'd shaken hands with the man.

Then all this would all be over before she knew it.

⚜

The next day, Eby thought she'd be productive and begin the process of going through the things that needed to be packed. She had great plans for finding her clipboard and cataloging everything. Maybe even taking photos. But she quickly became overwhelmed when she realized just how much stuff there was. Forget cataloging it. Where was she going to *put* it? She started by looking up nearby storage units in the town of Suley's thin phone book. But then she wondered who was going to move all these things, things she couldn't possibly part with, many of them bought on her honeymoon. So she switched gears and looked up movers. Then she wondered, if she was hiring movers, why didn't she just buy a house to move into and avoid having to move everything twice? But the only place nearby that was big enough to store everything she had—a house and thirteen cabins' worth of memories— was the old Rue-McRae Homestead in town, which had been turned into a visitor center years ago. It detailed the history of the town's settlers for anyone who was interested, of a rough-and-tumble group of people from the swamp, mostly displaced from Okefenokee over the past several hundred years. The Rue-McRae Homestead aside, it would take several normal-size houses to put all this furniture in. And she couldn't afford to buy several houses. Selling the lake acreage would pay off her first and second mortgages. But then, buying even a single house would leave her with no money to travel.

That made her think of Lisette, who had been banging around the kitchen for the past twenty-four hours. Currently, the scent of rising dough and hot berries was being sucked through the old air-conditioning unit and spread throughout the main house. This was Lisette's rebellion. She was cooking for guests who weren't coming. It was as if nothing bad could happen if she just kept going. Like a wheel in motion, she seemed to think no one could stop her, or make her leave, once she started.

Eby gave up trying to plan her departure for now and sat behind the front desk with a crossword puzzle. She couldn't do this alone. Lisette was going to have to help her. Eby would just wait for this hissy fit to pass.

The air conditioner turned off. The house ticked and settled. Eby sighed and set the crossword aside, then scooted her chair to the very edge of the desk, where she could lean back and see a corner of the window in the sitting room. She often did this, to watch a quiet corner of the lake. There were even scratch marks on the floor from years of pulling the chair to her daydream spot.

She was going to miss her daydream spot.

Giving up the money George had inherited fifty years ago had been the best thing she and George had ever done. But, as young and idealistic as they'd been, Eby still wished they'd squirreled a little money away, for times like this.

Times like this? She shook her head. She'd never in her wildest dreams imaged herself at seventy-six, forced to sell Lost Lake.

Seventy-six.

Good Lord, how did that happen? Yesterday, she was twenty-four making love under a bridge in Paris.

Suddenly, the front door flew open and two older women walked in in a gust of rose lotion and liniment oil. Eby gave a start and the front legs of her chair dropped to the floor.

"See? It's still here," said the woman with bright red hair. Makeup was caked into the fine wrinkles around her eyes, and she was wearing a cherry-print dress and four-inch red heels. She was helping a tiny old woman through the door. "She said she was *selling* it, not that it *was gone*. Can we go now?"

"No," the elderly woman said.

The redheaded woman closed the door behind them and stopped to wave her hand in front of her face, as if to cool off. "Okay, what's your plan?"

"I haven't figured that out yet," the old woman said. "All I know is that we didn't know last summer was going to be our *last summer,* so we didn't make it anything special. We've got to make this ending special."

Eby stood. "Selma, Bulahdeen—you came!" Eby had called them just yesterday to cancel their reservations. They were two of the three summer faithfuls she had left, the old-timers who came back year after year. Eby watched the door, waiting for Jack, the third, to come in. But he didn't.

"Bulahdeen called me after you canceled our reservations. She demanded I pick her up and drive her here," Selma said.

"I couldn't drive myself," Bulahdeen told Eby. "They took away my license last year."

"I'm sorry to hear that," Eby said. In her eighties, Bulahdeen Ward was the oldest of all Eby's guests. She was stooping like a fiddlehead fern now, curling into herself, making her appear that she was charging at life headfirst. She and her husband, Charlie, both former professors, used to come together to the lake until a few years ago. Charlie developed Alzheimer's and was now in a nursing home. Since then, Bulahdeen had been coming alone. She was a quiet force of nature, the peculiar southern lilt to her voice as old as low-country sand. Selma, tall and painted and standoffish, was Bulahdeen's every opposite. They were an odd pair. Bulahdeen had somehow, somewhere along the way, decided that Selma was one of her best friends. Selma vehemently disagreed. Bulahdeen didn't care.

"And *you* don't have to make such a big deal of it," Bulahdeen turned to Selma and said, pointing a bone-knobby finger at her. "It was on your way."

"I live in Meridian. *Mississippi*. You live in Spartanburg. *South Carolina*. That is not on my way."

"Don't give me that. You had nothing better to do."

"Speak for yourself, old woman. I've got another husband to catch." Selma was sixty-five but told everyone she was fifty, and she claimed to be an expert on men, though having seven husbands might mean to some that she was an expert on getting it wrong. Selma had a reputation for flirting with all the men who stayed here in the summers, in an offhand way, second nature, like the way a bird naturally flaps its wings when it falls. Thirty years ago, she'd visited Lost Lake with her third husband. She soon divorced him, like all the others, but then she kept coming back. No one understood why. She never seemed to enjoy herself.

"We stopped by town for some supplies before we came here," Bulahdeen said as she walked to the check-in desk.

"*Supplies* meaning Bulahdeen bought six bottles of wine," Selma said.

Bulahdeen hoisted her purse onto the desk, then leaned against it with a deep breath. "When I mentioned to some folks about you selling this place, they seemed surprised."

"Oh," Eby said. "Well, that's because I haven't told anyone yet."

Bulahdeen looked at her curiously. Her eyes were as cloudy as crystal balls. "Is it a secret?"

"Not anymore," Selma said dryly, still standing at the door, ready to make an escape.

"No, it's not a secret," Eby said. "It just happened so fast. And, really, there's no one in town I think would care. About the lake, I mean. Not anymore. The water park is now the biggest part of the town's income. Lost Lake isn't doing anyone any good anymore. Developing it will probably benefit Suley."

"What are you going to do?" Bulahdeen asked.

"Inventory. Then figure out where to move and where to put all this stuff. Then travel, maybe. George and I always wanted to go back to Europe."

Bulahdeen snorted. "I can guess Lisette's reaction to that."

"She doesn't want to leave." Eby's eyes shifted to the front door again, as if waiting for someone else to come through.

"Jack's not with us, if that's who you're looking for," Bulahdeen said.

"Now *he* I would have picked up," Selma said.

Eby turned to the wall of key hooks behind her. She hadn't

realized until that moment how much she'd been counting on Jack coming. She'd dropped hints. But Jack, for all his wonderful qualities, did not always grasp subtleties. Eby should have been clearer. *This was his last chance.* She grabbed two keys with heavy brass fobs attached. "Here are the keys to your regular cabins. I'll grab some linens and bring them to you. I haven't cleaned the cabins. Just giving you fair warning."

Selma walked over and took her key from Eby. "Yes, our last summer here is certainly going to be special."

Bulahdeen took her cabin key and picked up her purse. "Selma, has anyone ever told you that you complain too much?"

"No."

"Liar."

"So this is how I'm going to spend my summer?" Selma said, opening the front door and waiting for Bulahdeen. "Being insulted by the likes of you?"

"By the likes of me? Look who thinks she's so high and mighty."

"Watch out, old woman, or I'm going to leave you here."

"No, you're not." Bulahdeen reached into her purse and brought out a set of keys and shook them. "I've got your car keys."

"What are you doing with those?"

Bulahdeen cackled as she walked out the door.

"Bulahdeen, if you try to drive my car, I'll have you arrested!"

Eby walked to the kitchen with a smile. She was glad they came.

When she entered the kitchen, which she had to pass

through to get to the laundry room, Lisette was standing in front of an empty chair beside the refrigerator, her hands on her hips. She often did that—stare at that chair.

"Well, you'll be glad to know that Selma and Bulahdeen came anyway. All this food won't go to waste." Eby gestured to the colorful array of enamel-covered cast-iron pots on the stove in the remarkable kitchen, Lisette's domain. The appliances were cobalt blue, and the walls were stainless steel. Bright white lights shone overhead.

Lisette's father had passed away a few years after Lisette left Paris. He'd obviously forgotten to change his will, or he thought Lisette would finally come back. Or maybe he didn't even think of her at all, which was a strong possibility, given what Lisette had told Eby of him. Either way, Lisette had inherited half of her father's modest fortune. Her mother, the other half. Lisette's money explained the lovely kitchen in the otherwise shabby main house, and how Eby never had to worry about the cost of food. Lisette took care of all of that. To be happy, all she needed was a roof over her head and someone to cook for, which George and Eby had always given her.

Lisette raised her brows and gave her an *I told you so* look.

"You did not tell me so. They're just here to say good-bye." Eby hesitated. "Lisette, I'm going to need your help with inventory. I'm going to need your help with this move."

The fine bones of Lisette's jaw were set. She wrote on the pad around her neck, *I told you. I am not leaving.*

"But *I* am. Come with me. You can take the chair," Eby offered.

Lisette had never fully acknowledged that Eby knew about

the chair. She always gave a little start when Eby mentioned it, like a child caught doing something she shouldn't.

I am staying. Go away. I have lunch to make for our guests.

Eby left the kitchen thinking this would be so much easier if Jack had come. Now she had to find another way to make Lisette—and her ghosts—leave.

3

The roadside stand ahead on the highway had been promising fresh fruit, peach cider, and cinnamon pecans for miles. They had passed at least six signs for the stand, each hand-lettered and littered with exclamation points. Kate found herself looking forward to seeing the next sign, a tension building in her body that only the truly lost can feel, starting in her stomach and spreading to her shoulders and fingertips, where her hands clutched the steering wheel. In twelve more miles, there would be fruit. Ten. Eight.

Kate and Devin began to yell with each sign, the closer they got.

Six more miles!

Four!

Two!

Finally, like magic, the stand appeared, and Kate pulled to a stop in front of the gray shack on a dead circle of gravel just off the highway. Dust, gnats, and wavy heat surrounded the place like a bubble, as if it could float up at any moment and travel to another spot of land on another stretch of rural highway somewhere.

She cut the engine of the Outback, and the sudden lack of vibration made her limbs feel heavy. Devin jumped out and ran to the tiny front porch of the shack, which was covered with rusty advertising signs for RC Cola and Pink Lady apples. This reminded Kate so much of hot, sticky road trips with her parents when she was young. Her father would fill the tank with gas and drive until the gauge went down to half, then they would drive back. They'd scoured back roads all around Georgia, finding motels with pools, highway junk shops, and old fruit stands.

Kate had been thirteen when her father died. No more weekend road trips. No more hours spent after school in her father's video store, watching movie after movie. Her mother had gone a little crazy after that, like she'd pulled the IN THE EVENT OF AN EMERGENCY switch that the women in her family told her to pull if her husband ever died, and this was what happened. She wouldn't come out of her room for months. Kate had lived on bagels, sandwich meat, and microwaved popcorn for most of eighth grade. She had hidden when well-meaning neighbors knocked on the door, after the first time she'd let them in and they'd worried why her mother wouldn't see them.

There was still a place inside Kate that resented her mother's grief when her father died. She still remembered what her mother had said to her on the day Kate and Matt went to the courthouse to get married. *I hope you never lose him.* It had felt like a portent. Kate hadn't been as obvious about it as her mother, but, sure enough, she had still pulled that same switch. And she should have known that Devin had caught on. Children always know when their mothers are crazy—they just never admit it, not out loud, to anyone.

The summer afternoon was loud with the drone of insects. It throbbed through the trees like a pulse as Kate got out. The thick wet coastal-plain heat was trapped between sandy soil and low-hanging clouds, and it felt foreign and tight and new.

Once she met Devin on the porch, Kate opened the screen door and they both stepped inside. Box fans were roaring, moving the hot sweet air around and not letting the bees land on the bins of fruit. There were four customers talking with the loud voices of tourists. Kate had parked beside their cars. One was from Florida, the other from North Carolina.

The tourists turned and stared at Devin when the screen door slammed shut. She was dressed in cowboy boots, green lederhosen from last year's school play, *Heidi,* and fairy wings that were crushed from hours spent in the car. And she was now wearing her favorite zebra-striped glasses. She looked like an escaped summer-stock extra. When she had emerged from her bedroom wearing all these things that Cricket had told her to leave behind, Kate had smiled. But then she'd realized what it meant. Devin was treating this like it was her last chance to wear what she wanted, so she was going to wear *everything.* She didn't think Kate was going to sway Cricket on the matter.

Kate went to the ancient cola cooler. She took out a can of Pepsi for herself and a Cheerwine for Devin. There was a display of cinnamon pecans in paper cones beside the register, and she picked up two cones.

"Will that be all?" the old woman behind the register asked. She had small green gooseberry eyes.

"Yes. I mean, no," Kate said, taking the money out of her pocket. "I mean, could you tell me if I'm on the right road to Suley?"

"Yep," the woman said, making change. "Suley is about an hour south if you keep on the highway. But you're probably wanting to go to the water park in Suley. Fastest way there is to get back on the interstate."

Water park? She didn't remember a water park in Suley. "I'm looking for a place called Lost Lake."

The old woman shrugged. "Never heard of it."

"It might not be there anymore. It was sort of a camp, with cabin rentals."

"Oh. Well, camping would be in the old part of Suley. The old highway will take you there. Just keep heading south."

"Thanks."

Kate called to Devin, who had been talking to the tourists, and she and Devin walked back outside. Kate stood by the Outback and drank her Pepsi and ate cinnamon pecans while Devin ran as fast as she could back and forth across the gravel lot, trying to straighten her wings out with the wind. After about five minutes of this, breathless and sweaty, she joined Kate by the car and downed her Cheerwine and ate her pecans in record time.

Devin burped and Kate laughed, and they climbed back in the car and headed south.

Over the next hour, Kate grew more and more tense, though she kept telling herself to calm down. This was an adventure. She was alive and awake and in charge, and Devin needed to see that. A kaleidoscope of landscapes passed like a slide show—farmland, sandy pine barrens, cypress ponds. This is what Kate's mother had referred to as the "Wet South," as they'd made their way to Lost Lake the last time. She'd made it sound unexplored and exotic, something untoward and almost fearful. Someplace only Eby would choose.

But mile after mile, there was no Lost Lake. There was no camp.

Kate squeezed her tired eyes shut, trying to create moisture. She opened them quickly when Devin yelled, "Look out!"

Kate gasped and jerked the steering wheel sharply to the left to avoid hitting what looked like a large alligator, which had suddenly appeared on the gritty ribbon of highway in front of them. A car coming in the opposite direction honked, and she swerved back into her lane, skidding to a stop on the shoulder.

The blood had rushed from her face, and her skin had tightened from the near miss. She quickly turned in her seat to see the other car disappearing into the distance.

But there was no alligator there.

Devin was looking behind them also. "Where did it go?"

"I don't know," Kate said. They sat for a moment in silence. Kate finally took a deep breath and smiled encouragingly at her daughter. "How about we drive into Suley and try to find that water park? That sounds like fun." They'd come this far. She couldn't leave without giving her daughter something good to remember.

"*No*," Devin said, suddenly panicked. "I have to go to Lost Lake and have the last best summer, like you had!"

Kate reached over and touched Devin's fine hair. She could feel the warmth of her scalp through it, the delicate shape of her head. "Oh, Devin. I had plenty of good summers after that one. And so will you. But it's been years since I've been to this place. I've forgotten where it is. GPS doesn't even know. It's probably not there anymore."

"Mom," Devin said, confused, "we're *here*." She pointed straight ahead. Kate followed her finger to the small wooden sign in front of the car on the side of the road. Hand-soldered onto it were the words LOST LAKE—TURN LEFT.

Stunned, Kate looked across the highway.

There was the old gravel road, just a tiny break in the dense trees, leading to their destination.

※

The road to the camp was bumpy, and the overgrowth of trees made it seem like they were driving through a tunnel. The ground began to grow soft under her wheels; she could feel the pull and give. Suddenly, the road opened up and a large lawn appeared in front of them. The grass needed mowing, and the redbrick barbecue grills were starting to crumble. The picnic tables needed a good coat of paint to save them from rot, and the umbrellas were old and thin, meekly shielding the tables from the sun.

To the left of the lawn was a narrow yellow two-story house that leaned slightly to the side, as if giving room to something large passing by. To the right was Lost Lake itself, a dense round plop of gray-green water surrounded by trees with Spanish moss hanging from their limbs, like the long hair of ladies dipping their heads to sip from the lake.

"Wow," Devin said, her head darting around. "I didn't think it would look like this!"

"I didn't, either," Kate said as she slowly navigated the car around the driveway circling the lawn. They passed thirteen ramshackle cabins at the far end, painted in fading Halloween-storybook colors of black, brown, and orange, with mossy stone walkways in between. There were no signs that the cabins were occupied—no shoes left on the stoops, no folding lawn chairs propped against the walls.

Kate circled all the way to the spindly two-story house, then parked. When they got out and shut the doors, the sound echoed over the lake. There was the scent of something green in the air, like wet grass or peeled cucumbers.

She didn't know why she felt so disappointed. Of course the place would have changed. It was inevitable.

They walked inside, and a bell over the door rang. The place smelled of wet wood and cool air from the AC, like an old sea museum. There was no one at the old curved check-in desk in the small foyer, so they looked in the sitting room first, which was filled with dusty chintz furniture and a wall of built-in shelves, sagging with the weight of hundreds of books. Next they went to the informal dining room, where there were several mismatched café tables and chairs. The walls with faded purple wallpaper and the dark narrow floorboards looked scrubbed within an inch of their lives, as if, every day, someone diligently scrubbed back the damp.

"Hello?" Kate called.

No answer.

"Eby?"

Again, no answer.

"Are we the only ones staying here?" Devin asked as they walked back to the check-in desk.

"I don't think we're staying, sweetheart. I don't think it's open."

But then, as if in response, the scent of something savory curled over and tapped her on the shoulder. She automatically turned to look back into the dining room. It was still dark and empty, but now there was a single Blue Willow platter on the buffet table on the far side of the room. She could have sworn it hadn't been there before. She walked over to it. On it were several small ham-and-cheese puff pastries and two large slices of plum cake. Devin joined her, standing over the platter and inhaling deeply.

"Did you see who left this?" Kate asked her daughter.

Devin shook her head.

At that moment, the bell above the front door rang again and a tall slim woman in her seventies appeared in the foyer. She stopped when she saw Kate and Devin in the dining room, startled out of the reverie of her thoughts, which were obviously millions of miles away. Her silver hair was long, reaching almost to her waist, and she had it pulled back into a low ponytail. She wore jeans and a white T-shirt and jewelry made of large green stones.

She hadn't changed. Everything else here might have, but she hadn't.

"*Eby*," Kate said with a smile and a sigh, as if she'd been holding her breath, waiting for this to happen.

"Yes?"

"I'm Kate Pheris." Eby didn't respond. Kate shook her head and clarified: "I used to be Kate Snoderly. I'm your great-niece."

"Kate!" Eby said with sudden recognition. She laughed as she strode into the dining room and drew Kate into her arms. Kate hugged her back, feeling the sharp bones in her great-aunt's lithe frame. She smelled the same, like a vacation, like pretzels and taffy. "I can't believe it. You came back!"

When Eby pulled back, Kate said, "I'd like you to meet my daughter, Devin."

"Hello, Devin. What a lovely outfit," she said sincerely. She turned to Kate. "I'm overwhelmed. What are you doing here?"

"We're in the middle of moving, and this morning we found this postcard," Kate said, taking the folded card out of her pocket, "the one you sent after Mom and Dad and I left all those years ago. I didn't know about it. Mom kept it from me. Devin and I decided to take a road trip to see you again. To see if Lost Lake was still here."

Eby took the card and stared at it, a small change coming over her, as if she'd taken a step back from them without even moving. "Your mother and I left on a bad note. I regret that. How is Quinn?" she asked cautiously, handing the card back to Kate.

Kate blinked in surprise. But of course Eby wouldn't have known. "Mom passed away six years ago."

Eby's hand went to her chest and patted it softly, as if trying to calm something inside. "I'm so sorry," she finally said. "I . . . oh. I don't know what to say. Your father?"

"He's gone, too. Almost ten years before Mom."

"My dad died, too," Devin said. "Last year."

Eby focused on Devin, her brown eyes sympathetic. She reached over and touched Devin's shoulder. "That must have been very hard for you." Eby's gaze shifted to Kate with growing concern, as if Kate was newly fragile, as if the glue hadn't set and she might fall apart at any moment.

"We're okay," Kate said. "It's been a hard year, but we're okay." She was feeling awkward now, like they were unburdening their grief on a stranger. "I didn't mean to bring you bad news. We won't stay long. I just wanted to see you again."

"Won't stay?" Eby said. "Of course you'll stay! Let's tell Lisette you're here. She'll be so excited to have more people to cook for. It looks like she already set out some things for you, left over from lunch." She nodded to the Blue Willow platter.

Kate followed Eby. She didn't have to tell Devin to join them. Devin was spellbound. Eby led them through a swinging door into a surprisingly modern kitchen. It was like walking into another house entirely. It was windowless but bright, with stainless steel that sparkled.

Completely out of place was an old chair by the refrigerator. It was tilted back against the wall, as if someone were sitting there. Devin stared at the chair curiously.

A small woman, probably in her sixties, turned from the stove. Her hair was as dark and shiny as a wet otter's. There was a dramatic gray streak in it, toward the back, and it peeked out as she moved. "More guests, Lisette! Look who it is! It's my niece Kate! I told you she'd be back one day. And she brought her daughter, Devin."

Lisette gave Eby a look Kate couldn't decipher before she

smiled and, without a word, walked over and kissed their cheeks.

Eby said, "Kate, I don't know if you remember, but this is Lisette Durand. She's been my best friend for fifty years and the inimitable cook at Lost Lake for almost that long."

Kate didn't remember Lisette, but maybe she would later, like a figure forming in the fog. Bits and pieces of that summer were coming back to her. For years, she'd only had vague impressions, but very real emotions, about Lost Lake. She remembered feeling happy here. She could remember that very clearly. "Thank you for the food you set out for us," Kate said.

Lisette bowed her head modestly.

"Lisette's father owned a famous restaurant in Paris. La Maison Durand. Hemingway ate there once," Eby said. "She learned to cook from him. Her father, not Hemingway. I'll be right back with the linens for your beds."

As Eby disappeared down the hallway, Lisette lifted a small notepad tied around her neck and began to write: *Do not believe a word she says. Hemingway never ate at my father's restaurant. And my father taught me nothing. The turd. I learned everything I know from a handsome young chef named Robert. He was in love with me.*

Eby walked back into the kitchen with some folded plaid sheets under her arm. "Lisette can't speak," Eby explained when she saw Kate's expression. "She was born without a voice box."

"What's a voice box?" Devin asked excitedly, as if it might be something real, something tangible, a secret wooden box somewhere with Lisette's voice hidden inside.

"I'll explain later," Kate said.

"Come on, girls. Let's get you settled."

As they walked out, Lisette tore the note she'd written out of the pad and turned on a burner on the stove. She burned the note, and it disappeared in a *whoosh* of sparks and ash, like a magician's trick.

Devin walked out backward, to stare as long as she could.

"Grab your plate, and I'll show you to your cabin," Eby said as she took a key from behind the check-in desk.

They walked out together, and Kate led them to the Subaru. "Where is everyone?" she asked, opening the hatch with one hand, the plate in the other.

Eby turned and looked at the lawn. There was a wistfulness to her gaze, but also a small sense of frustration. "Two guests arrived, just before you. They're here for old time's sake. I've recently decided to sell. This is the last summer of Lost Lake."

Kate realized that they had landed in another big after-math in Eby's life, just like last time, when they'd visited right after George had died. It was like they were that strange de-bris that always washed up after a storm. "I'm sorry. We won't stay long."

Eby patted her cheek. The large green stone ring on her finger was cool and calming against Kate's skin, like a gypsy's touch. "You can stay as long as you'd like." She turned to the car. "You certainly brought a lot of luggage."

Kate looked into the Outback and for the first time real-ized how packed it was. "Devin, what is all this?"

"My luggage," Devin said. "You said I could wear what-ever I want."

"Did you bring everything?" In addition to their luggage, there were at least four duffle bags.

Devin shrugged. "All that could fit."

"We didn't even know if we were staying."

"I knew."

"I see the resemblance now," Eby said, smiling as she reached in for a piece of luggage.

4

The cabins weren't lakeside—the trees shielded them from the water—but the lake was nonetheless a palpable presence. Like heat from a fire, the closer to water you are, the stronger you feel it. The cabins were situated in a villagelike pattern, six on one side of the stone walkway, six on the other. Cabin 13 was at the far end, forming a little cul-de-sac.

Eby walked up the steps to cabin 13, which was painted a fading orange with black shutters on the windows. The roof arched to a point right above the door. She unlocked the door, and Kate and Devin followed her inside with their luggage. Kate suddenly realized that this was the same cabin she and her parents had stayed in fifteen years ago. She recognized the nubby red sofa and cheap landscape paintings, also the incongruously expensive pieces mixed in with them—the Tiffany lamp and the antique oak library table.

There was a back door next to the kitchen counter at the far end of the room. Devin dropped her bags and ran to it. "Mom, look at this!" Devin said, and Kate walked over and looked out the window in the door. She saw that there was a large pile of twigs and needles on the back stoop, as if some gigantic creature had made a nest there.

She opened the door.

"What do you think made this?" Devin asked.

"I don't know."

They heard the snap of a twig and stuck their heads out in time to see something that looked like the tip of a tail slowly swish away, disappearing around the corner of the cabin.

"Come out to the lawn at sunset," Eby said from behind them.

They both jumped and turned to her.

"We're grilling out tonight. I know the two other guests would love to see you."

"Are there alligators here?" Kate asked, putting her arm around Devin.

"At Lost Lake?" Eby laughed and shook her head. "No. People always think there must be. Truthfully, business might have been better lately if there were. But you have to go all the way over to Okefenokee to see any alligators. Come to the lawn for dinner?"

"Yes. Yes, of course," Kate said. "We'd love to."

Eby hesitated, staring at them like they were harbingers, like she was trying to figure out just what this meant. She finally turned and walked out, closing the door behind her. Silence stretched in front of them as Kate and Devin stood there, looking around the cabin.

Okay, they were here.

Now what?

"Come on, kiddo," Kate said, moving forward. "You have a lot unpacking to do."

&

After unpacking, they ate Lisette's ham-and-cheese puffs and plum cake with just their fingers, standing in the open front door. Kate stared at the quiet run-down camp in something that felt close to a trance.

Her family had spent a little more than two weeks here fifteen years ago. As soon as Kate had seen the books in the sitting room of the main house today, she remembered reading some of them, remembered taking them out to the dock and staying there all day. There had been many guests here but no young people, and she'd been bored.

But then she'd met a boy her age. He hadn't been a camp guest. He'd lived somewhere close by, in the woods. His name escaped her, lost somewhere in time.

There had been a whole other story going on with Kate's mother and Eby, one Kate had paid no attention to because she and the boy had spent the rest of those two weeks turning feral, roaming the woods around the lake from morning to night, making up stories and watching imaginary things turn real. The fog on the water in the evening became ghost ladies. They had names and personalities Kate couldn't remember now. The cypress knees protruding from the water were long-lost markers left by pirates, and treasure had been buried under them. They'd dived for the treasure every day, holding their breath longer and longer until they'd grown gills behind their ears. She'd been twelve years old at the time, a late bloomer, and everything had still seemed possible. After her family left—abruptly, Kate remembered—she'd gone back home, puberty hit, then her father died the next year.

Why did she have such good feelings about this place?

It was fairly simple, now that she thought about it.

She'd left her childhood here.

Kate turned from the door and took the plate to the kitchen sink, while Devin went to her room to decide what to wear that night for dinner. Kate went to her own room to make up her bed, but she flopped back on the mattress instead. A few minutes later, Devin came into her room, saw her sprawled out on the bare mattress, and climbed up next to her without a word.

Kate put her arm around Devin, then she reached into her pocket for her phone. She'd been dreading this.

She texted Cricket with one hand:

> *Don't worry when you get home today and Devin and I aren't there. I took Devin on a mini-vacation to see an old relative. Be back in a few days.*

Cricket immediately wrote back:

> *What relative? Didn't you read my list? Where are you????*

Kate sighed and typed:

> *I didn't read your list. Sorry. Devin and I found an old postcard from my great-aunt Eby in the attic this morning. We decided*

to visit her camp, Lost Lake, in Suley, near the Florida border.
Don't worry. We arrived safely. See you soon.

She turned off the phone so she wouldn't read what Cricket would say next, then she stared at the ceiling. There was no breeze, yet the dusty ceiling fan was slowly altering the rotation of its blades on its own, back and forth. There was an electric charge in the air. It made the hairs on Kate's arm stand on end.

"I like it here already," Devin whispered. "Can we stay?"

Kate leaned over and rested her cheek on top of Devin's head. "For a while."

"Do you think Dad would have liked it here?"

Kate felt her breath catch a little and hoped Devin didn't feel it. When Matt had been alive, Kate had done everything in her power to give him the life she thought he'd wanted. She'd always been tuned in to his cues, ready to turn even a hint into a full-blown wish. Matt hadn't really known how to be happy, but there had been something about him that had made everyone around him want to find it for him. "I don't know," she said, even though she really did. Matt would have hated it here. He'd hated vacations. He'd liked to stay close to home, where he could ride familiar streets and trails alone on his bike, earbuds in his ears.

"There's no place for him to ride his bike," Devin said.

"No."

Devin thought about that for a moment. "I still like it here, even if Dad wouldn't have. Is that bad?"

"No, sweetheart," Kate said into Devin's hair. "That's not bad at all. Your dad would want you to be happy."

"Alligators make me happy," Devin said right away.

That was new. "Really? Why?"

"Because they're here."

"There aren't alligators here, sweetheart. You heard Eby."

"I think there are."

"Okay, then. Watch your toes," Kate said, reaching down and making a snapping motion with her hand, biting at Devin's feet. Devin laughed and twisted away. But then she rolled back into Kate's arm, as if gravity had pushed her there. Right where she was supposed to be.

And that's how they fell asleep their first afternoon at Lost Lake.

It was twilight, and Eby, Bulahdeen, and Selma were on the lawn, each sneaking peeks at the walkway to the cabins, silent in anticipation, like waiting for a breeze to blow through the stagnant air. Bulahdeen and Selma had reacted with enthusiasm and feigned indifference, respectively, when Eby told them about Kate and Devin arriving that afternoon. But Eby could tell that they weren't quite sure what the girls' presence here meant. Eby wasn't even sure. It was so unexpected that Eby found herself wondering if it had really happened. Had she really seen them in the dining room? Had she really taken them to their cabin? Or had she just imagined it, daydreaming at the front desk again?

"Here they come," Bulahdeen said from where she was sitting at a picnic table, a jelly jar full of wine in front of her. Eby turned from the grill to see the girls materialize from the dark end of the walkway. Kate hadn't changed from her yoga pants and T-shirt so big it fell off one shoulder, revealing a racer-back tank. But Devin was in another costume, this time a tie-dyed T-shirt dress, red cowboy boots, a red cowboy hat, and a fringed vest. "She favors you, Eby."

"Kate or Devin?"

"Kate, of course."

"Although the child does seem to share your sense of style," Selma commented dryly.

"I'll take that as a compliment, from both of you," Eby said, watching the girls approach. Eby secretly agreed with Bulahdeen. Kate did favor her in some ways. Kate had inherited her green eyes from Eby's sister, Marilee. But her long nose, which was both elegant and awkward, and her coltish limbs—those were all Eby. Even her short choppy hair, flipping up at the ends in the humidity, was the same heavy chestnut color Eby's had been. When Eby had first met Kate, she'd seen in her a dreamy, bookish version of herself, and she had wanted so much to know her. But Kate's mother, Quinn, had left in anger that summer, and Eby knew from experience that there was nothing left to do but keep the door open and hope Kate might walk back through one day.

"You say she just showed up?" Bulahdeen asked.

"I tried to keep in touch with her, but her mother wouldn't have it. Apparently, today Kate found a postcard I sent her fifteen years ago. She decided to come see me."

"Atlanta is a long way to come just to stop by," Selma said, staring out over the darkening lake.

"What's that supposed to mean?" Bulahdeen asked.

"It means she wants something."

"Oh, hush," Bulahdeen said. "Don't listen to her, Eby."

When Kate and Devin reached them, Eby waved away some of the smoke billowing in front of her like a potion. "The hot dogs will be ready soon and hopefully not too burnt. These grills are unpredictable," she said. "Kate, Devin, I'd like you to meet Bulahdeen and Selma. Ladies, these are my nieces."

"Come here, baby. Sit with me," Bulahdeen said to Devin, patting the seat beside her at the picnic table. "Would you like a piece of candy?" She took a warm linty roll of Life Savers from her trouser pocket.

Selma had yet to acknowledge them, her gaze still on the lake. She was sitting alone at the next table, leaning back with her legs crossed and her skirt billowing down like a stage curtain. She was fanning herself with an old complimentary card fan from a wedding chapel in Las Vegas. Selma sniffed and suddenly put the fan down. Eby knew she'd been paying attention. "You call that candy? That's not candy. Come with me . . . girl," Selma said, as if she'd forgotten Devin's name already. "I'll give you some real candy."

"Can I, Mom?" Devin asked.

Kate automatically turned to Eby, and that made Eby smile. No one looked to her for direction like that anymore. People in town used to do it all the time. It had been the reason most locals came out here. Eby always used to know what to say, what to do. And the falloff had happened so gradually that she wasn't sure if the reason she stopped helping was because people stopped coming, or vice versa. Eby nodded at Kate, telling her it was all right. Selma made terrible first impressions with other women.

"Okay," Kate said to Devin. "But save it until after dinner."

"Selma, don't take that child into your cabin," Bulahdeen said. "It looks like a brothel in there."

"What's a brothel?" Devin asked.

"A place for only *beautiful* women," Selma said as she walked by them. Devin hurried after her like a cat following a string.

"Don't worry," Bulahdeen said as Kate watched them go. "Selma really does have better candy. But she's not doing this out of the goodness of her heart. She's doing this so she can specifically say, 'I've got the best candy here,' and make it a double entendre. Mark my words."

"Selma doesn't seem very . . . happy to be here," Kate said.

Bulahdeen shook her head. "Oh, that's just the impression she likes to give. She's come back every year for the past thirty years. I think she comes for the rest. She's been married seven times. I know I'd need the rest. But she only has one more to go."

"One more what?" Kate asked.

Bulahdeen leaned forward and said, "Husband. Selma has eight charms. Eight surefire opportunities to marry the man she wants. She's used seven of them. I'm anxious to see who she'll use number eight on. He's bound to be a big deal, being her last and all. He'll have lots of money. And he'll probably be old."

Kate looked to Eby again. This time, Eby just smiled. Kate hesitated, then said to Bulahdeen, "You mean eight actual, physical charms?"

"That's what she says."

"So she thinks she has magical powers," Kate said, her eyes going to where Selma and Devin had disappeared, probably

65

second-guessing her decision to let her daughter go off with this woman.

That made Bulahdeen laugh, and she reached over and patted Kate's hand. "Magic is what we invent when we want something we think we can't have. It makes her happy to think she's a femme fatale. We go along with it."

A minute later Devin came running back, delighted with a single piece of chocolate wrapped in gold foil. Selma sauntered after her.

"I've got the best candy here," she said, taking her seat back at the separate table, away from them.

"What did I tell you?" Bulahdeen winked at Kate. "Selma, there's not a man for twenty miles. Don't you ever turn it off?"

"Of course not," Selma said.

"She really does have the best candy here," Devin said. "I don't want her to turn it off."

"Out of the mouths of babes," Selma said.

Darkness fell, and the only illumination came from the umbrella poles wrapped in strings of twinkle lights, which Eby had found in the storeroom and brought out for one last summer. They created round dots of light across the lawn. As they ate hot dogs with brown mustard and dill potato salad on paper plates, they talked about the summers they'd had here. The summer it had rained every day and all the wallpaper peeled off the walls, and a carpet of frogs took up residence on the lawn. The summer it was so dry you could see the bottom of the lake, and guests waded out and found trinkets they thought they'd lost in the water years ago—coins with wishes still attached, old barrettes, hard plastic toy soldiers. Kate didn't say much, but she seemed to enjoy the stories. It relaxed her a little.

Eby kept glancing at her. Kate had said it had been a hard year after her husband died. That in itself wasn't unusual, not for a Morris woman. But the fact that she was here was significant. It showed some focus, some purpose, which *was* unusual for a grieving Morris woman. She had the look of someone stepping outside for the first time in a long time.

After they ate, there was silence, save for the thrumming of the nighttime wildlife, a strange sort of chorus that seemed to call from one side of the lake and answer on the other.

Devin held up the piece of candy Selma had given her earlier, and Kate nodded that she could have it now. The rattling of the candy paper caught Selma's attention. As Devin put the chocolate in her mouth and made a dramatic this-is-so-good face, there might have been a hint of a smile on Selma's lips, but it faded as quickly as it had appeared.

"This is almost how it used to be, with young people around. I'm going to miss this place," Bulahdeen said, filling her jelly jar with wine again. She always got a little tipsy at this time of night. Eby sometimes wondered if she came here because she could drink what she wanted and her children couldn't stop her. "You know what I'm going to do? I'm going to plan a party. For right here. With decorations and liquor and music. Yes! We'll say good-bye to this place with a party! Next Saturday. That's a good ending to this story. Not the best, but good enough." Bulahdeen foraged around in her purse until she found a notepad and pen, and she started writing.

"Will there be dancing at this party?" Selma asked from her table.

"Only if you want to dance with me," Bulahdeen said.

Selma sighed. "No, thank you."

A farewell party. Rattled, Eby got up and started collecting their paper plates and cups. Kate immediately stood and helped her. Devin wiped her hands on her dress and went to inspect a frog who was taking advantage of the bugs the twinkle lights were attracting. Selma leaned back as Devin passed her, as if afraid Devin was going to touch her with her chocolate-covered fingers.

"Do you still have that dance floor you and George used to bring out at night?" Bulahdeen asked Eby. "Those huge wooden squares that snapped together?"

"I just saw them in the storeroom when I brought out the string lights," Eby said. "I'd forgotten they were there."

"Those were some good times, weren't they? Dancing on summer nights." Bulahdeen swayed in her seat to imaginary music. "George even hired a band on the weekends. Remember that? Kate, will you and Devin come?"

Kate walked to the wooden trash can by the grills and put the remnants of dinner inside the plastic bag. "I don't know if we'll still be here."

"Oh. I thought maybe you'd be here for a while," Bulahdeen said. "To help Eby."

Kate turned to Eby. "Do you need help?"

"It's going to be a big move," Eby said, dumping the rest of the plates and cups in the trash. Too big. Too overwhelming.

"I'll be glad to help in any way I can."

Eby hesitated. At this rate, Lisette was going to be no help at all. But, at least with Lisette, Eby had an excuse not to do it. "Are you sure?"

"Devin's on summer vacation. And all our things are in our

new place by now. I'm supposed to start work at my mother-in-law's real estate office soon, but there's no fixed date."

"You're a real estate agent?" Bulahdeen asked.

"No. My husband and I ran a bike shop." She paused. "I sold it last year, after he passed away."

That sobered Bulahdeen a little. "I'm sorry."

"Well, if you're going to stay a while, I could certainly use your help," Eby said with resignation. A farewell party. Help with moving. It was all falling into place. She didn't admit to herself until now that she had thought that Kate and Devin showing up was some big sign telling her she shouldn't sell, that there was another way to save this place. It was silly, of course, because her family had never been a sign of anything good.

Bulahdeen took a celebratory swig of her wine and plopped the glass back on the table. "Good! That will make five people for the party," she said. "No—six! We'll have it during the day so Lisette can come."

Kate looked confused. "Lisette can't come out at night?"

"Lisette thinks evening meals are bad luck, so she doesn't like to be around food after sunset. That's why there's always been breakfast and lunch served in the main house, but never dinner. George built the grills for guests to cook out at night." Eby smiled as Kate looked to the main house, where one light was on upstairs, Lisette's bedroom light. A shadow passed by the window, as if she was watching them. "We must seem very strange to you."

"No." Kate shook her head. "It's what I remember most about this place."

The unmistakable sound of tires crunching over gravel was heard in the distance, and everyone turned. A pair of headlights soon flashed through the woods. Kate looked around for Devin, a slight panic in her voice as she called for her. Devin, who had lost interest in the frog, was jumping from one pool of umbrella light to the other across the lawn. She ran back to her mother. *That was curious,* Eby thought. *Who did they think it was?*

A dark blue Toyota appeared and circled around them, coming to a stop in front of the main house. A lean man in his sixties got out. He smiled and lifted his hand in a shy wave.

"That makes seven!" Bulahdeen said happily, writing his name down.

"If he'll be at the party, I might come," Selma said.

Bulahdeen made a *tsk*ing sound, not looking up from her list. "You know he's not here for you."

"It doesn't mean I can't dance with him."

"Who is that?" Kate asked.

"That's Jack Humphry," Eby told her. "He stays here every summer. He's been in love with Lisette for years. He knows this is his last chance with her. Look at that expression on his face. That is the look of a man who has finally woken up."

"I know that feeling," Kate said.

Eby wanted to say so much to her. She wanted to say that waking up is the most important part of grieving, that so many women in their family failed to do it, and she was proud of Kate for fighting her way back. But Eby didn't say anything. She could fix a lot of things, but family wasn't one of them. It was one of the hardest things she'd ever had to come to terms with. It was the very reason she'd left Atlanta. She squeezed Kate's arm, then pulled the bag out of the trash can and walked to the main house to greet Jack.

Because it was high time Lisette woke up, too.

5

In the inky stillness of the next morning, Lisette woke up and dressed quietly in the silks her elderly mother still sent her from Paris—cool slippery things that made her feel like she was covering herself with fresh air. For a while, after she left Paris, Lisette threw away her mother's packages on principle. Lisette was not the same vain pretty girl her mother had once known. But then Lisette started making an exception for the lingerie. It was not vain if no one but herself saw her wear them. She then put on a blue dress and a freshly laundered apron that smelled like the lemongrass soap Eby used for the camp's sheets and towels, the only soap that could take out the damp mustiness that wanted to cling to everything in this place.

She moved soundlessly downstairs to start breakfast, first cracking open the door to Eby's bedroom slightly to make sure she was still breathing. She had done this every morning since George died. Eby did not know. Eby did not like it when Lisette worried too much. Their relationship had always been disproportionate that way. It was only Eby, capable and confident, who was allowed to worry about Lisette, moody and delicate.

Lisette turned on the lights in her kitchen and began to work. Everything was quiet, too quiet. But she had forced herself over the years to become accustomed to morning, even though it was evening she used to truly love for its energy and restlessness. That, at least, she would acknowledge she got from her father. His restaurant had stayed open late, one of the latest in Paris, and it had attracted people of poetic and turbulent minds.

The ghost of Luc sat quietly in the chair in the corner, near the blue refrigerator, as he did every morning, looking as he did the last time she saw him over dinner when they were both sixteen, his good white shirt stained yellow from nervous sweat under his arms, his young face eagerly watching her every move. He was caught in the moment before she had handed him the note over dinner, the one that broke his heart, a note like countless others she had written before. She had not understood what it was like to be rejected, as she had never been rejected herself. She had been shocked to hear of his suicide the next day. What was she, a monster? No one should have the power to hurt another that fully, that completely. She deserved to die in the same way, because changing was out of the question.

Eby had saved her with her goodness. That was why Lisette had decided to follow Eby wherever she went, finally settling here at Lost Lake. Eby made her a better person. Lisette had no idea what she would do without Eby. It frightened her so much that she could not think of it. She could not see her life anywhere but here. She would never go back to Paris. What did Eby think would happen? That Lisette would see her mother and suddenly want to live with her again?

No. Never.

But without Eby, without this camp, all Lisette had left was Luc, and she did not want to accept that he was not enough, that he was sixteen and a ghost, neither of which knew much about living.

She turned on the small coffeemaker in the kitchen for herself and Eby, then got to work on the chive biscuits and fruit tarts, like the ones she remembered from a patisserie she used to go to as a child. They had loved her there, giving her sweets for free because she had been so beautiful. The child, Devin, would like them. It had been so long since there had been children here. It made Lisette happy. It made Eby even happier. Lisette knew that the only regret Eby had when it came to cutting ties with her family was that she never got to see her niece grow up. But then there was that summer George died, when her niece, Quinn, showed up, and Eby got to meet her great-niece Kate. Lisette thought that, finally, Eby would have children in her life like she had always wanted . . . but that had not worked out. Maybe now, the third time, the third generation, would be the charm.

Maybe the girls would make Eby want to stay. Or at least not go so far.

Lisette knew Eby wanted to go back to Europe. Eby and George had often talked about it. And when Eby dreamed of Paris, she always told Lisette in the morning. Lisette would always tense, hearing of it, but she said nothing. They were just dreams, after all. Lisette had no idea those dreams had meant so much to Eby. She had never suspected Eby would be willing to sacrifice Lost Lake for those dreams to come true.

Once everything was under way, Lisette turned on the large stainless-steel coffeemaker for the guests in the dining room and took the chairs off the tables, stopping at the window to look out. The mist from the lake was giving off its own odd light, as if it were alive.

Something caught her eye and she leaned forward, her forehead almost resting against the glass. Someone was jogging around the lawn in a hooded sweatshirt, shorts, and tennis shoes.

Despite her initial start at seeing anyone out on the lawn after a season of no guests, Lisette did not have to see his face to know who he was.

When had he arrived? Last night, probably. Eby had not told her.

She stepped back quickly and hurried to the kitchen and locked the door behind her. That was ridiculous. Why did she lock the door? It was not as if Jack would come in there. He was not that bold, that aggressive.

But, still, shy had its own form of aggression. She had no armor against slow, invasive feelings. They slipped straight to her as if through mouse holes. Jack had been working his way inside for years, as earnest and trusting as Luc had been.

She looked over at Luc, only to see him smile at her from the corner. He seemed to approve of this madness.

Lisette heard a shuffling sound and turned to see that Eby had entered the kitchen and was pouring herself a cup of coffee. She was wearing pink baggy pajamas, which only served to make her look taller and thinner.

"I take it Jack is out there," Eby said.

Lisette rolled her eyes as she pushed herself away from the door, where she'd been leaning against it, as if barricading it. She went to take the pastry shells out of the oven.

"He arrived last night. I know I said I'd take you into town for more groceries today, but I have all this inventory to do. Inventory you won't help me with. So Jack said he'd take you."

Lisette set the pastry shells down and quickly wrote on her notepad, *It can wait.*

"I don't think so. Bulahdeen has decided to throw us a farewell party. You might want to help her, or we'll end up with a lot of liquor and nothing to eat."

Lisette narrowed her eyes at Eby, then she wrote, *I know what you are doing.*

Eby read that and smiled. "Me?" she said, turning to go back upstairs with her cup of coffee. "All I'm doing is inventory."

Kate heard a knock on the door and opened her eyes. She sat up quickly on the wrought-iron bed and looked around, getting her bearings, remembering where she was. She stumbled into the living room of the cabin. She saw that Devin's bedroom door was still closed, and a sudden, irrational fear gripped her that Devin might not be there. But she opened her door and saw her sleeping on her back, her limbs spread out like points of a star. Her glasses were perched on her bedside table as if watching her, as if lonely for her.

Another knock at the front door. She went to it and unlocked it. Lisette was standing there in the morning light, holding a tray containing two plates covered with napkins, and a carafe of coffee.

The scent of something salty and doughy hit her, and Kate's mouth began to water. "Lisette," Kate said, surprised. "What is this?"

Lisette nodded to the inside of the cabin and Kate stepped back. Lisette walked in and set the tray on the scuffed round table near the kitchen corner. Kate watched her take the white napkins off the plates, revealing fruit tarts and biscuits and bacon.

She pulled a prewritten note and an envelope from her apron pocket.

The note read: *I have a favor to ask. Will you go today to the Fresh Mart in town and purchase some groceries for me? Eby was supposed to take me, but she said she has inventory to do. The money and list are in the envelope. Simply give it to the girl at the front desk. She will gather the things for me. There are more guests than I anticipated and Eby mentioned that Bulahdeen is planning a party. I will make a beautiful cake.*

"Of course I'll go," Kate said. "I'll be happy to."

Lisette wrote on the notepad around her neck: *Thank you. The fruit tarts are for Devin. They look like bright little jewels. Like her.*

"She'll love them. Thank you."

Lisette smiled and took the note from Kate, leaving her with the envelope. Then she walked out. Kate followed her and was about to close the door behind her, when she happened to look down to see a small curved bone on the top step of the stoop. Curious, she picked it up and held it up to the light. It was an old animal tooth of some sort, familiar in a way she didn't immediately recognize.

She took it inside and set it on the table as she sat down. She ran her hands through her short hair, then rubbed her face and looked at the lovely food on old mismatched floral plates.

Kate picked up the carafe and poured some coffee into a cup. She added sugar and cream until it was the color of caramel. Her mom used to take her coffee like this. *So sweet it could kiss you,* she used to say. As crazy as her mother had been, there were times after Kate's father died that she had seemed almost normal. When they could afford it, Kate and her mother would go to the movies, sneaking in candy and drinks so they didn't have to buy the overpriced things at the concession stand. They would watch television together every Friday night, with trays of dinner on their laps. Sometimes, her mother would braid Kate's hair on weeknights, then put her in a nightcap and let her sleep on one of her sateen pillowcases, so her braids would still be smooth in the morning for school.

Kate wished there had been more good times. Memories that would make going back easier.

She sat back and considered not returning to Atlanta. Of maybe hiding here forever. Silly daydreams. Of course it would never happen. Eby was selling the place. And Kate had to face the fact that the reason she'd agreed to live with her mother-in-law, Cricket—even though Matt wouldn't have wanted it, even though Cricket's idea of parenting didn't jibe with her own—was because she was fundamentally scared. She had plenty of money now, from the sale of her house and Matt's shop. She could do anything she wanted. She could move anywhere. But she'd never been on her own. She'd lived with her mother, then Matt. When Matt died, she'd discovered a void in her life she hadn't known was there. She missed her mom, and she missed her dad, but it took losing Matt for her to finally see just how isolated she'd been, like running out of rope. Cricket had stepped in and had filled that part of her daily existence for the past year, but they were each poor substitutes for what the other really wanted. But it was better than nothing. If Kate messed up, if she forgot something, there was backup. What if she fell asleep again for a year? What if she couldn't be the parent she needed to be for Devin? What if she couldn't do it alone?

She reached for a biscuit. She didn't want to think of that. For now, she and Devin would enjoy this place with its lackadaisical proprietor, its mute French cook, and guests with marriage charms and plans for a farewell party.

For now, they would enjoy their last best summer, which somehow felt like saying good-bye to a lot more than just the lake.

Jack Humphry sat alone in the dining room in the main house. The local newspaper was folded on the table in front of him. He'd read it through twice.

It was mid-morning now, and he could tell Lisette had begun to make lunch in the kitchen, something involving cinnamon. It was a calming scent, reminding him of mulled wine, baked apples, and winter nights.

He heard voices coming from outside, voices he didn't recognize.

Curious, he walked to the window and looked out.

Bulahdeen was sitting at a picnic table, scribbling in a notebook. She'd mentioned something about a farewell party that morning at breakfast, a party that would include just the lake guests, which Jack thought was okay. Bulahdeen was a sweet woman. She'd been a college literature professor long ago. Jack thought anyone who read couldn't be all bad. He had assumed that she would rather have her nose in a book than talk, but he'd been wrong. Sometimes she would walk up to him while he was sitting in the dining room and just talk and talk. Once he'd asked, "Don't you want to read? There are hundreds of books in the sitting room."

She had laughed and said, "I've read them all. I want to remember them the way they were. If I read them now, the endings will have changed."

He didn't understand that, but then English hadn't been his favorite subject.

Selma was sitting at the picnic table behind Bulahdeen. She was giving herself a manicure. Jack stepped back a little, hoping she wouldn't see him. He'd known Selma for thirty years, and he still couldn't figure out whether or not she was serious with her flirtations. This seemed to amuse her. He always tried to avoid her. But that had been easier to do when there had been more men around.

They weren't talking, so he didn't know where the voices

were coming from. Then he saw a tall young woman in a short floral sundress and flip-flops walking toward the house. There was a little girl with her, wearing a tutu and a pink bicycle helmet. She was talking loudly as she ran circles around the young woman. The little girl looked over at Bulahdeen and Selma, then asked her mother something. The young woman nodded, and the little girl ran over and sat by Bulahdeen.

It took Jack a moment to realize the young woman was still heading this way, that she was actually going to come into the house.

He ran back to his table and sat down.

Jack was not a social man.

Coming from an old family of dynamic Richmond southerners, he should have been. He had three older brothers—a lawyer, a television news anchor, and a horse breeder. He'd grown up overwhelmed by the noise of their booming voices. Sometimes, all Jack had wanted to do was cover his ears. He would slink around, looking for quiet corners. His parents had simply shaken their heads, figuring three confident sons were enough. Oh, he knew his parents had loved him fiercely, and even his brothers had had their share of bruises from defending him from kids who had made fun of him at school. But they hadn't expected much of him. He hadn't known what to expect of himself. He'd been an exceptional student, but when the time came for him to leave for college, he'd been paralyzed with indecision. He'd had no idea what to do with his life. He'd expressed this fear to his mother, who had kissed him on the cheek in his dorm room the first day of his freshman year and had said with a laugh, "Since you don't like looking people in the eye, why not focus on their feet?"

So he became a podiatrist.

It was the honest truth, but he found that when he told people that story, most laughed. It was his go-to joke when he absolutely had to attend a party or function.

He first came to Lost Lake when an older doctor at his practice in Richmond asked him to join him and his wife on their summer vacation. He had obviously felt sorry for Jack, who had alienated the nurses and staff in those early years because he'd been so bad at personal interaction. He'd gotten better, but it had taken years. The old doctor soon retired and moved away, but every summer Jack kept coming back to Lost Lake. He liked the quiet here. He liked how removed it was. He liked that, after a while, the summer regulars got to know him and didn't judge him for his shy nature and the way his eyes could never quite meet theirs. Most of all, he liked the quiet woman in the kitchen.

He had never known how silent a person could be. Lisette's presence was a comfort, and he spent most of his time in the dining room, near the kitchen door, near *her*. Sometimes when she cooked, she would bring him out little samples of summer borscht or smoked salmon tea sandwiches. She would set the food on the table in front of him, smile, then go back to the kitchen. One time she even reached out and touched his hair, but that seemed to shock her, and she never did it again.

Being around her was unlike anything he'd ever known. Wherever he went, everyone talked. Even at the ballet—where he went specifically to have the comfort of people around but not have to hear them—there were still words, buzzing around in whispers. Lisette not only didn't talk, she barely even made noise when she moved. Sometimes he wished the whole world was like Lisette. But it wasn't. That was something his mother always made sure he knew. The world was not like him and was not going to change for him. The trick to getting through life, she'd told him, is not to resent it when it isn't exactly how you think it should be.

When Eby had called him to cancel his reservation, to tell him she was selling Lost Lake, she had said to him, "But Lisette is still here and will be for the summer, in case there's something you want to tell her."

It didn't hit him at first. He'd been too focused on how his plans for the summer had changed. What was he going to do now? Where was he going to go? But that night he'd woken from a dream about a girl on a bridge, and realized it had been Lisette on that bridge, and if she jumped, he would never see her again. He'd always known where to find her, but after this summer, he wouldn't. Eby wanted him to tell Lisette something. He didn't know what that was. Was it something that would make her stay? He hated being unprepared for anything, but he still packed and left the next day.

That morning, his first morning at the lake, he'd woken up and gone for a jog, as he'd always done. When he'd seen the light flick on in the dining room, he'd gone inside. He'd sat by the kitchen door, waiting for Lisette to come out. When she hadn't—which was odd because she always seemed to sense his presence—he'd gone back to his cabin to shower and change. When he'd come back, breakfast had been set out for the guests, but still no Lisette.

Eby had asked him last night to take Lisette into town for

groceries today, and he'd happily agreed. He was curious
what it would be like to shop with her. Would it be like
walking around in a pocket of quiet while the rest of the
noisy world bounced off of them? He was sure he would enjoy that. When he had asked Eby that morning when Lisette
would be ready to go, Eby didn't know. Eby had left, saying
she had inventory to do in the cabins, so Jack had sat there in
the dining room the better part of the morning, at attention,
waiting.

He heard the front door open, and the young woman he'd
seen outside came in with a tray of empty dishes. She smiled
at him as she walked to the kitchen. She had wide interesting
features and a quiet way of walking that Jack appreciated. She
tapped on the kitchen door, then tried to push it open. But it
was locked.

Jack thought that was strange. Lisette never locked the
kitchen door. Was she all right?

"Lisette, it's me, Kate. I'm on my way out. I brought back
the dishes from breakfast," the woman called. While she waited
for Lisette to come to the door, the woman turned to him.
"You must be Jack. I'm Kate, Eby's great-niece."

He nodded, his eyes down. "Nice to meet you."

At that moment, a note was pushed under the door from
the kitchen.

Kate looked at it, surprised. It was just touching her toes.
She balanced the tray in one hand and bent to pick up the
note with the other. She read it, then said, "Hmm."

Jack wanted to ask her what the note said, but he didn't.

Kate walked over to the buffet table and set the tray down,
then she set the note beside it.

"It was nice to meet you too, Jack," she said as she walked back out.

When the front door closed, Jack stood and went to the buffet table. The note, in Lisette's pretty, spidery handwriting said, *Please leave the things on the table. I will get them later.*

She was obviously busy in there. He didn't want to bother her. But maybe she didn't know he was here. Maybe she had been waiting for him to knock on the door and call to her, like Kate had done. It was such a natural thing to do for most people.

Jack walked to the door and tapped on it. "Lisette? It's me, Jack. Jack Humphry. I got in last night. Eby told me you needed someone to take you to the grocery store. I just wanted you to know that I'll be out here, whenever you're ready."

After a moment, another note appeared from under the door: *I already asked Kate to get the things I need. You do not need to wait. I am sorry Eby has wasted your time.*

"I don't mind. I'll just read the paper. I'll be right here, by the door."

He knew she was still standing there, on the other side of the door. If he concentrated hard enough, he could almost see her form in the grain of the wood. Several seconds passed and he waited for another note from her. Nothing. He thought he should probably move away, but he couldn't bring himself to.

Suddenly, he heard the latch pull back, and he stepped away as the door flew open.

Lisette sighed and took the note he was still holding and gestured him inside impatiently. She poked her head out into the dining room to see if anyone else was there, then she made a beeline to the buffet table and took the tray and Kate's note into the kitchen. Setting them down on the counter, she then turned and locked the door again.

She wrote him another note: *You can stay in here with me. But you must not let Eby know. You must be quiet.*

"Of course," he said. "I'd like that very much. I'd like to watch you work." He turned to the only chair in the kitchen, but she grabbed his arm and shook her head, then held up a single finger, telling him to wait.

She disappeared down the hall and came back pulling an old squeaky office chair. She set it by the wall on the opposite side of the kitchen and pointed to it. He obediently sat.

She stood there for a moment, looking from the empty chair by the refrigerator, to him, then back again. She finally threw her hands in the air in frustration, as if she'd just had her own silent argument with someone and lost.

She took the notes she'd just written to the stove, then she burned them one by one.

He watched in amazement as her words went up in smoke.

Where else in the world could such a creature exist? Suddenly, Jack was no longer worried about where he would go when Lost Lake was gone. He was worried about where Lisette would go. Jack had learned to live among people out in that strange noisy world.

But somehow he knew Lisette could only live here.

✿

"Come on, Devin, let's go!" Kate called when she walked out of the house.

So that is the man in love with Lisette, Kate thought. Jack didn't say much, and Lisette didn't say anything at all. This might be interesting to watch, if Kate and Devin were staying longer. Jack seemed kind. He was craggy and athletic, with lines like parentheses around his mouth, as if everything he wanted to say was an afterthought.

"Where are you girls going?" Bulahdeen asked, looking up from her list as Devin ran to the car.

"To the grocery store for Lisette."

"Mind if I come along?" Bulahdeen asked. "I need to get some things for the party."

"We don't mind at all."

Bulahdeen put her notebook in her purse, then stood stiffly. "Selma, we're going to the store. I need to get more wine."

Selma was filing her nails at the next table. "Why do you need so much wine? Doesn't alcohol interfere with your medication?"

"I don't take any medication."

"That explains a lot," Selma said, blowing emery-board dust off her fingertips.

"Come with us," Bulahdeen said, shuffling over to her. "It's for the party."

"The party I'm not attending?"

"Didn't you say you forgot to pack your hand lotion? Now's your chance to get some."

"Unlike you, I have my own car. I can go get lotion any time. And maybe I don't even need it." Selma held her hands up, inspecting them. "This wet air is good for my skin."

Bulahdeen shrugged. "Suit yourself."

Selma watched Bulahdeen walk to the car. As soon as Kate helped the old woman into the front seat, Selma sighed and stood. "Why do I let you talk me into these things?" she asked, as if more arm pulling had been involved. Selma walked over. "Don't I even get the front seat?"

"No," Bulahdeen said, closing the front door.

Selma opened the back door and looked in at Devin, who was now in the backseat. "Scoot over . . . girl. Let's not wrinkle my dress."

"I like what you're wearing."

"Thank you. And that's . . . quite an ensemble you have on," Selma said.

"Thank you," Devin responded, quite proud of her ballet clothes, to which she'd added her cowboy boots and her bright pink bicycle helmet with the Pheris Wheels logo on it, which Matt had given her last year, shortly before he'd died. Devin wasn't a bike-riding kind of kid—she said the world went by too fast to see it when she was on a bike—but she had always enjoyed being with her father. Matt hadn't understood that. He'd been coming around in some small way when he'd given her the helmet, because he'd given it to her just to wear, just because he knew she liked it. But there hadn't been time enough for him to fully get it.

Kate smiled at her daughter in the rearview mirror.

"Seat belts on?" Kate called to her motley crew. "Okay, let's go."

After passing several neighborhoods of coastal-colored clapboard houses, Kate slowed as she approached the traffic circle in the middle of town. She didn't remember going into town the last time she was here, so it took her by surprise. The center of Suley was marked by a narrow silo, old and rusted, towering above the shops on the circle. It looked so completely out of place that she simply had to stare. The sign on the small park surrounding the silo said: SULEY GRANARY, BUILT IN 1801. Next to it was another sign that said: MEET SUE, THE OFFICIAL TOWN COW, EVERY SATURDAY FROM 9–1.

She found the Fresh Mart on the circle and parked in front of it. They all got out and walked into the store. It was a touristy market with a deli and a café and wooden floors that creaked. The whole place smelled like waffle cones. Bulahdeen went straight to the wine shelves. Selma floated around the produce section, acting bored, picking up a green bell pepper, then putting it down with a sigh. Kate and Devin went to the business counter and waited for the young woman with the blond ponytail to get off the phone.

"Why don't you go help Bulahdeen," Kate said to Devin. "Don't let her drop anything."

A few minutes later, the young woman finally got off the phone. "Sorry about that," she said.

"No problem." Kate handed her the envelope from Lisette.

The girl read the note inside, then looked up at Kate. "Are you staying out at the lake?"

"Yes. I came to see Eby. She's my great-aunt."

The girl reached up and pulled her ponytail tighter. She couldn't be more than twenty-one. "I don't think I've ever met any of Eby's family."

"It's been fifteen years since I was last here."

"Oh. Well, I'll box up the things on Lisette's list. It'll just take a minute," the girl said. "Lisette special-orders some strange foods from France, but she's a good customer. Not like some of the guests at Lost Lake. There's this one old woman who vacations there every summer. When she comes in here, she's so hateful to all the women, but the men fawn over her. My dad makes a fool of himself. I don't know what he sees in her. She has this hideous red hair."

"Do you mean Selma?" Kate nodded to Selma, who was now laughing at something the man stocking Bosc pears was saying.

The girl made a face. "That's her."

"She drove in with us."

"My condolences. Now the little old lady, I like. She always buys wine, and when the checkout girls ask for her birth date for the register, she always makes things up. October twelfth, 1492. July fourth, 1776." They both watched as Bulahdeen took her place in line at the checkout. She was carrying so many bottles that she had to lean back. Devin was hovering close behind her, as if to catch her if she fell. "I can't believe she's buying more wine. She was just in here yesterday."

Kate smiled and turned back to the girl. "She's throwing a farewell party for Eby."

"So it's true?" The girl asked. "Eby is selling Lost Lake? Yesterday, Bulahdeen said Eby was selling, but, you know, it's Bulahdeen. I didn't know if it was true or not."

"It's true. At least, that's what Eby says."

"That makes me sad. I haven't seen Eby in a while, but she was always nice to me. When I was in high school, she let me bring my boyfriends out to the lake, and we'd borrow one of her rowboats because she always said the middle of a lake was the best place to fall in love." The girl absentmindedly began to pick at the clumps of thick mascara sticking to her lashes. "When is the party?"

"Saturday afternoon, I think."

The girl nodded, then turned and grabbed a cardboard box from the stack behind her and went to get Lisette's special-order groceries from the back.

"I think I may have inadvertently invited the girl at the front desk to the party," Kate said, joining Bulahdeen and Devin in line. She took a few bottles from Bulahdeen's load.

"Oh, that's all right," Bulahdeen said. "The more the merrier."

"The more the merrier? What do you mean?" Selma asked, walking over to them. The four of them together drew some attention. They didn't look like your average tourists: an older woman in a tight red dress and heels; an elderly woman with her arms full of wine bottles; a toe-headed girl in glasses, a tutu, and a bike helmet; and Kate. All before noon.

"The owner's daughter. Brittany. She's coming to the fare-well party," Bulahdeen said.

"That girl hates me," Selma said.

"She might not if you stopped flirting with her daddy. You're not coming anyway. What's it to you?"

Selma shook her head and walked away. "It's nothing to me."

6

Minutes later, from the shop across the street, Wes Patterson watched a tall young woman walk out of the Fresh Mart. Her brown hair was a mass of short layers that, as she walked, fell loosely into her eyes. She pushed it away with her fingers, stopping to look around the circle as she did so. For a moment, staring into the distance, her hand holding her hair back, she had that look people often have on the beach, looking out into the expanse of the ocean. Like she couldn't believe there was just so much in front of her. She seemed a little lost. But she smiled and turned when the bag boy from the Fresh Mart said something to her. She opened the hatchback of a green Subaru, and the bag boy placed a large box of groceries inside for her. She tipped him, then helped an old lady carrying several bottles of wine into the passenger seat.

Her hair had been longer that summer when they were kids, the dark color an amazing contrast to her eyes, which were the exact bright green of summer morning grass. He couldn't stop staring. He'd recognized her immediately. He'd often wondered if he would, if he ever saw her again. She was older, of course, with curves and angles that newly fascinated him because they hadn't been there before. But he'd still know Kate anywhere. She'd given him the best summer he'd ever had, which he could never think of without thinking about the worst time in his life, which had come directly after.

She had a child with her. She didn't look much like Kate, but the girl was undoubtedly her daughter. There was just something so *Kate* about her. She was exactly the child he imagined Kate would have had.

What was she doing here, after all this time? He began to feel vaguely uncomfortable, like that moment you first realize you've lost your wallet. He actually reached back to feel if he still had his wallet in his back pocket and if his keys were still in the front.

She was with two guests Wes remembered from his years at the lake. That meant she was here to see Eby and it had nothing to do with him or the letter. That should have made him feel better, but it only made him more restless.

"Now that is a fine-looking woman," the older man sitting beside him at the counter said, having followed Wes's gaze out the large front window.

"She's a little young for you, don't you think?" Wes asked.

"Not the mother. The redhead," he said, watching Selma open the back car door and wait for the child to climb in first. Selma hesitated, as if knowing she was being watched. She smiled slightly, then ducked into the car, lifting her skirt high as she pulled her bare legs in last, giving them a show. "I've always had a thing for redheads."

"Has Deloris changed her hair color?" Wes asked the man.

"No, she's still a brunette," he said, taking one last bite of the slice of ham-and-pineapple pizza in front of him. He wiped his mouth on a greasy paper napkin, then tossed it onto the counter. "I'll be at the Water Park Hotel with Deloris and the girls for a few days. The lawyer is coming this weekend with the paperwork. I'm glad to be doing business with you, son. We're going to do great things with that property." He held out his hand.

Wes stared at the man's puffy hand for a moment before he said, "We'll shake on it when Eby sells."

He smiled. "Fair enough."

As his uncle walked away, Wes called, "Maybe we can all get together some time, you and me and Deloris and the girls. It would be nice to catch up."

"Right, right," Lazlo said without looking back. "We'll see what happens."

Wes watched as his uncle walked outside, batting at the air around his head as if an invisible plague of insects had just descended upon him. Once in his Mercedes parked at the curb, he took a handkerchief out of his trouser pocket and patted his unnaturally smooth face and neck with it.

Across the street, the Subaru was now gone.

"You're making a deal with the devil." An old man with a grizzly beard stuck his head out of the kitchen. It was Grady, the cook. He was sure to have been listening all this time. Everyone in the small restaurant, which was still decorated in early eighties pizza-chic from its previous incarnation as a pizzeria arcade, had been listening, leaning forward in their seats, speaking in hushed tones, their ears turning like owls' heads. This was bound to reach Eby soon.

"I know," Wes said, gathering his and Lazlo's plates and napkins from the window counter before one of the waitresses could do it. "But there's no reason for me to hang on to that land if Eby sells. My property is in the middle of her lake property. The only way it's worth anything is in connection to hers."

"I still can't believe she's selling," Grady said, shaking his head. "That place is an institution."

"Eby has helped a lot of people in this town over the years. If she wants to leave, if that's what she really wants to do, we should support her. Lost Lake isn't making money anymore."

"We should have supported her a long time ago, if it's come to this." Grady squinted his tiny brown marble eyes. "Can you imagine what Lost Lake will look like when it's developed? When your uncle built the water park and outlet mall, it completely changed the landscape north of the interstate. You'll keep him from doing too much damage this time, won't you?"

"Change is good, Grady." Wes handed him the plates.

The front door opened, and a young woman with a blond ponytail entered. "Well, it's official," Brittany announced dramatically. "I just heard it from her niece. Eby is selling Lost Lake."

"We know," Grady said. "We just heard, too. Wes is selling his property to the same developer."

"I'm depressed," Britt said, taking a seat at a nearby table. "I'll never have another boy take me out there. I'm never going to get married at this rate. Wes, let's make a pact. If we're not married by the time we're thirty, let's marry each other."

Wes laughed. Britt always flirted with him between boyfriends. For some reason, she seemed to consider him an odd sort of backup plan. Probably because he was nearby, one of only a few people their age who didn't go to work at the water park or outlet mall or who hadn't left town altogether. "I'm going to reach thirty long before you do."

"I'll be ready."

"Stop waiting, Britt. Go out there and get what you want."

"That's what I'm doing! I just asked you to marry me."

"I'm not what you really want," Wes said, patting her shoulder as he walked by her to the door that led to his garage below the restaurant. "I'll be out at Lost Lake if anyone needs me."

As he left, he heard Britt say, "I need cheese. Eby's having a farewell party on Saturday at the lake. I think I'll go, and kiss my youth good-bye."

"You say she's having a farewell party?" Grady asked. "Now that's a good idea. I'll whip up some chicken wings to bring."

❧

Wes turned off the highway onto the gravel road leading to Lost Lake a little too quickly, and gravel spit out from behind his wheels. He felt he couldn't get there fast enough. He needed to explain what was going on before anyone else had a chance to tell Eby. He owed her that.

He wanted her to know that all this, everything that was happening, started and ended with her. Lazlo was family, sure. And that blood connection meant something to Wes. More than it should, considering his uncle had never really been around when Wes was growing up. But Eby and, by extension, the lake were everything good about his childhood. Wes and his brother, Billy, used to come here every day, walking from their cabin in the woods. When Wes's mother left, his father had seethed with resentment, hating his circumstances and everyone who had done him wrong, until that was all he thought about. Inside he was no longer human, just churning flames. He turned to alcohol and then, almost inevitably, violence. Eby was the one who mended Wes's and Billy's clothes and gave them breakfast before school and threw them birthday parties, inviting their classmates to the lake. Lisette served pistachio and rose water ice cream and cakes made of dark chocolate.

After the fire, after he lost his brother and father, Wes moved away from the family property, and then there had been Daphne, his foster mother, who had been everything good about his teenage years.

If not for those two old women, Wes was sure he would be either dead, drunk, or incarcerated by now.

He and Eby still kept in touch. He'd see her sometimes in town. Every once in a while she'd stop by the restaurant to have a slice and catch up. But this was the first time in years that he'd been out here. As the lake came into view, he saw that the place had aged dramatically and seemed to have grown smaller. Everything felt precarious, as if one good rainstorm would wash it away.

He parked at the main house and went directly inside, finding Eby at the front desk. She had her back to him, reaching for a cabin key on the wall of hooks. Curiously, she had dust on the back of her head and on the backside of her clothing, as if she'd been lying on a rug that hadn't been vacuumed in a while.

His throat thickened as he watched her. She'd always been a thin woman, but she seemed so fragile to him now, as reedy and brittle as dried grass. It had almost killed him to lose his foster mother four years ago. He didn't want to lose Eby too. He knew the end of Lost Lake didn't mean the end of Eby, but he was still going to miss her, miss knowing where to find her. He should have checked in more. He should have come out here before now. If he had, he would have seen how much repair work the place needed, and he would have fixed it. There's a point where anything can be saved. The trick is knowing when. And he had missed it.

But if this was what Eby had decided on, then it was the right decision. Eby didn't make bad choices. Everyone knew that. There wasn't a person in town who hadn't found him- or herself driving out to the lake because life had become too crowded or too noisy, their marriage was a wreck, or they hated their boss. And they always sought out Eby. They would sit in the dining room and have coffee and snack on something Lisette was experimenting with in the kitchen—lemon curd or yogurt sorbet or corn soup. It hadn't been unusual to see Eby walking the wooded trail around the lake with someone from town, heads together, deep in conversation. There was even a cabin at Lost Lake, number 2, where harried mothers would come to stay for a night of blissful silence, no questions asked. Eby had a reputation for fixing things. If people really wanted to change, she knew what to do. She would jump off a bridge after you if she thought she could help.

Somewhere along the way, though, they'd forgotten how much they'd needed her. They should have told her sooner. Wes should have told her sooner.

Key in hand, Eby turned and saw him standing there. "Wesley! Hello! I'm just . . . um, going through the cabins, doing inventory." She paused, looking at him curiously. "What are you doing here?"

"Lazlo wants my land too," Wes said quickly, just to get it all out. "I'll be investing in this development. It just happened, just today. And I wanted to tell you first. Lazlo's never had any interest in my land until now. And I haven't done anything yet. I'm waiting for your deal with him to go through first, just in case you decide not to sell."

Eby smiled at his outburst. "That's sweet of you, Wesley. But you don't have to wait. I'm not going to change my mind."

"Lazlo doesn't think you will."

Eby searched his face. "But you do?"

"I want you to do whatever makes you happy, Eby."

"And I want the same for you," she said, walking around the desk. She drew him into a fierce hug. He held her lightly, afraid he might break her. She pulled back and saw his hands were covered in dust from her clothes. "The cabins haven't been cleaned in a while," she said as she brushed his hands. "Now, are you sure you want to give up your family land?"

"Nothing but bad memories and a burned-out cabin there," he said, shaking his head. "I'll be glad to get rid of it."

"What about your good memories?" she said, putting her cool hand to his cheek.

"All my good memories are here." He looked away, embarrassed.

At that moment, the door opened and he stepped back to keep from getting hit by it. From behind the door, he watched Kate and her daughter enter in a blast of chatter, filling the air with the scent of shampoo and sunblock and raspberries and onions. Kate was carrying the large open cardboard box full of groceries from the Fresh Mart. He was surprised that he'd gotten here before them.

"Kate!" Eby said, surprised. "What are you doing? What is this?"

"Lisette asked me to pick up some groceries for her," Kate said, shifting the box in her arms. "We would have been here sooner, but we had to go back because Selma forgot to buy hand lotion."

"Lisette asked *you* to pick this up? I thought Jack had taken her. So she's been here the whole time? That imp! She's probably been tiptoeing around so I wouldn't hear her," Eby said, turning on her heel and striding to the dining room, where she was soon heard banging on the kitchen door, demanding that Lisette unlock it.

"Here, let me take that," Wes said, stepping out from the other side of the door. "It looks heavy."

Kate yelped and almost dropped the cardboard box. Wes reached out and grabbed it.

The little girl laughed. "He scared you!"

"Yes, yes, " Kate said, embarrassed. "Very funny."

"You should have seen your face!"

"I'll just take this to Lisette," Wes said.

"Thanks," Kate said, and he watched her brow knit, studying him. Now that he was closer, he could see that she was paler than he remembered, like she didn't spend a lot of time in the sun anymore. Some freckles he hadn't known were there were visible along her nose. She saw something familiar about him, but it didn't click. It was for the best. He turned away and heard her say to her daughter, "Scoot, you. Let's help Bulahdeen with her bottles."

They left, taking with them that chattering breeze, leaving the house in still silence. Eby had stopped knocking, and there was something in the air in those few moments before Lisette opened the door to the kitchen and Eby said, "You're not sixteen anymore." And Bulahdeen came in with several bottles of wine and said, "Wes! I haven't seen you in years! You need to come to our party!"

Something that had felt almost like hope.

⚹

"What is that *god-awful* noise?" Selma asked as the guests began to congregate on the lawn for dinner. Earlier, everyone had retreated to their cabins during the hottest part of the after-noon, but now they were emerging like nocturnal animals from their cool caves, their noses to the air, in search of suste-nance.

Kate, who was standing by Eby and shucking corn to be placed on the grill with the hot dogs, suddenly became aware of a steady pounding echoing over the water. She looked to the van that was still parked in front of the main house, a white van with HANDYMAN PIZZA written on the side and a logo of a smiling burly man wearing a tool belt and twirling pizza dough in the air.

Eby was either having some handyman work done or hav-ing a lot of pizza delivered.

"Wes decided to fix some warped boards on the dock while he was here," Eby explained. "He said some of them looked too dangerous to walk on. I told him he didn't have to. There's no need to spruce this place up, now that I'm selling." She said this regretfully, and Kate was beginning to wonder if Eby was truly on board with selling. Kate had looked for Eby earlier, thinking she would help Eby with the inventory that seemed to be weighing so heavily on her mind. But Eby had been nowhere to be found, almost like she was purposely avoiding it. And as gung ho as Bulahdeen was with this farewell party, Eby wasn't participating in the planning and was saying as little about it as possible.

"Maybe he's doing it for the party," Bulahdeen said from her seat at a picnic table. Devin was sitting beside her. Jack had quietly joined them and was showing Devin a coin trick. "I invited him."

"Did you?" Selma asked, walking by. "Maybe I'll come after all, now that men are going to be there. Do you dance, Jack?" She trailed her fingertips along his shoulders as she passed.

"No," he said, slipping out from under her hand.

Kate asked Eby, "Are you talking about the man who was in the house earlier today? The one in the yellow shirt?"

"Yes."

"He looked familiar," Kate said.

That made Eby laugh. "He should. The two of you were as thick as thieves that summer you were here."

That made Kate jerk her head around, her eyes going to the dock. "That's him?"

"You know, Wes asked me for your address after you and your family left. I think he missed you." Eby took the ear of corn out of Kate's hands. "Why don't you go ask him if he wants to stay for dinner."

Kate nodded and wiped her palms on the sides of her dress. Did that seem too eager? She walked across the lawn to the dock. He was about halfway down, on his knees, hammering nails into a new pale board. He hadn't fixed just some of the boards. He'd replaced nearly all of them.

A memory hit her suddenly. The last time she'd seen him was right here. They'd been sitting on the end of the dock with their feet in the water. Something had been changing between them, something that only the passage of time had made clear. From almost the very beginning, she'd known Wes had liked her, liked her in that way boys like girls. She hadn't really minded, as long as it hadn't interfered with their adventures. But slowly, as the days had passed, she'd begun to feel something like a summer fever coming over her, a sickness. It had emanated from somewhere near her trembling belly and had evaporated hotly from her skin whenever he was near. Sitting there on the dock that afternoon, Wes had shifted slightly and his bare leg had accidentally touched hers. It had taken her breath. *What is this?* she remembered thinking, almost panicked. *What has changed?* She'd tried to keep it from him, this affliction, because she'd wanted things to stay as they were. She'd been having so much fun. Completely oblivious, Wes had turned to her to ask a question, but then he'd stopped, looking at her curiously as she'd held her breath and stared at him, at the glints of red in his hair, at the scar above his right eyebrow, at his eyelashes, so light they were almost blond.

He'd known then. He'd seen the change, that this strange sickness had taken her too. And he'd looked so *relieved,* like the way he'd looked the first time he'd set eyes on her, reading on the dock. It was as if, finally, he could share all that he'd been keeping inside. Finally, someone understood.

His eyes had gone to her lips. *What does that mean,* she'd thought. *What is he going to do? Why has all the air left my lungs?*

He'd slowly leaned his head in toward hers.

And that's when her mother had called her from the lawn, startling them both and making them jump away from each other. Kate had gotten up and told him she'd be right back. She hadn't known at the time that her mother had packed all of their things and that they were leaving.

She'd never seen that boy again.

He was a big man now, broad shouldered and long limbed. She smiled, thinking of how fast he'd been growing that summer when they were twelve. He'd been gangly with arms and legs that seemed to stretch second by second, as if he were made of putty.

"Excuse me," Kate said as she approached. He didn't hear her. "Excuse me!" she said, louder. No response.

She stopped a few feet away from him.

"Wes!" she yelled.

He finally stopped and craned his neck around to look at her with blue eyes that were so achingly familiar, now that she felt something unknotting in her chest. It really was him. His hair was a russet shade, like an autumn leaf, and it was stuck to his forehead with sweat. His color was high, with vivid pink slashes of exertion on his cheeks. His presence was just so vital, so *centered*. She wasn't expecting that. She remembered him being the Sancho Panza to her Don Quixote that summer. He'd gone along with everything she'd wanted to do. He'd happily let her take the lead and stayed in her shadow.

He smiled when he saw her, then he put down his hammer. "Sorry, I didn't hear you."

He stared at her, brows raised, until she realized he was waiting for her to speak. "Oh," she finally said. "Eby wants to know if you'd like to join us for dinner."

"Sorry, I can't. Not tonight. I didn't know it had gotten so late." He lifted his face to the sky. The setting sun in the distance resembled a bright orange ember, as if a candle had just been blown out. "What time is it?"

Kate took her phone out of her pocket. She turned it on to see the time, and as soon as she did, she saw all the missed texts and voice mails from Cricket. There were dozens of them. She was going to have to call her back soon.

"It's almost eight," she said, returning the phone to her pocket.

"Thanks."

He started to turn, but she stopped him by suddenly thrusting out her hand and saying, "Hi, I'm Kate. You probably don't remember me."

He stood. His hand was large and calloused, folding around hers like wrapping paper. "I know who you are," he said, nicely but blandly. Milk and white rice. She knew that tone very well, that politeness ferociously guarding something else. Her mother-in-law was an expert at it. "I sent you a letter, years ago. Did you get it?"

"Eby just told me that you'd asked for my address. It never came." She paused. "Or, at least, I never received it. My mother might have hidden it from me."

He gave her a strange look. "Why would she do that?"

"She and Eby had some sort of argument that summer.

That's why we left so suddenly. I just found a postcard Eby wrote me years ago that my mother kept from me. When I get back home, I'll look for your letter. I wish I had known. I had a great time here with you."

"If you find it, just throw it away."

"Why?" Kate asked, surprised. "What did it say?"

He shook his head. "It's been a long time."

He had come into his own with a confidence and presence that he hadn't had before. But he'd lost something, too. She wasn't quite sure what it was. Maybe, like her, he'd changed too much, left too much behind.

"Mom!" Devin called, running toward them. Her cowboy boots clunked on the dock boards as she approached. Kate didn't have a quiet child. Devin could make noise in a room made of cotton. "Bulahdeen said to tell Wes that there's cocktails if he'll stay. Is that a bird?"

"Cocktails are grown-up drinks. Cockatiels are birds." Kate put her arm around Devin's shoulders. "Wes, this is my daughter, Devin. Devin, this is Wes. I met him the summer I came here when I was twelve. We were good friends."

"Wes," Devin asked breathlessly, her eyes wide, "have you ever seen any alligators here?"

He smiled. "No. Sorry."

"Devin is newly interested in alligators," Kate explained.

"When my brother was about your age, he was obsessed with alligators," Wes told Devin. "He even called himself Alligator Boy, and he wouldn't answer to anything else. He was determined to turn into an alligator when he grew up. He had it all planned out. One day he would wake up with a tail. The next day his alligator teeth would come in. This would go on for days until he was finally a whole alligator and no one, especially our father, would recognize him."

Alligator Boy. Kate had almost forgotten about him. He had tagged along wherever they went but rarely said anything. It had been easy to forget he was even there. "Billy," she said, suddenly remembering. "His name was Billy."

"Yes. And you were the one who made up the story about him turning into an alligator," Wes said. "He loved that."

"Did he really turn into an alligator?" Devin asked, her voice quiet with awe.

"No. He passed away a long time ago in a house fire. But he wanted it so much that, if he had lived, I bet he would have."

"I'm sorry, Wes," Kate said, and put her hands in her pockets awkwardly. She felt her phone—and the scratch of something sharp against her knuckles. She took out the small curved bone she'd found on the stoop.

"What is that?" Devin asked.

"I found it this morning. I didn't recognize it at first, but it looks like an animal tooth, like the kind Billy collected in a big box. Do you remember that?" she asked Wes. "He used to carry that box around wherever he went."

"He called it the Alligator Box," Wes said, staring at the tooth in her hand. "It was lost in the fire."

"Is it an alligator tooth?" Devin asked Kate.

Kate shook her head. "Probably not."

"I bet it is!"

"Would you like it?" Kate said, offering it to her daughter. Devin looked excited and was about to take it, but Kate saw the moment it clicked that this nice man had a brother who collected things like this. A brother who was now gone. She stepped back and said, "No, I think Wes should have it."

Devin was one great kid. Matt had rarely seen it, but Kate always had. She wasn't going to fall asleep again and miss another year. She was going to be here for every moment. For the first time since waking up, she knew that clearly, without fear. She smiled at Devin while extending her hand to Wes.

"That means a lot to me," he said sincerely. "Thank you."

Suddenly, something knocked hard against the dock below. Tiny ripples fanned out on all sides of the water around them, like petals. They all looked down, as if waiting for something to appear, but the ripples gradually died away, leaving the water once again calm and inscrutable.

"It's been doing that all afternoon," Wes said with a laugh, when he saw that Kate was standing perfectly still, her arms out slightly, as if the entire dock was going to collapse under her feet. "There must be a floating tree trunk stuck under there, knocking against the support columns."

"Can we dive down there and see?" Devin asked.

"No. Go tell the others that Wes can't stay," Kate said. "I'll be there in a minute."

Devin ran back to the lawn, calling, "Bye, Wes!"

He waved, and they both watched her go.

"Is your husband here with you?" Wes asked as he turned to place his tools back in his toolbox. He clicked it shut and picked it up with one hand, still holding the tooth in the other.

"No. He passed away last year." Kate turned and walked back up the dock, still not entirely convinced it wasn't going to collapse.

Wes fell into step beside her. "Now it's my turn to be sorry."

They walked in a familiar silence. There was a muscle memory there, forged by repetition fifteen years ago. It felt nice to be this comfortable around a person again. Kate used to make friends so easily as a child, like everyone was made of magnets, instantly drawn to one another. As she got older, it seemed like those magnets turned and forced everyone away from a specific area around her.

They stopped on the lawn. Wes put the tooth in his pocket and shifted his toolbox from one hand to the other. "How long are you staying?"

"I don't know," she said. "I just wanted Devin to see this place. I have such good memories here. I wanted her to have them, too."

"Maybe I'll see you again, before you leave."

"I'll say good-bye this time, I promise."

Wes nodded. She wondered if he was thinking about that almost-kiss, or if he even remembered. Was she just projecting old feelings onto him, like a movie on a wall? The boy who had given her that last best summer was now this handsome unfamiliar man. And yet, she *knew him*. She knew him in that way you can only know a person you remember as a child, like if you cracked away the adult shell, you'd find that child happily sitting inside, smiling at you.

Without another word, he waved to everyone on the lawn, then walked to his van.

"Kate, will you get the butter from the kitchen?" Eby called. "I forgot to bring it out."

Kate turned and went into the house. She tapped on the kitchen door, then entered and saw that the kitchen was closed down for the night. She glanced at the old chair beside the refrigerator as she opened the door and took out the tub of butter. When she closed the door, she paused because the chair was now leaning back against the wall on two legs.

Hadn't it been on all four just seconds ago?

Puzzled, she left by the back entrance so she could take the cardboard box from the Fresh Mart, which Lisette had left by the door, to the garbage bins. After recycling the box she turned the corner, but then stopped short.

Wes was at the back of his van, out of view from the people on the lawn. The back doors of the van were open, and he had put his tools inside, alongside a pile of the old dock boards he was obviously going to haul away. He had taken off the yellow long-sleeved T-shirt he'd been wearing, which was wet with sweat, and was in the process of putting on a black long-sleeved T with the Handyman Pizza logo on it. An angry river of scars covered his back and arms, the skin shiny and rippled from what looked like an old severe burn.

She quickly stepped back behind the house before he could see her.

She leaned against the wall for a moment. Behind her fond memory of him that summer fifteen years ago, she was now also starting to remember bruises, and how Eby gave him and his brother boxes of food to take home with them, but how reluctant they were to go in the evenings. She pushed herself away from the wall and walked back around the other side of the house.

Eby was still by the grill, putting the hot dogs on a plate.

Kate stopped beside her and said, "Wes mentioned something about a fire and how his little brother died. What happened?"

Eby's brows rose. "I'm surprised he told you. He never talks about his brother." They watched as Wes's van pulled out and disappeared down the driveway. He honked twice in good-bye.

Kate waited for Eby to say more.

"It was the summer your family came here to visit, a few months after you left," she said. "Wes's father owned the property next to Lost Lake, and he and Wes and Billy lived there, on basically nothing. Their home life wasn't good. George and I tried to help out as much as we could. That father of theirs was a hateful man. The fire burned their cabin completely. Wes was the only one to get out alive. He's been through a lot, but he turned into a remarkable young man. I'm very proud of him."

"I can see that." Kate smiled, looking to where he'd just driven away.

But she understood now—the change in him. The change in them both.

Neither one of them was the same after that summer.

After Devin had gone to sleep that evening, Kate took her phone and walked outside. She couldn't put this off any longer. She had to call her mother-in-law. Kate hadn't answered any of her calls or texts since they'd arrived yesterday.

She walked down the steps of the stoop. The lights were out in Bulahdeen's cabin. Jack's cabin was also dark. But Selma was apparently still awake. As Kate walked past, she heard music coming from inside, something jazzy and seductive. Billie Holiday maybe. She picked up her pace, disturbing the low-lying fog in puffs and swirls. She hadn't bothered to put on shoes. Lost Lake had a different feel to it this deep into the night. There was more mystery, and it was easier to believe in things you couldn't see. She and Wes had spent a lot of time out here in the dark.

She walked down to the dock where, just hours earlier, she'd come face-to-face again with the person responsible for her best memories here. She smiled as she looked out over the lake. The fog was moving and curling over the water, creating shapes. It made her think of the story of the ghost ladies she had made up. Ursula, Magdalene, and Betty—those had been their names. Remembering that made her look behind her, as if expecting Wes to be there.

Muscle memory again. She shook her head, then turned on her phone. There had been two more texts since she'd last checked a few hours ago. Another from Cricket and one from Kent Harwood. Kent and his husband, Sterling, bought Pheris Wheels from Kate after Matt died. They had been two of Matt's best customers. Kent's text read:

We saw the commercial today! It was nice to see Matt. And you and Devin look great. Come by and see us sometime!

She had no idea what that meant. She'd call Kent later. Right now, she needed to get this over with.

In two rings, Cricket picked up and said, "It's about time, Kate! I cannot tell you the trouble you've caused me. Are you on your way back, or do I have to come get you?"

She'd been anticipating worry. Cricket's anger caught her off guard. "Trouble?" Kate asked. "What are you talking about?"

"I had a film crew waiting for you when you were supposed to move in! Didn't you read my note?"

"No, I didn't read your note," Kate said, frowning. "Why would a film crew be there?"

"Because we're filming new Pheris Realty commercials. The first one aired today."

Kate went silent. She lowered herself to sit on one of the squared-off pylons.

"That was part of what I wanted to talk to you about. I told you I had big plans to discuss with you later, and you *leave?* Who does that?"

Who does that? Kate thought. Someone who doesn't want to be a part of Cricket's big plans, that's who does that.

"I've finally decided to throw my hat into the ring. I'm running for Congress. My team decided a few months ago that a series of new real estate commercials would be the perfect way to reintroduce me to the public, only this time with you and Devin "Moving On" with me. I received a lot of condolences after Matt died from people who were fans of the old commercials. They wanted to know what happened to him. What his life turned out like. This will show them. It will be a nice tribute to him. It will make a lot of people remember him—and me." Silence. "Kate?"

It still amazed Kate that when Cricket did talk of Matt, she did it so plainly. Her grief wasn't fresh. Cricket had mourned Matt a long time ago, when she'd lost him to Kate. It was the reason why, a few months after his death, Cricket had been so matter-of-fact about getting rid of all of Matt's clothes. Kate had let her; at one point she'd even tried to help, stopping sometimes to tell Cricket a story behind a shirt or a pair of shoes. Cricket hadn't liked that and had told Kate that she could handle this on her own. Kate had seen it then, just briefly, Cricket's jealously that Kate knew more about her son's life than she did. Kate had saved only one item of Matt's clothing from Cricket's purge, that T-shirt with the moth on it, hidden in a sewing bag somewhere among her things back in Atlanta.

"That's what this past year has been about? Getting you ready to run for Congress?" Kate finally said. She couldn't fully wrap her mind around it. She'd always known Cricket was unreadable, but she never imagined that *this* was what she'd been hiding.

"Of course not. It's been about getting you and Devin through this difficult time," Cricket said, sounding just like she did in her commercials.

"But you've known about this for months? Why didn't you say anything? I've gone along with *everything* you wanted me to do for the past year, Cricket. Why did you still feel the need to blindside me with this?"

Cricket made a sound of disbelief. "Selling your house for, frankly, more than it was worth, putting your daughter in private school, letting you move in with me, giving you a job—these are things you just *went along with*?"

"I didn't want any of it," Kate said loudly, and the ghost ladies on the lake seemed to turn to her. "And I don't want to be a part of this either, Cricket. Matt wouldn't think of new commercials as a nice tribute to him. He would hate them. He would never want Devin to be in them. Did you give any thought to that?"

"Do you really want to go there, Kate?" She said it so easily, like she'd been practicing taking this sword out of its sheath in one long smooth movement. "You and I both know that what's best for your daughter has not always been your primary concern."

And there it was, the thing Kate had feared most. Cricket brought up the incident with the scissors. Kate had been waiting for this for a while. And now that it was out in the open, now that it had been acknowledged, it felt so far away, like something she'd done a lifetime ago. Why had she been so afraid of this? Why had she been so afraid to acknowledge her grief? Just because Cricket had bottled it inside, waiting to air it on TV, didn't mean Kate had to.

"I can't believe I was starting to feel guilty about not calling you, because I thought you might be genuinely worried about us."

"Well, Kate, of course I was," Cricket said, trying to make her voice go soft.

116

"My great-aunt is selling Lost Lake, and she needs my help sorting everything out this summer. I'll let you know when Devin and I will be returning. I'll call you in a few weeks."

Kate hung up the phone. Cricket immediately called her back. She ignored the call and connected to the Internet and searched for this new Pheris Realty commercial. She found it easily.

It was thirty seconds of Cricket talking about her real estate company, with flashbacks to the old commercials featuring Matt. Kate had forgotten just how lost he'd looked back then. It made her want to save him all over again. At the end of the commercial, Cricket was standing outside Kate's mother's house, beside her real estate sign with the SOLD placard on top of it. "After my son died in a tragic accident last year, my daughter-in-law and granddaughter needed me to sell their home and help them on their new journey in life, which I did." She held up a framed photo of Kate and Devin, one she'd obviously taken from Kate's album. Kate was smiling, holding Devin, with the sun behind them. Matt had taken that photo a year and a half ago, at a bike race their shop had sponsored. "Pheris Reality—" Cricket said as the commercial closed, "we still know about moving on." Then there were the words *To be continued*.

Kate put her hand over her eyes and let out a sob. For a few moments, her chest heaved and tears ran out from under her fingers. Why she'd fallen in love with Matt, how much she had tried to help him, how much she had wanted to make him happy—it all came rushing back to her. The reason she'd worked so hard and committed so much to a life she didn't even want was because of that boy on TV. She'd wanted him to finally have that place where he belonged. And she found herself crying as much for herself as for him, because she knew—knew with all her heart—that as much as she had loved Matt and had wanted the world for him, he had never truly felt the same way about her. She had spent seven years married to a man who hadn't cared for her nearly as much as she'd cared for him. And she'd begun to resent it.

The phone started ringing again. Cricket. Kate was so angry and full of grief at that moment that, without thinking, she hauled back and threw the ringing phone into the lake, where it landed somewhere near the ghost ladies with a soft *plop*.

She stood there, stunned. She couldn't believe she just did that.

She ran her hands through her hair, pushing it out of her eyes. They were going to have to go back to Atlanta. She knew that. That was their home. And she was going to have to face Cricket. But she was not going to be in any commercials. She was not going to support Cricket's burgeoning political career. Cricket had spent so much time behind the scenes in politics that it had never occurred to Kate that she would ever step in front of the camera, though it made perfect sense. Kate didn't know why she was so surprised. She had money, looked great on TV, came across as sympathetic but had firm opinions, and she had hair that didn't move. She had wanted Matt to go into politics, but now that he was gone, Kate figured Cricket had decided she was just going to have to do it herself. Matt had told Kate once that Cricket had made him run for class president and major in political science because she'd been prepping him for something big. He'd said it in an *I showed her, didn't I?* kind of way, something that al-ways made Kate think that his life with her was just a way of getting back at his mother.

But Kate was tired of sacrificing her happiness for someone else's dreams. She'd done it for her mother when she was a teenager, and she'd done it for Matt. She'd done it all willingly, but never again. For the past year, she'd been scared that she couldn't actually live her own life, that she was someone who was inherently incapable of it. She was scared of being a bad parent. Scared of being alone. Scared to *grieve*. Not anymore.

This, she thought, was where her real life was going to start. She didn't know where it was going, but it was going to *start* here, where she used to know herself so well, where no one else's rules made sense but her own.

She looked at the water and sighed.

Apparently, her new life was going to start without a phone.

7

The next morning, Devin woke up early. She didn't know where she was, and she sat up quickly. But then it came to her. The cabin. Lost Lake. Her eyes went slowly around the room. It reminded her of a hut, the kind a banished princess would live in, hiding from a wicked witch. She liked the thought of being banished. That way, she'd never have to go back. The bed was old and white, with a scene from the lake painted on it. The dresser was fat and round and had glass knobs that looked like cloudy diamonds. The wallpaper was peeling, and she got a splinter in her foot from the uneven floorboards last night, but all in all she couldn't have dreamed of any place better.

Her dad wouldn't have liked it here. But her dad wouldn't have liked moving into Grandma Cricket's, either. Her dad had only really liked his bike shop, and Devin didn't like it there. She missed him, but not the way her mom seemed to miss him. She wondered if her mom missed him because she didn't remember him. Devin remembered him very clearly.

She would test herself every once in a while and, yes, she could still recall everything about him, right down to the way he smelled, a sharp combination of soap, summer sweat, and tire rubber. She had a fanny pack that had belonged to him, and inside she kept a photo of him and a Paracord bracelet he used to wear all the time, which she'd sneaked out of her parents' room the day Grandma Cricket decided to clear all of her dad's clothes out of the house. She kept it around in case she ever needed it, in case she started forgetting.

Everything was quiet. Her mom obviously wasn't up yet. She threw the covers off and walked to the window in her bedroom. She pulled and straightened her Wonder Woman T-shirt and her pajama shorts with the strawberry pattern on them, which had gotten uncomfortably twisted in her sleep. She stopped at the window and looked out, yawning. Bright mist from the lake was threading through the spaces between the cabins and lying low over the lawn in front of the main house.

A tang of barbecue charcoal was in the air, left over from where they'd cooked on the grills last night, and it made her hungry. She turned to go to the kitchen, to see if food had magically appeared like it had when she'd woken up yesterday. She'd liked those fruit tarts, which she'd never had for breakfast before.

But something caught her eye outside the window, and she stopped.

There, walking down the path toward the lawn, was an *alligator*.

It was huge and green-black and walked in a slow, swishing motion. Its wide, stiff tail left a trail in the dew. It was the most beautiful thing she thought she'd ever seen. She watched it walk all the way to the lawn, then it stopped. Minutes, hours, days passed. What was it doing?

It slowly turned its long bumpy head, teeth baring slightly, and looked back at her.

Follow me.

She sucked in her breath. It turned and ambled left, toward the lake, then out of sight.

Devin ran out of her room and into her mother's. "Mom!"

Kate's head was covered with a pillow. "Hmm?"

"Mom!"

When her mother didn't answer, Devin couldn't wait. She ran out of the bedroom, then out of the cabin, leaving the door wide open. She darted barefoot down the path, exhilarated. She turned when she got to the lawn and ran down to the lake. Her feet pounded on the new boards Wes had laid down as she ran all the way to the end of the dock. Her breathing was heavy, and it sounded loud over the water. She looked around, turning in circles, trying to find it. The lake had no beach; the water simply butted up against the ground, forming a muddy ledge.

Where was it?

She pushed her tangled hair out of her face, and that's when she realized she'd been in such a hurry that she hadn't put on her glasses. She used to wear an eye patch, back when she was little. She'd loved it. As she grew older, she got to wear it less and less as her lazy eye improved, until finally the doctor said she didn't need it anymore. He was wrong. Sometimes she still put it on when her mother wasn't looking. She was convinced she saw things better with her lazy eye, better than other people. If she put her hand over her good eye, she could find the back of an earring lost in the rug. She could find where Grandma Cricket hid her secret stash of M&M's in her office, and the T-shirt that had belonged to her dad that her mom still kept hidden.

She put her hand over her right eye and slowly looked around. It only took moments, and there it was. The alligator had swum out to the middle of the lake, and all that could be seen was the top of its head and its tiny black pebble eyes. It was so still, the water didn't even move.

"Hi," she said, going to her knees.

It immediately submerged itself.

"No!" she called. "I won't hurt you!"

She wanted to scream in frustration. She didn't know what to do, short of jumping in, which she knew she shouldn't do. She wiggled on her stomach to the edge of the dock, then she put her fingers in the lake. She moved them back and forth, waving a greeting in the water. She smiled when she felt its rough skin glide under her fingers, like a cat arching to be petted.

The alligator's eyes appeared above the water again, several feet away.

It said something to her, and she blinked in surprise.

"What box?" she said. "I don't see a box."

The alligator disappeared under the water, resurfacing even closer to the dock.

The Alligator Box, it said.

It disappeared again. Minutes passed and Devin finally sat up. Her head felt swimmy from dangling it over the dock. Suddenly there was a tremendous splash and the alligator seemed to jump right out of the water. Midair, its body arched as if in a spasm, flinging its head in the direction of the dock. Devin heard a small clacking sound as she was sprayed with water. The alligator fell back into the lake with a great splash.

Devin looked down and saw that it had tossed her what looked to be a wet knobby root the size of a large ice cream cone. She picked it up. She'd rather have had a tooth, like the one her mom found and gave to Wes, but she'd take what she could get. After all, how many people got gifts from alligators?

"Devin!" her mother called. Devin turned. Uh-oh. She knew that tone of voice.

"I'm here," Devin called back. "I'm fine."

Kate slid on the wet grass as she crossed the lawn. Her short dark hair was sticking up in spikes from sleep. It made her look like an elf. Devin remembered when her mother cut it. It took a long time to get used to it, waking up in the mornings and not recognizing her. First her father died, then her mother changed her appearance so drastically. Then Grandma Cricket came into their lives, and Devin had to go to a new school, and they had to sell their house and move in with Grandma Cricket. It was strange, when she thought about it. Her dad was at peace, but no one else was. For almost a year, her mom had floated around, not really present, not happy, not anything. Devin had hated it.

But now, Devin could see her start to change. It was hard to trust at first, but her mom was happier here. Devin was happier here. And what a strange set of circumstances it was that brought them to this place. It almost scared her, how much could have gone wrong. What if they hadn't seen the alligator on the road? What if Devin hadn't found the postcard? She'd been playing in that trunk of clothes almost all her life, and she'd never noticed that corner of paper, tucked almost completely into the lining.

They were *meant* to be here.

"What are you doing out here so early?" Kate asked when she reached Devin. She knelt in front of her. "How did you get so wet? And look at you—you're barefoot."

Devin leaned forward and said softly into her mother's ear, "I saw the alligator."

Kate smiled and ran her hands up and down Devin's arms, as if to warm her. "Sweetheart, there aren't alligators here."

"Yes, there are!" Devin insisted. She held out the root as proof. "It gave me this. I'm not sure what it means yet."

"I see. That was nice of him." Kate met Devin's eyes. "Okay, make me a real Devin Promise. You will not leave the cabin alone like this again." Devin Promises were what Devin and her mother had agreed were the most serious promises to make. You made them, you kept them.

Devin sighed. "I promise. But I *tried* to get you up first."

Kate stood and took Devin's hand. "I know you did. The trick is to wait for me. Then we both go."

"Okay," Devin said, looking over her shoulder as they walked away.

The alligator watched her go, then dipped under the water and vanished.

That afternoon, Eby was gazing at the ceiling in cabin number 9. There was a water stain here that looked like a bicycle wheel. It had been here for years, growing progressively larger. It had appeared the year George died. Back then it had looked like a tiny black beetle, and she used to come to this cabin and stare at it, sometimes swearing it would move, that it would run around the ceiling and spell out words like *hope* and *love* and *real*. But then she would blink and the words would go away. The stain was in the corner of the room, and its moisture had caused the coral wallpaper to peel away from the top. She'd always meant to fix that tiny leak, but then she'd thought, *What if the ceiling wanted to tell me something else?* So she'd left it.

This cabin also had a truly magnificent sleigh bed, antique and handcrafted. The camp was scattered with antiques from Eby and George's halcyon days, hidden like secret treasure among the cheaper stuff. The vanity next to the yard-sale dresser was one George had bought on their honeymoon, an antique with inlay, the mirror slightly smoky, as if it would magically show you the most beautiful version of yourself if you asked. But she'd never asked. Her sister Marilee had been the beautiful one in their family. Even so, George, who had risen to the top of Atlanta's eligible bachelors when he'd unexpectedly inherited his estranged grandfather's money, had chosen Eby over her. Oh, Marilee had tried to win him. But she would have had to overcome a lifetime of teasing him in school about his red hair and bad teeth. Eby had always been kind to him, in love with him most of her life because he drew the most beautiful things with pencil and paper during classes. He was a dreamer, like her. And he'd wanted to marry her when he'd inherited his money, much to everyone's surprise. He could have had his pick of beautiful belles. He could have had Marilee, before she'd fallen in love with Talbert, the gas station attendant. But he'd loved only Eby.

You didn't need a mirror to tell you that you were beautiful when you had proof like that.

There was a knock on the door, then she heard Kate call, "Eby?"

Startled, Eby sat up on the dusty bed. She thought she could come here in secret. She thought Kate would be like everyone else and fall under the siesta spell that summer afternoons at Lost Lake were famous for casting.

After an initial panic, she decided not to bother getting off the bed. She'd been caught. There was no use trying to hide it. "I'm in here," Eby said.

Kate walked in. She was wearing cutoff shorts and a quirky gray T-shirt printed with a giant bicycle that looked like it was parked on top of a tiny old-fashioned circus. The two large Ferris wheels from the circus below magically rose up and morphed into the bicycle wheels. PHERIS WHEELS, ATLANTA, GEORGIA was written underneath it.

Eby found herself studying Kate. She had a face that people liked to look at, just to figure it out. Pretty, yes, but not symmetrical, her eyes a little too wide, her nose a little too long. She was thin, but a thin that could only go so small, stopped by good muscle and big bones. All the women in their family had sturdy frames. They weren't made to break, but most of them did anyway, blown down by that perfect storm called love.

"I saw that the number nine key was missing off the key wall, so I figured you were here," Kate said. "I was just wondering about the inventory you said you wanted to do. I want to help all I can before we leave."

"Thank you," Eby said. She patted the dusty bed, and Kate crawled up and sat beside her.

"What are you doing in here?" Kate asked as she looked around the room.

"Thinking, mostly."

"About what?"

"Lots of things. Today I was thinking about George. When we first bought the camp, we spent a year doing repairs. Then, when we were ready to open, George drove far and wide in every direction, leaving brochures anyplace a store owner would let him. The brochures had a photo of us on the front. Our first guests were unconventional—free spirits and hippies. We seemed to attract oddballs, and we didn't know why. Don't get me wrong. We loved it. But I'll never forget the first summer Bulahdeen and her husband arrived. She said they chose Lost Lake because of the brochure. She said that she took one look at the photo of me and George and thought, *I'm a misfit like them, so maybe I could be happy there, too.*"

That made Kate laugh. "She was right. Misfits need a place to get away, too. All that trying to fit in is exhausting."

Eby looked over at her great-niece. Her smile changed her entire face, widening her lips and crinkling her eyes. What was she doing here, hiding out with a bunch of old people? She should be moving on, living her life the way it was meant to be lived. She'd gotten through the hard part. Happiness now was inevitable, if she just let it happen. "You said you were in the middle of moving. Aren't you in a hurry to go back to your new place?" Eby asked.

Kate's smile faded. "It's complicated."

Eby waited.

Kate folded her legs in front of her and picked at the strings of her cutoffs. "I was paralyzed, living in the house I'd shared with Matt. So my mother-in-law helped me sell it. I actually made a lot of money. But, instead of finding another house to live in, like any normal person would, I decided to move in with my mother-in-law. I let her take over, and it wasn't the right decision. I realize that now. I need to clear the air." She took a deep breath and turned to Eby. "So, yes, I have to go back. But, no, I'm not in a hurry. I'm here for you. I can stay all summer, if you need me to. I don't think Devin would object."

Eby smiled. "You can stay as long as you like."

"Devin said she saw an alligator this morning. I found her on the dock, damp with lake water, holding an ugly root she said the alligator gave her. If he's giving her gifts now, I'm never going to get her to leave."

Eby wedged a pillow behind her and sat back. "You used to give your mother fits here at the lake, too. Disappearing all day, coming back smelling of lake water, bugs in your clothes. Sometimes you and Wes would have a frog with you. A couple of times you even captured scorpions in a jar. Your mother used to make you sleep with a shower cap full of baby powder on your hair to get the lake smell out."

Kate laughed. "I'd forgotten about that."

Eby hesitated before asking her next question. She was better off not knowing, because there was nothing she could do. But leaving Kate's mother when she was a little girl was one of the hardest things Eby had ever done. "How was Quinn? I mean, was her life good?"

"She was happy when my dad was alive," Kate said. "After he was gone, she hated to be alone. When I was in high school, I stayed home most nights so she wouldn't get so anxious. She was pretty much my best friend back then. Then I met Matt in college, and we moved in with her when I got pregnant. She liked having Devin around. I think that was the happiest she'd been since Dad died."

"The house you sold, was it the pink brick house on Dora Cove Road?"

Kate looked surprised. "That's the one. Mom's house. I didn't know you'd ever visited."

"I didn't," Eby said. "George and I bought that house for your grandmother when her husband died. Your mother was only about three at the time."

"*You* bought the house?"

Eby nodded. "Just before we left Atlanta. We bought my sister the house and a car. Gave her some money. Set up a small trust for Quinn. Then we gave the rest of the money away to charity and moved to Lost Lake."

Kate sat back against one of the pillows, and a puff of dust rose up around them and sparkled in the air. "Why did you give the money away? Mom would never explain it to me."

Eby shrugged. "I doubt she truly understood. No one did. Our family has a history of wanting money. Wanting it, never having it, never able to keep it. George grew up without money, and he'd been happy without it. When we got back from our honeymoon, everything just fell apart. My mother and sister wanted so much. Expected so much. And nothing was ever enough. George and I realized we didn't need the money, and my family wouldn't leave us alone as long as we had it. So we gave it away. And they never forgave me."

"But Mom must have," Kate said. "She must have wanted to bury the hatchet, by coming here that summer after George died."

Eby hesitated. "I don't want to speak badly of your mother," she said, looking at Kate kindly. "I know she had a hard time growing up in the shadow of her mother's grief. And I know she must have loved you. I could tell the first time I met you that you'd had a childhood full of love. She let you express yourself. Like you do with Devin."

"It's okay," Kate said. "I want to know."

"Quinn grew up with a very negative impression of me. I think she wanted the satisfaction of seeing me grieve the way her mother grieved." Eby waited for Kate to interrupt her, to protest, but she didn't. "I was devastated when George died, but I had Lisette and the lake guests and the town, and they didn't let me go to that place, that dark place. I had a support system, which is what the women in our family sorely lack after they fall in love. They get married and want nothing but that one person. But relying on one person for your every need is so dangerous. One set of hands isn't enough to keep you from falling. Quinn didn't like that I wasn't going to sell the lake and have extra money to share with her. She didn't like that I was going to be okay. She didn't expect that. It was just one more thing for her to resent."

Kate took a moment to process that. "I can't believe my dad let her come here to do that."

"I don't think he knew. When he figured it out, he made you and Quinn leave with him."

Eby was surprised how easily Kate accepted what Eby had told her. But it all made sense when Kate said, "She was never the same after he died." Quinn was as high-strung as her mother had been. And Quinn had obviously been as torn up after her own husband died. Kate had seen it, and Eby was sorry that she had.

"It's the Morris curse."

"It almost happened to me—when Matt died," Kate said quietly, looking up at the ceiling. Eby wondered if it was telling her anything.

"But it didn't," Eby said. "If we measured life in the things that almost happened, we wouldn't get anywhere."

They stayed there, side by side, for a while. Eby decided, once she sold Lost Lake, that she would stay in touch with Kate. This felt good, to finally be able to be in a room with her family and feel nothing but camaraderie, where conversation and moral support were the only things asked for and given freely. It took fifty years for this to finally happen.

Kate stood and dusted herself off. She put her hands in her pockets and considered Eby for a moment. "It's not official, is it? You haven't signed over Lost Lake yet?"

"Not yet."

"So it's still a thing that almost happened."

Eby smiled to herself. She caught on quickly. "For now."

"So no inventory yet."

"Not *physical* inventory, at least. Now, *mental* inventory; I'm doing a lot of that."

"What are you going to do," Kate asked, "when you sell?"

"Travel," Eby said. "George and I always wanted to go back to Europe."

"What about after?"

"After what?"

"After you travel, where will you come back to?"

Eby laughed. "I haven't thought that far ahead."

Kate's brow lowered. She looked like she was going to say something, then thought better of it. "I'll leave you to it." She turned to go, then stopped. "Thank you, Eby."

"For what?"

"For being a misfit." She smiled. "You give the rest of us hope."

Amsterdam, The Netherlands
Winter 1963

*I*t *was one of* the coldest winters on record, and the snow fell
in sheets. It thrilled Eby to no end. She'd seen very few snow-
falls in her life. It was so cold the canals froze solid, and she
and George would skate on their shoes for hours, finding
cubbyhole restaurants along the way to fortify themselves
with alcohol and stew. The girl from the bridge in Paris,
whose name they discovered was Lisette, followed them most
days, but she tired of the cold. It didn't amaze her as much as
it did Eby. George had written to Lisette's family in Paris the
moment they realized Lisette had followed them to Amsterdam. Lisette wouldn't tell them how old she was, but she
couldn't be more than sixteen. Her family was bound to be
worried. Lisette's father wrote back to George in French,
which the man at the desk in the hotel translated for them.
Her father said Lisette was moody and stubborn and would

not come home until she was ready. Maybe, her father said, this would make her grow up.

Eby was secretly glad for Lisette's presence. Eby liked to think she understood the girl better than anyone. She understood her frustration. She understood that the hardest times in life to go through were when you were transitioning from one version of yourself to another. And Lisette was doing just that. Eby had managed to glean that Lisette's parents had sent her to a school for the deaf when she was young, but Lisette had run away from it. Her world was not quiet, and she could not live among those for whom it was. She'd never learned sign language, so her only source of communication was through notes. Her pockets were full of crumpled pieces of paper. Every night she would stand on the balcony of her room and light a match to each note, letting it fall in the snow to the frozen street below. She started losing weight, only eating what she herself was allowed to cook. And never, ever, would she eat an evening meal. It was, Eby discovered, because Lisette had broken her dead lover's heart over dinner, and now the thought of it literally made her nauseated.

There were hints, though, that Lisette was improving. It became routine for Lisette to walk along the sidewalk as Eby and George skated on the canals. She watched them closely, clapping her chapped hands loudly to warn them if Eby and George were getting too close to careless children on sleds.

That particular day, as Eby and George skated, they broke out into an impromptu dance. George let Eby step away from him, holding her hand as she executed a twirl that went so well and felt so good that she immediately twirled again. She kept twirling, so fast that George lost hold of her and she spun like a whirling dervish down the canal, George racing after her. He finally caught her by the waist and ending up twirling along with her, caught in her tornado. They finally lost momentum and George fell onto his backside, taking Eby with him, her legs straight in the air. Eby rolled over and looked at George. The moment their eyes met, they started laughing. It took them a few tries to get up. Several strangers got involved, Amsterdam natives in beige shoes and beige pants, with brightly colored scarves around their necks. Finally, they made it up, like support walls being hoisted in a barn raising, and everyone cheered. Eby turned to see Lisette doubled over, laughing so hard her body was heaving. No sound came out, but there was such joy and such release. By the time Eby and George made it off the canal and walked over to her, Lisette was on her knees, tears frozen to her skin. When she finally looked up at Eby, she was exhausted but purged. She looked like she felt something other than guilt for the first time in months.

That was the moment Eby knew that Lisette was going to be all right. Lisette had been following them because she was looking to Eby as an example of what true happiness was. She was trying to learn from her all that she'd never been taught. It was a remarkable realization to Eby, that we are what we're taught. That was why Morris women were what they were. It was because they knew no different. Eby had forged new ground, and it made her feel powerful and useful. It fed her lifelong need to make things right. There was a certain hubris to it, though. And she would soon learn her lesson. Lisette was changing because she wanted to. When it came to Eby's family, no amount of love and no amount of money would change people who didn't want to change.

They made their way back to their hotel, cinnamon cheeked and watery eyed. Later, Eby and George were going back out for dinner. Getting lost in Amsterdam during a snowstorm was exciting because of its danger. Buildings began to all look the same, snowbanks hiding storefronts and sometimes entire streets. She and George had once had to find refuge in a strange family's home overnight. The family didn't speak English, and she and George didn't speak Dutch. They'd played games with the children and slept on the kitchen floor. It had been wonderful. But Lisette had been beside herself when they'd finally showed up at the hotel the next morning.

That afternoon, Lisette went up the stairs to her room while Eby and George stopped at the front desk for their mail. They'd spent enough time in Amsterdam that their Paris letters were catching up with them, and it was always Eby's least favorite time of the day. Eby took the letters to the small round sofa in the lobby, while George, as he did every night, asked for food to be delivered to Lisette's room, even though she never ate it. When she got hungry enough, Lisette would sneak into the manager's kitchen early in the morning and stealthily make something, leaving sugar-crusted palmiers and cracked bread for the employees to find later, convinced the feast was made by elves.

A letter from Eby's sister, Marilee, was on the top of the stack. Resignedly, Eby opened it.

> Eby,
> Surely you've heard by now. Mama said she wrote. *Everyone* has written. It's been two weeks since Talbert died. *Where are you?* Why are you being so selfish?

Mama has tried to call, but that stupid hotel where
you're staying acts like they have no idea who you are.
Now you're forcing me to write to you, when I can
barely even hold a pen. What do you want me to do,
beg? I need you, Eby. My husband is dead and I don't
know what to do. Quinn won't stop crying. She
doesn't understand why her aunt Eby isn't here when
everything is falling apart. You need to be here. Talbert
died in *your* house. This is your fault. Come home and
make it right.

Marliee

Eby let the letter drop to her lap, suddenly numb to the
bone. Talbert, dead? It couldn't be. He'd been so young and full
of life. Eby remembered him at her and George's wedding, the
way he'd made her sister smile, the way he'd taken her to the
dance floor and held her close, making Marilee forget her jeal-
ousy. He'd known how to navigate her vain and troubled
moods. Marilee had always been high-strung. Talbert had been
good for her. His love for her had been a balm on the wound of
their mother's disappointment that she didn't marry better.

Eby looked at the other letters, all forwarded at the same
time from Paris. They glowed greenly, as if lit within, all
bearing the same bad news. She wanted to slap them off her
lap, like spiders.

"What's wrong, Eby?" George asked, walking over to her.

She silently handed him the letter, then stood, letting the
others fall to the floor. Home. They had to go home. Marilee
sounded frantic in her letter. But mentioning Quinn had been
deliberate. Eby loved that child. From the moment she was

born, Eby had tried to be an anchor for her, letting her know that she didn't have to become the crazy that was their family. That she could be whatever she wanted to be.

George read the letter, then rubbed his face with his hand. "It might take a few days. Roads are closed with the snow." He turned and went back to the desk. He took the letter with him. She never found out what he did with it. She never saw it again.

As Eby stood there, agonizing over her sister's loss, she realized her grief had a personal edge to it. This was it. The end of their dreamworld. She knew it was going to happen, she just didn't realize it would happen so quickly. She thought the decision to leave would be theirs, that months and months from now, when they'd seen everything they could see twice, George would turn to her and say, "Let's go home" in a way that made home sound like a haven, a place they wanted to be.

They left two days later. Lisette had wanted to go with them, but Eby said no. Eby told her to make amends with her own family before something like this happened to her. They left Lisette crying silently, the force of her emotion nearly rattling the lampshades and shaking loose icicles on the eaves outside. Eby ran back to her and hugged her one last time. "We are conduits for happiness," she whispered to her. "Remember that."

The trip back was uncomfortable and jarring, like that moment you wake from a dream and have no idea where you are, what is real. The air in Atlanta was humid and warm when their plane landed. As the taxi drove them away and sweat began to stain her pink silk dress, Eby kept turning around as if winter was just behind them, still in view, as if she could still see swirls of Amsterdam snow.

They didn't stop by their house first. George had bought the place, a neoclassical mansion that had once belonged to a mayor of Atlanta generations ago, in the months before they married, but they had never actually lived there. They'd slept there on their wedding night, on a bundle of blankets in the dining room in the cavernously empty home, laughing just to hear the echo and jokingly calling out to any ghosts. They'd left for Europe the next day. They'd sent home enough furniture from their honeymoon to fill the place, and Eby had imagined, when they eventually returned, that her days would be spent going through crates and remembering their trip fondly. She would carefully decide what would go where, which memory she wanted in the study, in the hallway, in their bedroom. It was what was going to make being home bearable.

What had actually happened was that her sister, Marilee, had used the key Eby had given her in case there was an emergency (Marilee's suggestion) to make the house her own in the eight months George and Eby had been away. Soon after they'd left on their honeymoon, Marilee's husband Talbert had been unable to pay their rent, and they'd been kicked out of their apartment. Marilee had then decided that it would be okay to move into George and Eby's home. It had just been temporary at first, but the longer George and Eby had stayed away, the more comfortable Marilee had become.

Thinking back to the letters Eby had received in Europe, she'd thought it odd how many of her friends had told her how beautiful the house was. Eby had assumed they'd meant from the outside. But they'd all actually been inside. Marilee had been throwing parties there nearly every month. And she had unpacked all the crates of furniture that had been delivered and had decorated the house herself.

One of the last things George had shipped home was an extremely heavy Louis XV marble-top dresser. When it had arrived, Marilee had loved it and had wanted it in the bedroom she and Talbert were sharing. The two of them had tried to push it up the grand staircase by themselves, but Talbert had lost his grip, then his footing, and he'd fallen back down the stairs, the marble-top dresser landing on top of him. It had killed him before Marilee could get the neighbors over to help her. He had died in front of three-year-old Quinn.

Eby had learned this when she'd finally been able to reach Marilee on the phone when they'd arrived in London the day before. The first thing out of Eby's mouth had been, "Why did you leave Quinn there alone with him?" She'd been aghast that the poor child had been subjected to such a thing.

It had been the wrong thing to say.

"*She'll* forget! What about *me*? I just lost my husband! I was there! I saw it happen!"

Eby had heard Quinn crying in the background. They were staying with Eby and Marilee's mother, in the tiny turquoise house for which George had paid off the mortgage before they'd gotten married. His first wedding gift to her.

"Fix this," Marilee had said. "You have *everything*. If you had just given me some money before you'd left like you did with Mama, none of this would have happened! If you had just come home when you were supposed to! And why did you have to send that stupid, awful dresser?"

The taxi Eby and George rode in from the airport came to a stop in front of Eby's mother's house.

"Why don't you want me to come in?" George asked, taking Eby's hands in his own.

"That will only make it worse." Showing up with her own husband after Marilee had lost hers would only fuel Marilee's madness. All her life, Eby had been tiptoeing around her family, her calm nature antagonizing their volatile personalities. She wanted to make them happy. She wanted to steady them. And now, so full of the confidence she'd gained on her honeymoon, she wanted to change them. She could make them better. She was sure that she could.

"Whatever they need, I'll do for them," George said.

"I know you will. Thank you."

George took a deep breath as if smelling the air for the first time, how foreign it was now. "I can't believe we're home."

"Me either," Eby said, squeezing his large hands and stepping out of the cab before she changed her mind. "I'll call you when I need you to pick me up."

She stepped onto the front porch and waited for the taxi to pull away. This was the first time in almost a year that there was measurable distance between them, and the farther he was away from her, the stronger she felt the tension, like a rubber band pulling tautly, ready to snap. She wanted to run after the taxi. She wanted to dive into his arms and make this all disappear. Instead, she turned and, through the window, saw her mother, Marilee, and Quinn sitting stoically in front of the television, three stunned figures. She took a deep breath, knocked on the door, then entered.

The moment she did, the hysterics started again.

Eby looked good, and Marilee hated her for it. And whenever little Quinn got too near Eby, cautiously happy to see her, Marilee would pull her away and tell her that her father would be alive if it weren't for Aunt Eby. It took three days of sleeping on the couch, wearing the same clothes, for Eby to finally look sufficiently bad enough for Marilee.

In the days they spent apart, George arranged for a tombstone for Talbert. He had already been buried, but there had been no memorial service, so George organized one for him. George also met with a realtor to find Marilee a home. Lastly, he destroyed the dresser, burning it outside and burying the marble top under the magnolia tree in their backyard.

The night of the memorial service, George was shocked to see Eby so bedraggled. Marilee had insisted Eby wear a black dress, an ill-fitting one that belonged to their mother. Marilee had wanted to shine, to be the beautiful widow. And she hadn't wanted anyone to ask Eby about her honeymoon. The moment anyone approached Eby in the chapel, happy to see her back, Marilee would wail and call attention to herself. Once, she even pretended to faint.

George took Eby home after the service, despite Marilee's protests. Eby had been too tired to argue with him. She would make it up to Marilee the next day.

He'd left every light in the home on for her so it would look cheery. But when they walked in, they both knew.

"We can't live here. We're going to have to sell this place," Eby said as George closed the door.

"I know."

"I suppose it's for the best." Eby sighed. "It doesn't feel like home."

"We'll find it, Eby. I promise. Look at this." He reached over and took a postcard from a stack of mail piled in a large basket by the door. "A friend told me about some investment property down south—a lake and some cabins. I'm going to take you there for the weekend, just to get away for a while."

There was a photo on the postcard of people enjoying a summer day at a swampy lake—a woman with a white parasol, a boy in overalls, a girl in a pink swimsuit. The words *Welcome to LOST LAKE Georgia* were written on it. It was an old photo, but Eby had the strangest feeling looking at it. Like she was seeing her future, which was silly. She couldn't go there. She didn't have the strength to leave, knowing she had to come back. "Lisette would like this," she said sadly. "Someplace warm."

He kissed her neck gently, as if she would break. No one had ever thought Eby was delicate before. Only George. "You need a drink."

He disappeared around the corner into the dining room. Eby stood in the open foyer and looked around. The house was immaculate but decorated all wrong. It wasn't at all how Eby had imagined it. This was how Marilee wanted it. That damn dresser wasn't even supposed to go upstairs. Eby had intended for it to go here in the foyer, with a nice mirror above it. She had imagined the sound of her keys as she tossed them there every time she walked inside, a pleasant *clink* against the marble.

She staggered to the staircase and sat down. She put her head in her lap, exhausted. She had woken up several times the past few nights, wondering where she was. Paris? Amsterdam? And where was George? In those few frightening moments before she remembered, she thought she might have an inkling of what her sister might be going through, and it made dealing with Marilee in her present state of mind a little easier.

Sitting there, nodding off, Eby wondered if there was a form of mental illness that wasn't biological but learned. Eby could remember her own mother on a downward spiral after her husband died. And even now, their mother was feeding Marilee's beautiful grief with outrage of her own that Eby had stayed away so long. They were wounded. They were victims. If only they had everything they'd ever wanted, then they'd be okay. But because they didn't, it was everyone else's fault.

It was suddenly too overwhelming to think of what it was going to take to make them happy. She loved little Quinn so much, but the child looked at her with such fear now. Who does that to a child? Who chooses this over happiness? She missed Europe. She missed how hopeful she was there. She missed the comfort of Lisette. Already this was too hard. Already her family was controlling things and spending George's money.

There was a knock at the door, and Eby's head shot up.

George walked into the foyer. In his hand he had a highball glass filled with amber liquid. "Who on earth could that be?" he said, going to the door and opening it. There was a pause. "I don't believe it," he said.

"Who is it?" Eby asked, half afraid it was Marilee or her mother, bringing their resentment and grief back to Eby as if returning something Eby had mistakenly left behind, like a scarf.

George stepped aside with a smile, and standing there in a green dress with her hair tied back with a length of white ribbon, was Lisette.

She took one look at Eby and ran to her, hugging her with all the strength in her tiny arms.

Several months ago, Eby had saved Lisette's life.

And Eby would always contend that, at that moment, Lisette had returned the favor.

PART 2

"A MAGICAL EXPERIENCE"
– George and Eby Pim, PROPRIETORS

Welcome to
LOST LAKE
Georgia

8

Lost Lake
Suley, Georgia
Present day

*E*by *didn't show up* for lunch. The guests ate without her, as-suming she was just too busy with her inventory. Lisette set out browned chicken, warm butternut squash salad, blue po-tatoes, and blackberry bread with a crust of sugar that looked like ice crystals.

When the phone in the foyer rang, everyone's forks froze halfway to their mouths. They sat motionless, startled, not only because this was the first time the phone had rung since they all had arrived at Lost Lake, but also because Eby wasn't there to answer it. When it rang again, they looked at each other curiously, like jungle natives marveling at technology. Even Lisette walked out of the kitchen and stood there as if wondering what to do.

"I'll get it," Kate said, taking her napkin out of her lap. She got up and walked to the foyer. She reached over the desk and picked up the receiver. "Hello?"

"Hello?" A female voice said. "Is this Lost Lake?"

"Yes."

"But this isn't Eby."

"No, I'm Kate. Eby's niece."

"Oh, good! You might be able to help me. I'm Lara Larkworthy from the Ladies League. We heard about Eby's farewell party and we wanted to know what we could bring. I know Grady is bringing chicken wings. And I heard Mavis Baker is bringing her famous chowchow."

Kate hesitated. "All I know is that Lisette is making a cake."

"So you don't need dessert. Good. I'll tell the ladies. One more thing. My husband wants to know if his bluegrass band can play at the party. When they were boys, Eby used to hire them to play for her guests on the weekends. He wanted to play one last time for her."

"Sure," Kate said, though she wasn't really sure at all. "I guess that will be okay."

"He'll be so happy! Thank you for your time. I hope to meet you on Saturday!"

Lara Larkworthy of the Ladies League hung up.

Kate put the receiver back in the cradle, then walked back to the dining room.

"I think we have a problem," she said.

"Who was that?" Bulahdeen asked.

"Someone from town. She asked what her ladies group could bring to the party. She also asked if her husband's band could play. I think this party is going to be a lot bigger than we thought."

Lisette immediately wrote something on her notepad and showed it to Jack.

"Lisette says she'll need someone to go to the grocery store for her again," Jack said. "And she'll need someone to help her make a bigger cake."

"I'll go to the store for you," Kate said.

"And I'll help with the cake," Jack offered. He even stood up, as if volunteering for military duty.

"I knew it!" Bulahdeen said with a cackle. She slapped the table's surface with the palm of her hand, making the silverware jump. "Just when you think you know the ending, it changes."

Selma patted her mouth with her napkin, leaving a smear of lipstick. "No, really, you should look into getting that medication."

Bulahdeen ignored her. "I taught literature for nearly forty years. The books I read when I was twenty completely changed when I read them when I was sixty. You know why? Because the endings changed. After you finish a book, the story still goes on in your mind. You can never change the beginning. But you can always change the end. That's what's happening here."

No one responded. She looked frustrated that they didn't understand.

"Kate," Bulahdeen said, "Eby's not really doing inventory, is she?"

Kate reached up and rubbed the back of her neck. "Not really. No."

"Eby doesn't want to leave. We all know that."

"I don't think it's within our power to stop her," Jack said. "Is it?"

"Of course it is!" Bulahdeen said. "We've been coming back year after year, but have we ever truly let Eby know how much this place means to us? Does she really know how much we appreciate her? What have we been doing? We've just been hanging around, like we were waiting for this to happen, for Eby to finally give up. No more! I bet the whole town is coming here to tell her how much they love her. This isn't a farewell party anymore. This is a make-Eby-stay party!"

Selma stood. "You can put a tuxedo on a goat, but it's still a goat."

"No, it's not," Bulahdeen said. "It's a completely different goat when you put a tuxedo on it."

"You're feeling your oats today," Selma said as she walked out.

"You bet I am. This is going to be great. There's a lot more to do. I need to make another list." Bulahdeen dove into her purse and began to rummage around in it, murmuring things to herself.

Confused, Devin turned to Kate and whispered, "Is there going to be a goat at this party?"

※

Eby spent time in cabin number 2 today, the cabin she always reserved for young mothers who wanted to get away from a screaming baby for a while. She'd fallen asleep on the fainting couch in the living room, and when she awoke, the sky was so low and dark that she thought for a moment she'd slept the day away. She lifted her wrist and looked at her watch. It was an hour past noon. She'd missed lunch, and her stomach began to growl.

She slowly sat up. Her knees popped, and she rubbed them before standing and going to the window. The picnic-table umbrellas were swaying in the wind, and leaves were rushing across the lawn, following one another frantically, as if they knew of a safe place to go. The sky was the color of old pewter. A flash of lightning illuminated the tree line at the far end of the lake. These flash storms happened a lot around the lake. They never actually produced rain, just a lot of drama. It took years to realize that. George and Eby used to scurry around and secure things and bring in tablecloths and food when the sky grew dark and the wind picked up, until they finally understood that nothing ever happened. Rain, when it came to Lost Lake, was like an old woman watering her garden. It always gave plenty of warning. It was always steady. And it never made a lot of noise. George used to laugh and say that when one of these flash storms in the distance finally produced rain at Lost Lake, it was time to worry.

Eby left the cabin and went straight to the lawn, feeling the wind blow wildly through her hair and the electricity in the air bounce around her. She stretched her arms out and lifted her face to the sky. She closed her eyes and waited. Her heart was beating quickly, alive. Her hands tingled with energy, as if forming something solid she could ball up and throw.

She waited. And waited.

Minutes later, she felt the wind die down, then she felt

the light on her face. The storm had passed without a drop of rain.

She opened her eyes and dropped her arms.

Okay.

So it wasn't time to worry yet.

Eby walked to the main house. The dining room had been cleared from lunch, so she went to the kitchen. Lisette was bringing out a variety of cake pans and intricate-looking pastry tools. Her father might have been a famous chef, but everything Lisette knew about pastries was self-taught, and she was exceedingly proud of that.

"I fell asleep doing inventory and missed lunch," Eby said, going to the refrigerator and grabbing a handful of grapes. "Where is everyone?"

Lisette wrote, *Jack will join me soon. He will help me with this cake.*

"Jack? Here in your kitchen?" That made Eby's brows rise. "What does Luc think of this?" Eby gestured to the empty chair in the corner.

As always, Lisette became uncomfortable when Eby spoke of Luc.

Eby knew all too well that there was a fine line when it came to grief. If you ignore it, it goes away, but then it always comes back when you least expect it. If you let it stay, if you make a place for it in your life, it gets too comfortable and it never leaves. It was best to treat grief like a guest. You acknowledge it, you cater to it, then you send it on its way.

Lisette had let Luc stay for far too long.

I am not speaking to Luc.

"He agrees with me, doesn't he? About you and Jack."

You and Luc are both trying to make me happy without you. How does that work, exactly? How can I be happy without you?

Eby read that and shook her head. "There aren't a finite number of things that can make you happy. There's more than just me and Luc. I'd wager Luc would agree with me."

Lisette rolled her eyes and wrote, *Why should I listen to either of you? Luc is a child, and you are an old woman.*

That made Eby laugh. "*I'm* old? You're no spring chicken, missy."

Lisette threw her hands in the air, a very European expression of exasperation, something she hadn't lost in fifty years spent in the American South. No matter how hard she tried, and she did try, Lisette would always look not-from-here. You didn't need to hear a voice or an accent to figure that out.

"Where is everyone else?" Eby said, taking a slice of blackberry bread from the tray before Lisette put it away.

Lisette sighed and wrote, *Planning your party.*

Eby turned before Lisette could see her reach up and touch her chest, touch that fluttering under her skin. The guests were throwing her a farewell party. Jack had come for Lisette. Wes was selling his property. She had put all of this in motion. She knew it was for the best. She couldn't save this place.

She walked to the front desk and sat down, leaning back to check once more for rain, but finding only sunshine. The lake was telling her not to worry, that everything was going to be all right, but she still had an uneasy feeling.

Why else would she still be looking for signs that she should stay?

※

When they reached downtown Suley, Kate left Lisette's grocery list with the young woman at the business counter at the Fresh Mart again. She said it might take about thirty minutes, so Kate and Devin strolled down the sidewalk around the circle, looking in windows of antique marts, galleries, tea shops, and bookstores. The last few buildings were townie businesses—a law office, a print shop, a real estate office with a dance studio upstairs—and Kate almost turned to go back. But Devin wanted to walk all the way around.

That's when they saw Handyman Pizza, the last building on the far side of the circle.

Kate stopped on the sidewalk in front of the window. Just like on Wes's van, HANDYMAN PIZZA was stenciled on the glass, along with the caricature of a smiling burly man in a tool belt. At this angle, the sun was shining against their backs, turning the glass into a mirror.

"It smells *really* good in there," Devin said. She leaned forward and cupped one hand on the glass, trying to look inside.

"We just had lunch."

"I hate to tell you this, Mom, but I don't like butternut squash. I mean, *I'm eight years old,*" she said, in the same tone she would have used if someone had asked her to drive a car.

Kate laughed and opened the door.

They entered, and whatever Kate had expected, it wasn't this. The floor was black and white tiles, but the rest of the place was an explosion of neon colors. The walls were plastered with movie posters and record album covers from the 1980s. On the far back wall was a bank of old-school video games. PAC-MAN, Donkey Kong, Frogger.

She and Devin took a seat at the counter. It was a busy

place, obviously a local hangout. When a waitress in blue jeans and a Handyman Pizza T-shirt approached them, Kate quickly scanned the chalkboard wall with the menu written on it. She ordered a slice of cheese pizza for Devin and two iced teas.

"Haven't seen you here before," the waitress said as she poured the iced tea into two plastic cups. "Are you visiting the water park?"

"No, Lost Lake."

The waitress's eyes widened. "You're Eby Pim's niece! I heard you were out there for a visit."

Kate was surprised. "You did?"

The waitress laughed. "Small town. I'm coming to the party. Be right back with your slice."

In minutes, Devin's pizza was in front of her, and she dug in.

Kate sipped her tea, aware that people were watching them curiously. There was some commotion in the kitchen, and suddenly the door swung open and Wes stood there, his eyes finding them immediately.

"I told you she was out there," a male voice from inside the kitchen said.

"Hi, Wes!" Devin said, strings of cheese stretching between her mouth and the pizza slice.

"Nice place you have here," Kate said. He was dressed in soft, worn jeans and a long-sleeved T. His hair was a lighter red than it had been, wet with sweat the day before yesterday. It made him seem more real, here in a place that wasn't the lake. It was the first time she'd ever seen him outside that context, and it was strange to realize that her fond feelings for him were the same here as they were there. It wasn't just situational. It was *him*.

He walked over to them, looking a little embarrassed by his entrance. "Thanks."

"Can I ask you a question?"

He leaned against the counter. "Sure."

"Why do you call it Handyman Pizza when it's totally eighties in here?"

He smiled. She could see the boy inside best when he did that, guard down. "That confuses a lot of people the first time they come in here. When this building went on the market, I wanted it because it has a large alley garage entrance downstairs, which was perfect for me because I'd finally saved enough to make my handyman business a brick-and-mortar company instead of one I ran out of my foster mother's house. There are three stories. The third floor is my apartment." He pointed his thumb at the ceiling. "The man who owned the place before me ran this restaurant here on the street entrance. He called it Flashback Pizza. I didn't have any interest in running a restaurant, so I thought I would lease the space out. But the restaurant was popular with the locals, and they campaigned to keep it open. The previous owner had died suddenly, and people kept putting his vintage green high-top sneakers on the steps outside my apartment at night. Sometimes I'd find them in the garage downstairs. A couple of times they were even in here in the restaurant when I came down from my apartment in the mornings, on the floor at that table"—he indicated a neon orange table in the corner—"like he'd just been sitting there, then got up and left."

A man whose whole face seemed to be made of whiskers

appeared in the doorway to the kitchen. "I keep telling you, we didn't do it," he said. "It was his ghost. He wanted the place to stay open. He was buried in those shoes! Hi there, Kate, I'm Grady. Tell Eby I'm bringing chicken wings to her party, okay?"

Kate smiled and nodded, but Wes ignored him. "Thus Handyman Pizza was formed. Two businesses in one. I have an employee and a dispatcher for my handyman business downstairs. And I kept the employees of the restaurant here, which Grady oversees." He nodded to where the cook had disappeared back into the kitchen. "But there are weird cross-overs, like when people call for a handyman and ask that a pizza be delivered, too. Or when customers in the restaurant bring in broken lamps, and eat here while the lamps are re-wired downstairs."

"That's very clever," Kate said.

"I just fell into it," Wes said.

"You always were pretty easygoing."

Wes snorted. "Meaning I let you boss me around."

Devin finished her pizza slice and said, "Hey, Wes, look what the alligator gave me." She lifted the knobby piece of wood she'd set on the counter earlier. She carried it around with her like a flashlight everywhere she went. "I think it's a clue."

Wes took the piece of wood and gave it due consideration. "A clue to what?"

Devin shrugged. "Something the alligator wants me to find."

"It looks like part of a cypress knee," he said, handing it back to her.

"You know . . . it does," Kate agreed.

Devin looked excited. "What's a cypress knee?"

"It's the part of a cypress tree root that sticks out above the ground or water. Your mom and I used to go diving around the cypress knees at the far end of the lake, looking for treasure."

"Not that you can do that," Kate added quickly. "It's too dangerous. My mother would have had a fit if she'd known what I was doing. I remember how tangled those roots were underwater. It's amazing we didn't get trapped."

"But we grew gills, remember?" Wes said.

Kate actually reached up and touched a place behind her ear. "I remember."

She also remembered the story she'd made up about the three girls who went swimming in the cypress knees and got trapped, about how they had stayed there forever and grown up underwater, their hair floating like seaweed as they watched their parents look for them every day. And how, when they were grown, they figured out how to harness the fog and appear above the water. Ursula, Magdalene, and Betty. The ghost ladies.

Devin hopped off her stool. "Let's go back to the lake. I want to check out these knees!"

"Are you coming to Eby's party?" Kate asked as she stood. She called for Devin to wait by the door.

"I'll be there," he said.

"So will most of the town, apparently. It's snowballed into something bigger than Bulahdeen expected."

"I can come out later today, if you'd like. I can help get the place ready."

"I think everyone would be grateful for that," Kate said.

"Mom, come on!"

Kate smiled as she walked away. " I'll see you then."

❦

"Does she know you're a part of this development deal, the one that's going to take Eby's property?" Grady asked, his timing perfect as he poked his head out of the kitchen the moment Kate and Devin left.

Wes shrugged. "Unless Eby has told her, no."

Grady hooted. "You're going to be in hot water when she finds out."

"Why?"

"Has it really been that long?" Grady shook his head. "I keep telling you, you need to date more, son."

"I date enough."

"Going bowling with me doesn't constitute dating. You never even buy me dinner."

Wes grabbed a wipe from under the counter. He paused, then asked, "What makes you think I'm even interested in Kate?"

"That right there, what just happened, is called *attraction*. A-trak-shee-un. Look it up in the dictionary."

Wes smiled and turned to buss the counter. Grady knew that Wes had had girlfriends in the past. Not that they'd ever lasted very long. Everyone his age always seemed to be in such a hurry to leave. His longest relationship had lasted two years. He and Anika had fallen in love their senior year in high school. But not long after graduation, Anika had started making plans for them to leave. They had jobs that could travel, she'd said. He could fix anything, and she could waitress anywhere. His foster mother Daphne had encouraged him to do whatever his heart told him to. The problem with that was that his heart didn't belong to Anika. Not all of it, anyway. A big part, sure. He did love her. But he also loved Daphne and Eby and the town. And Billy.

It really all came down to Billy.

If he left this place, he would have to leave his brother. And he couldn't do that. He and Billy had been inseparable. Wes had never minded changing his diapers or teaching him to swim or walking through the woods with him to the lake every morning. Everything Wes did, Billy did. Everything Wes liked, Billy liked. Wes had almost died trying to find him in that burning house. But he couldn't. He couldn't find him. Maybe he was still looking for him. Maybe he always would be.

There had never been a single force, a single person, who could compete with that memory, with that place in his heart. Except Kate. She'd made him want to leave all those years ago. Even then, he'd been planning to take Billy with him. But even she couldn't make him leave now. Not that that would ever happen. No matter what Grady said, what he and Kate had now was just a memory of something good.

It, and she, would be gone before he knew it.

9

The groceries were ready when Kate and Devin walked back to the Fresh Mart, and Kate tipped the bag boy who helped load Lisette's boxes into the Subaru. Devin had already buckled herself in, and Kate was about to get behind the wheel when she heard voices coming from inside the store. A window cleaner on a ladder was squeegeeing the glass above the door, leaving the doors open.

"Why do you keep coming in here? He's *married*." Kate recognized that voice. It was the young woman with the ponytail at the business counter—Brittany.

"I don't see your father complaining," Selma said as she walked out. She didn't see Kate standing there. Her skirt swished with agitation, and her heels clicked so hard on the sidewalk that they sparked and made black burn marks on the concrete. The air around her was charged with a bright red electricity that every woman recognized. So did every man, but for entirely different reasons.

"What's the matter with Selma?" Devin asked.

"Nothing," Kate said, climbing into the car. "She's just in a bad mood."

"The alligator likes her."

"Does he?" Kate asked absently as she started the car.

"He likes everyone. I think he's upset that he might not see them again. He doesn't want them to leave."

"Even Selma?"

"He thinks she's pretty."

Kate turned to back out of the space. "Well, that means he's definitely a he."

They were a few minutes ahead of Selma in arriving back at Lost Lake. When Selma arrived, she got out of her red sedan and walked to her cabin without a word.

Kate and Devin had just started unloading the groceries when Kate heard Selma call, "Kate! Oh, Ka-ate!"

With a box full of vegetables in her hands, Kate turned to see Selma now standing on the front stoop of her cabin. "Yes?"

"I want to take a long bath and I don't have any clean towels."

Kate nodded to the main house. "I'm sure Eby has some in the laundry room."

"I'll wait here," Selma said. "You said you were helping Eby, right? Eby usually does this."

Kate and Devin took the first load of groceries inside. "I'll be right back with the rest," Kate said to Lisette. "I have to run some towels over to Selma first. What is it with women like that?"

Lisette shook her head slowly and wrote something on her notepad. *She is lonely.*

"She doesn't act lonely."

Lisette smiled and wrote, *None of us do. Not even you.*

⚘

Minutes later, Kate knocked on Selma's door. Selma called for her to come in. When Kate entered, she saw that Selma had already changed into a Chinese dressing gown and was lying on the couch, reading a magazine. The cabin seemed hazy but not by smoke. The haze had a scent, like a perfume.

Scarves were draped over lampshades. High-heeled shoes lined the hearth of the fireplace. There were open hat boxes strewn around, but they didn't contain hats. One contained candy; another, hundreds of tiny makeup samples; another, inexplicably, bottle caps. Kate stood at the door and held out the towels.

Selma tossed the magazine aside in a truly impressive show of ennui. "Just put them in the bathroom. And take the old towels with you."

Kate went to the bathroom, set the new towels on the sink, and came back out with the used towels, which were covered in makeup. She walked to the front door, about to leave, but then stopped and turned. "I saw you at the Fresh Mart today. You were having an argument with the girl there."

Selma sighed. "She doesn't like me."

"Why not?"

"Because I flirt with her father. The man who owns the

store. He's married. It's what I do. All my husbands were married when I met them." She rubbed her bare ring finger distractedly. "But she doesn't have anything to worry about. If I'd wanted him, I'd have used my last charm to get him by now."

Kate opened her mouth, then closed it. Finally she had to ask, "*All* of your husbands were married?"

"Strange, isn't it? But those are the rules," Selma said.

"You have rules?"

"I didn't make them. They've been there since time immemorial."

"So why didn't you stay married to any of them? You obviously went to a lot of trouble to get them."

Selma frowned, then stood. "It's never what I think it's going to be." She gestured to seven picture frames on the mantle, some large, some small, each photo of a smiling man. The youngest was an old photo of a man in his twenties, the oldest was a recent photo of an elderly man. "Those are my husbands," Selma said. "I keep them around to remind me what not to look for the next time."

Kate watched Selma walk over to the mantle. She picked up a small jewelry box. It was chestnut in color with tiny flecks of ivory inlay on top. On its own, it was completely innocuous, and Kate would have thought nothing of it. But the way Selma picked it up and cradled it made it alive somehow. Kate stared, fascinated. She could feel its pull.

"Do you know what this is?"

"No," Kate said, shifting her weight and swallowing.

"The secret to my success," Selma said, holding out the box and opening it slowly in front of Kate.

Kate leaned forward and looked inside. She frowned when she saw that it was empty, save for a small heart charm sitting on the black velvet lining. "What is it?"

"Ha!" Selma said, snapping the box shut, making Kate jump back quickly. "I knew it. Only women like me know what it's for."

"What do you mean?" Kate felt a little light-headed, like she'd stood up too quickly.

"It's a charm. My last one. I'm saving it to use on my last husband. He will be old and rich, the last one I will ever need."

Kate wondered if Selma clung to this idea of charms the same way Kate had clung to Cricket, because when you run out of rope, you grab the first thing within reach. When Selma divorced one husband, maybe the charms comforted her with the fact that she wouldn't have to be alone for long, that another one would come along soon.

After standing there awkwardly for a moment, holding the dirty towels and watching Selma smile and stroke the box like a cat, Kate turned and left the cabin. Once outside, she stopped on the stoop. She took a deep breath of lake air and felt her head clear. She looked back at the door she'd closed behind her and wondered if understanding Selma was really possible.

Maybe she really was magic.

Selma put the box back on the mantle. She didn't understand why she acted this way. She couldn't seem to help herself. And she had been this way for so long that she didn't think she could be any other way. Not that she wanted to. Her mother had hated it, had hated what Selma had become, but Selma didn't care. She wasn't her mother. That was all that mattered.

Selma tried not to think of her mother, but when she did, she felt pity. She was a fading photo from the past—thin, transparent, disappearing from the window at the kitchen sink, where she would always stand and wait for her husband to come home to her.

She didn't like to think of her father either, but when she did she felt anger, sometimes longing. But he too was a whispery figure of her past, consisting mainly of the scent of newspaper ink.

The only thing from her childhood she really liked to think of, what she remembered in striking detail, was the endless string of women with which her father had cheated on her mother. She remembered the hems of their dresses, the curl of their hair, the color of their eyeshadow, the marks their jewelry left on their skin. When she was very young, she'd had no idea who they were, these strange women who would show up at their front door, looking for Selma's father. Selma's mother would slam the door in their faces, but Selma would sneak out and follow them down the sidewalk, entranced by these painted creatures and the music created by their bracelets. They'd always had bracelets.

When Selma was older but still too young to stay at home alone, her father would take her to bars on nights her mother drugged herself into a stupor with sleeping pills. Hidden in a corner, drinking Virgin Marys, Selma would watch her father interact with these women. It hadn't been her father who had called the shots, though. These women had all the power. How charmed they'd been. How potent to the people around them.

Ruby, a beautiful woman with dyed black hair and the largest bosom Selma had ever seen, had been the woman who had finally made Selma's father leave her mother. The others, Selma realized now, had just been playing with him, batting him around like a cat with a stunned mouse. They hadn't wanted to marry him, because if they had, he would have left long before then. Selma had been thirteen when this happened, and she had loved going to visit her father and Ruby's apartment in downtown Jackson. Selma had been on the cusp of womanhood, and Ruby had been all that Selma had wanted to be. Ruby, in her better moods, would show Selma how to apply makeup, making her lips so pink she looked like she'd just taken a bite of a cupcake. It had felt that way, too, sticky and thick. It had been during one of these makeup sessions that Selma had asked Ruby about her bracelet.

Ruby had stepped back and held up her hand, making the four heart charms jingle. "Women like me have exactly eight times in our lives to get the man we want. This is how we keep track." She'd rattled the bracelet again. "I had eight charms. I have four left."

"What happens to the charms?"

"They disappear the moment we decide on the man we want, the moment we know. The first few men are usually out of spite. We use them to steal the men of women we don't like. The last four are usually for money. The very last one is the last chance to get exactly what we want. Is it money? Is it revenge? Is it love? Is it a family? It's the most important charm."

Selma had listened with rapt attention. "Do you have to use them all?"

Ruby had laughed, a sharp sound like a barking seal. "Darling, why would you waste them?"

Selma had tried desperately to process it all. She'd wanted to know everything but was afraid it was too much, that she didn't have what it took to understand. Boys had just started to intrigue her, and she had trouble thinking beyond finding one to hold hands with. That was all. Just one. That had been all she'd wanted. "If you fall in love, can you just keep using the charms on the same man?"

"Of course not," Ruby had said, and her condescending tone had wounded Selma. "Who could love one man that long?"

"So you're not going to stay with my dad?" Selma had asked.

"No. Be still," Ruby had said, putting a row of false lashes on Selma's eye. "Your mother and I used to go to the same school, a long time ago. She used to make fun of me, she and her friends. She used to think she was so much better than me. Now look at her. Her life is pitiful, and I can have any married man I want. I guess I showed her, didn't I?"

Selma had felt a shudder go through her. Ruby had felt almost dangerous at that moment. Selma had always hated the powerlessness of her mother. And she'd hated how her father always seemed to get his way with no consequences. Ruby was better, stronger, than them all. Ruby would always win. "I want to be just like you," Selma had whispered, her voice trembling. Even if she hadn't really understood, even though it had confused her, she'd *known*.

Ruby had lifted Selma's chin with her fingers, her face just inches from Selma's. "Just by saying that, darling, you already are." She blew into Selma face, her breath warm. Something came over Selma. She was different now. She could feel it. "Eight charms. That's all you get. It seems like a lot a first, but you'll soon see you'll have to pace yourself. You're going to be the envy of all women. Any married man who feels a sliver of attraction to you can be yours. You're going to lead a charmed life."

Ruby had left four months later. Two weeks after that, Selma had received a package in the mail from her—a bracelet with eight charms.

Selma's father went back to her mother. She made his life miserable. He continued to cheat. But they realized they were stuck with each other. Selma might as well have become invisible, so focused were they on their hatred for each other.

When Selma turned eighteen, she'd used her first charm to marry an army sergeant who had married a classmate of Selma's the year before. They were home on leave, and Selma had hated this girl, how she gloated that she was free of this place, how she said that all the other girls were rotting here while she saw the world. Selma had shown her. And that first time she'd watched a charm disappear, knowing she was going to get exactly what she'd wanted, had been *wondrous*.

At first Selma had been giddy with her power and had married foolishly, just as Ruby had said. Her third husband was stolen from a cocktail waitress who had spilled a drink on her. The later ones had been for more practical reasons.

But with all that Ruby had told her, there had been two things Ruby had failed to share. The first was that the effect of the charms was fleeting. She could get any married man who was attracted to her to leave his wife and marry her, but she couldn't make him stay. Five years was the upper limit, though there was a rumor among their kind that one of them had managed seventeen years on a single charm. Information was hard to come by. While they instinctively knew one another when they crossed paths, women like her didn't share their secrets easily.

Selma went to the window in her cabin and watched Kate walk away. Kate threw a look back over her shoulder. Selma knew that look very well. Hundreds of women had given her that look over the years. She wasn't immune to it.

That was the second thing Ruby had failed to tell her. That those looks would always hurt.

And that, by choosing to be the woman she was, she would never again have female friends.

10

L isette and I brought in the rest of the groceries. Can I go down to the lake?" Devin asked her mother, running up the path toward Kate as soon as she came out of Selma's cabin. That heavy, beautiful-lady scent hung in the air around her. Selma's cabin was surrounded by it, like a force field. Devin imagined that if she threw rocks at it, they would just ricochet off.

"No," Kate said, shifting the towels in her arms. "Stick with me for a little while. I don't think Eby has done any laundry lately. It might be backing up."

From behind them on the path, someone said, "I'll watch over her."

It was Bulahdeen. Devin liked her. She wasn't much taller than Devin, so Devin had a weird impression of her being a very old little girl. She was wearing dark sunglasses that took up half of her sweet, wrinkled face.

"Please, please, please?" Devin said, jumping up and down.

Kate smiled. "Okay. You two keep an eye on each other. Thanks, Bulahdeen."

Kate walked into the main house, and Devin turned to Bulahdeen. She held up the root the alligator had given her and said, "To the cypress knees!"

"You want to see the cypress knees? Okay, this way," Bulahdeen said, directing her to a trail that led around the lake, so close that the water nearly reached the bank in places. Cypress trees leaned over it, draping moss to the water like a curtain.

Devin walked backward in front of Bulahdeen as Bulahdeen peppered her with questions about her school and her family, which Devin didn't want to talk about, because that was her old life and things were different since leaving Atlanta. Her life had changed so much, had been in a constant state of flux for almost a year. It was like spinning around in circles with your eyes closed. Once you stop, the world still feels like it is going too fast. Then, after a while, you realize nothing is spinning anymore—that everything is perfectly still.

That's what Lost Lake felt like.

Bulahdeen stopped a lot during the walk—to toss branches out of the pathway or to show Devin a mushroom or a nest. Everything that shone attracted her attention like a magpie. It seemed to take forever to get even halfway around the lake. Devin became anxious to get to the cypress knees, so she ran ahead of Bulahdeen. Bulahdeen called her back in a tone that brooked no defiance. Devin slowed down and matched her pace to Bulahdeen's, learning it, making sure she remembered it.

Finally, Bulahdeen said, "There they are! The only place on the lake where you can see them."

Devin looked out over the water. They didn't look like knees. They didn't even look like roots. They looked like the ancient spires of Gothic buildings sticking out of the top of the water, like there was a church under the lake and she and Bulahdeen could only see the top of it. They were clustered in a section close to the bank, no more than a foot or so out of the water. She got as close to the edge as possible and looked down. The water moved slightly, and she thought for a moment that she saw a flash of something electric blue at the bottom. But, then again, the water was so murky that it was hard to tell just where the bottom was. She didn't see any evidence that the alligator had been here, or that whatever it was he might want her to find was hidden anywhere. She even put her hand over her good eye and looked around.

She thought it would be more obvious than this.

Her shoulders dropped. She was tired. Fatigue suddenly settled over her like someone encasing her in glass.

The alligator had kept her up most of the night, tossing things up against her window. *Tic tic tic.* It had driven her crazy. She'd finally turned on her light and gone to the window. When she'd opened it, the humid nighttime had air rushed at her, as thick as soup. The light from the window had spread a fan of light on the ground below, and there he'd been. When he'd seen her, he'd opened his mouth and turned his head, giving her a sideways glance that was almost mischievous.

"Don't you *sleep?*" She'd asked him.

He'd made a hissing sound and flung his head around again.

"I can't come out. I promised my mom."

He'd walked a few steps away. His strange, scaly feet with toes that ended in long claws had scratched against the dirt.

"I don't know what you're so upset about. You're the one who won't tell me where the box is. If it's such a big deal, tell me."

He'd walked out of the light, frustrated with her.

Devin had closed the window and crawled back into bed. But the moment she'd turned out the light, the *tic tic tic* had started again. She'd put her pillow over her head, but he hadn't let up until the lime-colored sunlight broke through the trees, and that's when Devin had finally dozed off.

"What are you thinking about, baby?" Bulahdeen said from behind her.

"No one believes me about the alligator," Devin said, turning away from the lake. "And Mom even saw him on the road coming here! I'm not making him up. Do you believe me?"

Bulahdeen smiled. "Sure I do. One person alone can't do it. I've learned that. But two people? That's a done deal. If two people believe in the same thing, it's automatically real."

That made Devin feel better. "He wants me to know things, then he won't tell me. It's frustrating."

"He's an alligator. And they're single-minded, those alligators. They don't focus on much except what's right in front of them."

"You're right," Devin said. "He needs my help."

"Where to?" Bulahdeen clapped her hands and rubbed them together. "Anything else you want to see?"

"No. We better get back. I think I heard Wes's van. He said he was coming by to help get things ready for Eby's party."

"Now that's good news! Hot diggity. Let's go talk to him."

Bulahdeen scooted off at a fast clip, her arms pumping at her sides like she was power walking.

Devin hesitated, looking out over the cypress knees once more, before running to catch up with Bulahdeen.

She needed to find this box quickly. She had the strangest feeling that they were running out of time.

*

As soon as Wes arrived, Bulahdeen charged at him from the trail beside the lake and asked if he would set up the dance floor. Of course he agreed.

He remembered every summer weekend George would bring out the large squares and set them on the lawn and snap them together like a large puzzle. Wes had even helped him a few times. There had been live music on the weekends, and in the evenings Wes and Billy would linger in the woods to listen. Eby would put colorful Chinese lanterns in the trees and launch tiny boats with candles out into the lake. Those nights, more than most, they hadn't wanted to go home. They'd just wanted to listen to the music and watch the people dance as lights twinkled, and imagine that this really was their home.

With Jack's assistance, Wes brought out the floor squares from Eby's storage room, and together they spent the better part of the afternoon putting them together. The damp had gotten to them, warping them in some places.

Wes caught sight of Kate a few times. She was wearing the same shorts and bright green tank top from when he'd seen her earlier at the restaurant, but now sweat was making the ends of her hair turn up in curls. She was obviously helping with housekeeping that day, taking towels and sheets back and forth to the cabins. He'd been so busy watching her that he'd once hammered his thumb with his mallet. Jack had given him an understanding look. Some women just make you forget yourself.

When they were done, Kate walked to the lawn to inspect their handiwork. She put her hands on her hips and nodded. "Very nice," she said, which made Wes feel ridiculously proud of himself. Seriously, it was pitiful.

"We were going to put the canopy up but noticed that moths had gotten to it," Wes said, gesturing to the folded canopy on the ground.

"I can mend it tonight," Kate said. "Would you have time to come back tomorrow to help put it up?"

"Sure," he said, and the thought of plans with her made tomorrow seem so far away. It had felt that way fifteen years ago too, when he couldn't wait to see her in the mornings. He hadn't been able to sleep, knowing that in just hours they could start their day over again. Past and present. The lines were getting muddy. "I'll repair these grills tomorrow, too, and maybe sand some places on the picnic tables and benches so people won't get splinters."

Kate smiled at him, her eyes on his face, going to the scar above his eyebrow where his father had once hit him and Wes had fallen against the woodstove. When they were kids, he'd told Kate he'd gotten the scar rescuing a heron caught in some moss.

Evening began to fall, and Eby came out with hot dogs

and hamburgers to grill. When she saw the dance floor, she shook her head. "I can't believe Bulahdeen talked you into doing that."

"It was my pleasure," Wes said, realizing he hadn't actually left the dance floor yet, like he was somehow holding court over it. "I loved watching the guests dance when I was a kid. Maybe I'll dance on it myself this time. I always wanted to."

"I like to dance," Devin said. She'd been sitting with Bulahdeen all afternoon, knocking the cypress knee she held against the table absently as she stared at the water. She was restless, the way Kate used to get restless when it rained, like something was holding her back.

Wes held out his hand to her. "Then join me."

Devin ran onto the dance floor, and they did some robot-style moves that made Kate laugh.

Selma was sitting at one of the picnic tables, watching them with detachment. "My second husband was a dance instructor. Did I ever tell you that?" she said to no one. She suddenly stood and took Jack by the hand. "Dance with me."

"I don't know how to dance, Selma," Jack said, panicking.

"And they do?" she asked, gesturing to Wes and Devin.

"Hey," Wes said, in mock offense.

Selma dragged Jack onto the floor and began to execute some complicated move that involved Jack putting his leg between hers and spinning her around.

Jack promptly fell and twisted his ankle.

Selma just stood there and looked at him, then she sighed at the injustice of it all and went to sit back down while everyone gathered around Jack.

"I'll get some ice," Eby said, rushing to the house. She

returned with not only ice but Lisette. Lisette didn't have on shoes, and her toenails were painted a surprising color of orange. Her dark dress was buttoned wrong, as if she'd hastily dressed, and through the missed buttonholes, some bright yellow lingerie could be seen. Her hair was pushed back with a headband, wet in some places, like she'd just washed her face. Everyone suddenly stood still. It was as if she was a wild animal who had lost her way and they didn't want to startle her. Lisette never came out to the lawn at night.

They had gotten Jack's shoe off by this time. Lisette took the ice pack from Eby and set it on Jack's foot. She looked up at him worriedly, darting her head back frequently to look at the grills where the hot dogs and burgers were now sizzling.

"It's okay," Jack said. "It's not broken. You go inside. I'll be fine."

Lisette looked relieved. She hurried back into the house as if the smoke from the grill were chasing her, as if she might just get sick from it.

The group helped Jack to his cabin, and they ended up having dinner in there with him. Even Selma joined them. She never exactly apologized, but she had gotten up and refilled Jack's drink once, which everyone figured was as good as it got with Selma and contrition.

Later, color high from laughter, they all said good night to each other, and Wes helped Eby and Kate take the dishes and trash back to the main house. Eby went upstairs, and Kate and Wes walked back outside. The umbrella lights were now off, and Devin was trying to catch fireflies in the dark.

They stood side by side and watched her. Wes could feel Kate's arm graze his. When he was twelve, this was what he had lived for, a brief touch from her—their legs as they sat on the dock, their hands as they both reached for something at the same time. He'd known she hadn't felt the same way, not until that very last moment, just before she left. It had been floating around the lake for years now, that longing they'd left behind. But it too had grown. There was a different tenor to it now, something grittier, more lusty and heavy. He couldn't deny that he had stared at her legs as she'd walked around to-day, studying the way they moved. She was small breasted, and after careful consideration, he was fairly certain that she didn't wear a bra. He wondered what it would feel like to kiss her, what she tasted like with Bulahdeen's wine on her lips. Things would never be as simple as they had been. And yet . . . here they were, barely touching, and he found himself thinking that he would be perfectly happy to stay here all night like this, with just the feel of her arm against his.

"Well, good night, Wes," Kate finally said, her voice slightly breathy. "See you tomorrow."

He nodded.

Kate called to Devin. "The alligator says good night, too, Wes!" Devin said as they walked away.

When Wes got into his van, he sat there for a moment.

This had been the best summer night he'd had in a long time, and it left him afraid that it was happening all over again, that he was going to fall in love and wish for a life he couldn't make happen, because that life could only ever exist here for a single moment, with Kate.

Maybe it was for the best that Eby was selling, that he was getting rid of his own land. You can't spend your whole life unhappy, just waiting for a moment of something perfect. Wes had already made his life into something good.

This was just a place.

And Kate was just a girl he'd once known.

He needed to let them both go.

Lisette loved the flavors of old, simple recipes, ones made so often that their edges were worn down and they tasted soft and sure of themselves. They made her think of her *grand-mère,* who had lost her husband and two of her sons in the war. She had cried every day for a year, walking the same stretch of road from her home to the train station, waiting for them to come back. Her tears fell as black stones to the ground, and to this day those stones lodged themselves in car tires and let all the air out slowly in a wail. People called it Sorrow Road. Lisette had very few memories of her *grand-mère* and her house in the country. She remembered the bread she had baked there in a sooty black stove. And she remembered her *grand-mère* once holding out her spotted, papery fingers and telling Lisette that old hands made the best food. "Old hands can hold memories of good things," she had said.

That made Lisette look at her hands as she stood there at Jack's door that next morning, holding a tray of food.

She had old hands now. Sometimes it came as such a surprise. Interacting with Luc could make her believe she was so much younger sometimes.

Jack opened the door. He was wearing khaki pants and a pink polo shirt with the name of a symphony on it. On anyone else, it would have looked prissy or pretentious. On Jack it just seemed sincere. She had not seen him jog around the lawn that morning, so she had decided to bring him breakfast. "Lisette? Is this for me? Come in."

She walked in. She had been in this cabin many times, just never when Jack had been occupying it. Sometimes, when he left for the season, she would help Eby clean the cabin, and she would always look for things he left behind. But he was so meticulous that he never forgot anything. There were signs of his life that drew her eye now, making her curious. There was a photo of him and his three brothers on the kitchen counter, next to several bottles of vitamins. An iPhone was on the coffee table, with a ladies handkerchief next to it.

"That's Selma's," Jack said, when he noticed Lisette looking at it. "Everyone ate in my cabin last night."

Lisette nodded as she set the tray down on the table. Jack walked over to her, limping slightly. "Thank you for this, but it wasn't necessary. I could have walked to the main house. I decided to forgo my morning jog, though."

Lisette's eyes went to his wrapped ankle.

"It's fine," he said. "Just a mild sprain. Trust me. I spend a great deal of time with feet."

She felt uncomfortable, like she had just revealed more about her feelings than she had wanted to, like last night, when she had run back into the house. She had gone back to her room and then realized her bra could be seen through her buttonholes. She had touched those buttonholes worriedly, wondering if anyone had seen.

"Will you sit with me?" Jack asked, pulling out a chair for her.

She nodded and sat, though she did not know why. She had not intended to stay.

Jack sat beside her and poured coffee. He did not feel the need to fill her silence with talk. She had always liked that about him. Her silence made most people nervous, but it seemed to comfort him. Perhaps that was why she liked him so much. She had never been a comfort to anyone but Eby. And that had been a long time ago.

The first time she had set eyes on Jack, he had been in his late twenties and he had been sitting in the dining room with an older couple. The camp had been full in the summers back then, and she and Eby had had to replenish the breakfast buffet several times every morning. At one point, they had even had to hire a waitress to help. Lisette remembered that morning in vivid detail. Her hair had still been long, and it had been braided. Her dress had been yellow. She had been carrying a plate of chive biscuits. She had entered the dining room and had been walking to the buffet table when she had seen him. Startled, she had stopped. For one fleeting moment, she had thought it was Luc. He had the same hair, the same nose. Only he'd been dressed in different clothing. It had made her smile, thinking Luc had moved out of the kitchen, that he had changed clothes and had decided to join the living. But then Jack had looked up at her, and she had seen the differences. He was not Luc. For some reason, the realization had been devastating. It had been at a time in her life when she had begun to feel like she had wanted to move forward. She had not missed breaking hearts, but she had missed feeling loved by a man, the weight of his body, the smell of his skin. And every time she had seen children at the camp, she had felt her heart squeeze a little, telling her it was still there, that it was possible to love again.

But it was not to be. She had walked back into the kitchen and had seen Luc there in his chair, looking at her with such sympathy. He was not going to move on until she let go of him, of her guilt. And that was one thing she could not do. If she lost that, she would lose the thread that had sewn her new life together. She would become that careless, cruel person she had been before.

The feeling of wanting to move on had not lasted long anyway. She had still been young. The older she got, the less she wanted it.

Still, she looked forward to seeing Jack every summer. She liked seeing him grow older. She kept waiting for him to bring a wife. For there to be children. Grandchildren. But he remained single, and she grew close to him. She had not wanted to, but it had happened anyway. Had she been kinder to Luc, he would have grown into a Jack. He would have been quiet and kind and successful.

"What will you do when Eby sells?" Jack suddenly asked, as if he had been carrying on a conversation with her in his head and he was now letting her in on it. "Where will you go?"

Lisette lifted the notebook from around her neck and wrote, *Nowhere. I will stay here.*

He read that and nodded, as if it was the answer he had been expecting. He sat back and looked into his coffee, as if there were secrets there. More silence.

Lisette pointed to the eggs on the plate and mouthed the word *Eat.*

"Oh, right. Of course." He set his cup aside so quickly that the coffee sloshed over the rim onto the table.

With a smile, she handed him his fork, then picked up his napkin and cleaned up the coffee while he ate.

He kept sneaking glances at her. Finally, his eyes on his plate, he asked so sincerely that it felt like a lullaby, "Will you have dinner with me one night? Maybe after the party? I know you have a lot of work to do."

He had his fork suspended in midair, waiting for her reply. She paused, then wrote something on her pad. She reached over and showed it to him. *I will break your heart.*

He put down his fork and made a face. "Oh, that's right. I forgot. Never dinner." He turned to her and said, "How about lunch?"

There was a sense of tightness in the room now, filling the space. Attraction was like that. It filled. It poured into you like batter into a pan, sticking to the sides. Lisette stood abruptly.

"Lisette?" Jack called as she ran out, knowing he could not chase her. She tripped and fell on her hands just as she reached the end of the path.

She got up quickly and went to the kitchen through the back of the house so no one would see the great spectacle she was making of herself, running away from the sweetest man on the planet because she thought her presence might poison him somehow, like it had done with Luc. Luc was leaning back in the chair when she entered. He watched with great interest as she angrily scrubbed her hands at the sink. He was smiling at her, as if he knew what had just happened. Smiling as if it made him *happy*.

⚜

She had said no, of course. Jack was embarrassed. Not that he'd asked her out, but that he'd asked her to dinner first. He knew her better than that. He knocked himself lightly on the head with his hand. *Stupid, stupid, stupid.* She never ate dinner. In all the years he'd been coming to Lost Lake, Lisette had never come out to the lawn at night for barbecue and cocktails. When the sun set, she was always in her room, the single light from her window like a wink. Most of the summer faithfuls knew how Eby had saved Lisette, how she'd been sixteen and about to commit suicide because, over dinner, she'd broken the heart of a boy who had loved her. There was part of Jack, a part tucked back behind everything he treated so logically, that understood why the boy had taken his own life, because he understood how powerful an attraction to her could be. She was enchanting. He loved the notes she wrote in her pretty handwriting, the way she smelled, like oranges and dough, the savage blackness of her hair.

It suddenly occurred to him.

Was that what he was supposed to tell her? Was that what Eby meant?

It seemed so simple. He thought she knew.

But what if she didn't? What if she didn't know he loved her?

He frowned at another possibility. He felt fear heat his ears, the same fear he felt when he had to go to a place he'd never been to before or speak in front of people. It made him want to run, to avoid the embarrassment altogether.

What if she *did* know, and it didn't matter?

What if she didn't love him back?

⚹

"Wes!" Devin said, and Kate watched her run up to him.

The sun was setting behind the trees, streaking over the water. The heat had gone from boiling to a soft, wet simmer. Devin had been sitting on a picnic table since Wes had arrived, elbows on her knees, chin resting on her hands, waiting, waiting, *waiting* for him to finally stop working. She watched as he first put up the canopy Kate had mended last night, then fixed the barbecue grills. Kate was sure that he could feel her daughter's impatience as surely as if she'd thrown it and hit him with it.

"I want to ask you something," Devin said, almost sliding to a stop. "Did you and your brother live someplace close by?"

"Yes, we did," Wes said. "About a half mile from here. Through the woods." Wes pointed to the east side of the lake. "But the house is gone now. It burned down."

Devin turned and squinted in that direction. She put her hand to her good eye and covered it, something she often did when she was looking for something. She'd been doing it most all her life. She saw that Kate was watching, and lowered her hand. "Is there, like, a trail or something?"

"There used to be. My brother and I walked it here every day."

"Will you take me there?" Devin asked, turning back to him.

That caught him off guard. "Take you there?"

"Yes. Can we go on a hike through the woods?"

"Devin, you can't ask him to do that," Kate said, walking over to them. Her hands were stained green and brown from pulling up weeds in Eby's neglected planters in front of the main house.

"But *I'm* not asking," Devin said. "The alligator wants him to."

"That sounds ominous," Wes said, taking off his tool belt.

Devin looked over her shoulder at Kate. "What does that mean?"

"It means it sounds like the alligator wants to eat him," Kate clarified for her.

"No!" Devin said immediately. "It's not like that. He's friendly. And he really, really likes you, Wes. Out of everyone here, he talks about you the most."

Kate's brows dropped in confusion. "He talks about Wes?"

"All the time."

"Okay, let's do it," Wes said.

"Really?" Devin said.

"Never argue with an alligator," Wes said.

Devin nodded at him seriously. "Exactly."

So the three of them headed off to the lake. "We'll be back before dark," Wes called to the others. "I'm going to show them the path to the cabin."

"Be careful," Eby said. She'd been waiting for Wes to

finish with the grills before she started dinner for the guests. She was now lighting charcoal in one. "Do you have your phones with you?"

"Mine, um, accidentally fell into the lake," Kate said.

Wes took his out of his pocket and held it up. "I have mine."

Once they reached the path around the lake, Wes ducked into the woods and soon found the trail. After a few minutes of walking, Kate began to notice some markers on the trees. "What are all these plastic tags?" she asked Wes, reaching out to touch one of the small bright ties that were deliberately attached to some low-hanging limbs.

"They look like survey markers," he said. "Did Eby have her land surveyed recently?"

"Not that I know of."

The trees began to thin the farther they walked, becoming more uniform, more evenly spaced, as if they'd been deliberately planted years ago. Kate realized that they were all pine trees, and all of them had identical scars on them, reaching high into their trunks. The bark of the trees seemed to peel away in a V shape, like a curtain parting, and inside were even, whispery lines that looked like they were made by ax cuts. There was something magical about this place, about the uniformity of the trees, like they were dancers in costumes, frozen the moment before their first step.

"What are these marks on all these trees?" Kate asked.

"They're called catfaces," Wes said, walking at a brisk pace, like he was passing through the bad side of town. "That's how I always knew we'd crossed from Eby's property onto ours."

"I don't remember us ever exploring this part of the woods," Kate said. "I think I would have remembered this."

"I kept us on Eby's property to avoid my dad. I think I knew her land better than my own."

"Why are they called catfaces?" Devin asked.

Wes talked while he walked, so Kate and Devin couldn't linger. Instead, they walked while looking up, periodically tripping over branches and roots. "Because those scars where the bark is peeled away look like cat whiskers. Generations of my family were turpentiners. They tapped these trees for resin. The catfaces are the hacks they made to get to the veins of the trees. Turpentining used to be a huge industry in this area. When the industry dried up, there wasn't much to do with this land."

A short time later, they broke through some brush and suddenly found themselves in the curve of an old dirt road. Kate was out of breath.

"The road leads to the highway, that way," Wes said, pointing left, not stopping. "This way leads to what remains of the old cabin."

They walked a short distance up the road to where there was a grassy bare spot containing an old stone chimney, looking as if it was standing inside an invisible house.

"And here we are," Wes said.

Devin ran to the clearing. Wes stayed at the very edge, as far back as he could get without disappearing into the trees.

Kate walked over to him, pushing her sunglasses to the top of her head. She was the one who was winded, yet he was the one who looked like he was about to pass out. "Are you okay?"

He managed a smile that didn't quite reach his blue eyes. "It's been a long time since I've been here."

"Oh, God. Wes, I didn't realize. Is this the first time since the fire?"

"No," he said, lowering himself to the ground and leaning against a tree. For a big man, he moved easily, deliberately, aware of his body and its proximity to those around him. He brushed some dirt off his hands. "The last time was when I was nineteen. I said good-bye to a lot of bad memories."

He still didn't want to be here. She could tell. He'd done this just for Devin. And knowing that he'd done this for her daughter, at a cost to himself, made her stomach feel strange, trembling slightly the way it did those last days at the lake all those years ago. Sometimes she thought she'd forgotten what selflessness looked like, until she ended up here again.

She sat beside him, stretching her legs out and leaning back on her hands, trying to cool the places where sweat collected, in the crooks of her elbows and the bends of her knees. "Who owns this property now?" she asked.

"I do."

"You kept it all these years? Why?"

"I don't know." They watched as Devin kicked around in the dirt and looked under rocks. "Is Devin looking for something specific?"

"Your guess is as good as mine. She's not talking to me about it." Kate stared at her daughter for a few more moments, then turned back to Wes. "Thank you for bringing her here."

"The trail wasn't as hard to find as I thought it would be.

Some guests from the lake probably found it and walked it over the years. Not lately, though."

Kate frowned. "When did the camp start going downhill? When did people stop coming?"

He shrugged. "The hotel by the water park was built about fifteen years ago. That, combined with the economy, Eby's aging guests, and the fact that Eby doesn't advertise, just started taking its toll, I guess. I hadn't been out to the lake in a while, so I didn't know how bad it had gotten. If I had known, I could've helped. Repair work is what I do. When George was alive, he used to take care of all that."

"What was he like?"

"George?" Wes smiled. "He wasn't tall, but he was big shouldered. You could hear his laugh across the lake. He liked steaks and liquor. He loved entertaining. And he loved Eby. He would pull her into his lap when he was sitting at a picnic table, and she would kiss him before insisting he let her pass. He called it a toll."

"Why do you think Eby didn't sell after he died?" Kate asked.

"I don't know. She was devastated when it happened. But there were a lot of people around her during that time. It kept her busy. She liked that. She's always liked that. She and George were very social."

"When was the last time she left Lost Lake? I mean for a trip or a vacation?"

"It's been years." Wes raised an eyebrow. "Why?"

"I think Eby wants to leave. But the more I think about, the more I'm convinced she doesn't want to sell." There. She

193

said it out loud, and it didn't sound as outlandish as she thought. There was something more going on with her great-aunt. Eby's decision to sell wasn't as straightforward as she was letting on.

Wes shook his head. "I think it's too late."

"She hasn't signed anything. She told me."

"What I mean is, it's not just a matter of wanting to stay. There's a matter of capital, too," Wes said tactfully.

"Oh. I see." She sat up and pulled her knees to her chest. It never occurred to her that Eby couldn't afford to stay.

Several quiet minutes passed. The thought had been immediate. She kept pushing it away, but it kept rolling back to her. Could she? Would she? Was it possible? Would Eby even let her?

"I know that look. You always got that look on your face before you jumped out of a tree or poked a snake and ran. What are you going to do now?" Wes asked suspiciously.

That made her laugh—that he knew her on such a level. "I'm thinking, what if I offer to buy Lost Lake, or at least buy into it? That way Eby won't lose it. She can come back to it. Everyone can come back to it." She turned to him and asked earnestly, "Does that sound crazy?"

"Yes," he said without hesitation.

That made her laugh again. "Good. Because if it made sense, I'm not sure she would agree to it."

"Kate . . ."

"I haven't said anything about it to her," she said quickly. "Maybe I won't. I don't know. When I think about it, it makes me happy. That's a good sign, right?"

"What about your life in Atlanta?" Wes asked, giving her the strangest look.

"What about it?"

"Your friends. Devin's friends. Family. Job. You're just going to leave it all?"

She finally understood. "Oh, you thought I meant I'd buy into Lost Lake and move here."

"That's not what you meant?"

"No. But . . ." Kate allowed herself to enjoy the thought. "Maybe I could. That doesn't sound any more crazy than just giving Eby the money and leaving."

He looked away. "Giving up everything isn't as easy as it sounds."

"Only if you have a lot to give up. The only thing that matters is Devin. And I think she'd be happy to stay here forever."

"It's getting late," Wes said, suddenly standing. "We should get back."

Kate stood and called to Devin. When Devin ran over to them, Kate asked, "Did you find what you were looking for?"

"No. This would be so much easier if I was told what I'm supposed to find instead of just being given stupid clues."

They followed Wes, who had already started off back down the road, running away from whatever ghosts he had here.

"You just said a mouthful, kiddo."

꽃

After dinner, no one was in any particular hurry to leave. The evening held them down the quiet way a mother puts her hand on her infant's chest to lull it to sleep. At least half an hour passed in silence, and they all remained seated, staring off into the distance.

But then Devin got up when she saw a frog. And Jack got up to show her how to feed it dead moths. Eby and Bulah-deen started cleaning and clearing. Kate had told Wes about "accidentally" throwing her phone in the lake, and he asked her to walk down to the dock to show him. Maybe he could retrieve it. Only Selma remained motionless, nursing the last of her drink, ignoring everyone, as she was wont to do. But Kate could feel her eyes on them, curious, as they disappeared into the darkness.

When they reached the dock, the blackness of the water made it look like silk, billowing as if pulled from a bolt.

"It's out there in the middle of the lake, near the ghost la-dies," Kate said, pointing in the general direction she remem-bered throwing it. "I don't think it's retrievable."

"I don't know. We dove for a lot of treasure back then. The lake isn't that deep."

"It's not worth it. Besides, according to Devin, there are alligators to think about." Kate paused. "You know, when Devin mentioned earlier that her imaginary alligator talked about you, it startled me a little. I know she misses her dad, but she dealt with the transition so well, better than any of us. She always seemed to have him with her emotionally. I just . . . Why would her alligator talk about you and not him?"

Wes shook his head gently. "She's not going to forget him, if that's what you're worried about. If Devin's obsession with alligators is anything like my brother's, then it's harmless. It was just his way of dealing with things."

"What sort of things?" she asked as they walked back to the lawn.

"Our father, mostly. Alligators are powerful, and Billy was powerless. I think it helped him to imagine a way of being in control, when our childhood was full of such chaos."

They got to the lawn in time to see Selma floating down the path toward her cabin. The light from the lawn touched her red dress, making it glow with strange images, like a slide show as she moved.

They stopped and watched for a moment. "So, are you ever going to tell me what was in that letter you sent me?" Kate asked, thinking for just a moment how her life might have changed if they'd kept in touch, how *his* might have.

"It was a long time ago," he said. Kate waited until he finally shook his head and smiled. "Great plots and schemes from the mind of a twelve-year-old boy. I wanted to move to Atlanta."

"Really? What happened?"

"The fire happened."

There was no going back after that. There was nothing to do but let those words sweep them through the years and land them solidly back in the present, older, wiser, different.

Kate finally said, "Don't you wish you could take a single childhood memory and blow it up into a bubble and live inside it forever?"

He shook his head. "You can't live on a single memory," he said as he walked away, toward his van.

"Wes," Kate called. "You haven't said anything about my offer to help Eby. What do you think?"

"I think it's very generous," he said. He got to his van and stopped. "But you can't save everything, Kate. Sometimes it's best to just move on."

11

Bulahdeen sat on the couch in the sitting room while Kate dusted the bookshelves. It was an afterthought, a last-minute decision that the main house should look presentable in case anyone at the party decided to come inside. Lisette kept the dining room spotless, but the sitting room had an air of neglect, as if Eby had walked out of it one day, to get a cup of Earl Grey or to answer the phone, and had never returned. There was even a book laying open on one of the chairs, a fine film of dust on its pages and a tiny spiderweb along its spine.

Every once in a while, Kate would peer out the window to see if Devin was still on the dock. Today, the last day before the party, Wes was outside scraping the driveway with a grading attachment he'd secured to the front of his van, so that people arriving tomorrow wouldn't spin out or get stuck in the uneven road when they parked. The dust he kicked up had sent Selma running to her cabin earlier, her handkerchief dramatically over her mouth as if she were fleeing a forest fire.

Jack was in the kitchen with Lisette, helping her put the finishing touches on the cake. Eby had disappeared into one of the cabins, as she had for the past few days, while the party preparations were going on, emerging around dinnertime, dust in her hair, as if she'd crawled through a secret passageway, a portal from past to present.

There was an undeniable sense of anticipation in the air. No one knew exactly how many people were coming, but there was a possibility of it being something big. Kate found herself hoping that it would be, that it would be something grand, that it would be all that Bulahdeen wanted it to be. Kate had been waiting for the perfect time to approach Eby about helping her financially, and the more she thought about it, the more she was convinced that tomorrow would be it.

"I remember reading this book here, on the dock, fifteen years ago," Kate said, picking up the book Eby had left on the chair.

Bulahdeen took a bite of the ham-and-Brie sandwich Lisette had brought her earlier. Lisette seemed to instinctively know when there was someone hungry nearby. She had appeared holding a plate with tiny violets painted on it as soon as Kate and Bulahdeen had entered. "I learned to read by that book," Bulahdeen said, chewing her sandwich in tiny bites, like a squirrel.

"You learned to read by *Jane Eyre*?" Kate asked. "You must have been a very advanced reader."

Bulahdeen shook her head. "Actually, I got a late start. We were so poor I didn't even know I was supposed to go to school until I was seven. Then I couldn't get enough of books. That's why I taught literature. It always made me feel sneaky and giddy. Like I was getting away with something. I always thought that, at any moment, someone was going to tell me to put down my books and get a real job."

"Have you read all of these?" Kate asked, indicating the wall of bookshelves.

"Every one."

Kate laughed. "Eby should update her library, then."

"No, I've read enough." Bulahdeen finished her sandwich and licked her fingertips. "I never thought I'd say that, but it's true."

Kate put *Jane Eyre* on the shelf and continued to dust. "Why do you keep coming back here, Bulahdeen, when everyone else stopped?"

"Because life is my books these days. And every summer here is a new chapter. Ever read a story that you simply can't imagine how it will end? This place is like that. The best things in life are like that. My husband has Alzheimer's. You'd think that would be the end of that story, wouldn't you? A brilliant man who loses his mind. The End. But, every once in a while, when I'm visiting him at the nursing home, he'll turn to me and suddenly start talking about Flaubert. Then he'll ask me how our sons are doing. As long as he's still there, as long as this place is still here, the story goes on."

Kate smiled as she looked out the window again. Devin was still on the dock, the cypress knee in one hand, her other hand up, shielding her eyes from the light as she looked across the lake. She was wearing her green bathing suit, white shorts, and a blue polka-dot capelet. She looked like a pint-size superhero on watch.

Kate turned back to Bulahdeen, only to find she'd stretched

out on the couch and had fallen asleep with the plate on her stomach. Kate continued to clean, wiping off table surfaces and combing the dust out of pillow tassels.

The rumbling outside stopped, and the sudden silence left a buzz in her ears.

"Selma will be so disappointed now," Bulahdeen said, her eyes still closed. "There's one less thing for her to complain about."

Kate started to respond, but she suddenly felt dizzy.

She grabbed the back of a chair. She thought she heard a splash, and there was a sensation of darkness behind her eyes. She looked to Bulahdeen, but the old lady hadn't moved. What was happening? She tasted lake water in the back of her throat and felt a clamminess along her skin. She wiped her face, and her hand came away wet, with tiny grains of silt. She'd never experienced anything like it before.

She went to the window and looked out again. Devin was gone.

She ran out of the house to the lawn and looked around, panicked without any reasonable explanation why.

Wes had just gotten out of his van. The dust he'd stirred up from the driveway was settling around them like flour.

"Devin," Kate said to him. "Where is she?"

"I don't know. Why? What's wrong?"

"I don't know. I think . . ." That's when it occurred to her. *"The cypress knees!"*

In the few seconds it took Kate to turn, Wes had shot off like a stone from a slingshot, down to the lake and around the trail. It didn't take long for her to catch up with him. He didn't hesitate when he reached the group of cypress knees and jumped into the water and vanished.

You can't save everything. Wes's words echoed in her head.

Through the murky water, Kate thought she could see the billowing of Devin's blue capelet. She lost her breath when it floated to the surface without her. But almost immediately after, Wes broke through the water. Devin had her arms around his neck, and she began to cough. Kate's knees gave out as Wes walked out of the water with her and handed her over to Kate.

Kate held on to her daughter tightly. She was so small that it felt like Kate could wrap her arms around her twice. With all the loss Kate had experienced lately, this was the un-imaginable one. This was the one she knew she couldn't live through. She closed her eyes and felt the tears sting.

"There's something down there," Wes said, sloshing back into the water.

"What?" Kate said, her eyes popping open. "Wes, wait!"

But he took a deep breath and went under again. Kate could remember the maze of roots down there. It was like swimming through a scribble.

"Mom, you're squashing me," Devin finally said.

Kate pulled back. She angrily wiped at her eyes. "What were you doing out here? I told you not to go swimming around these roots!"

Devin looked taken aback at Kate's tone, as if it never oc-curred to her that Kate would react this way. Devin had an agenda that made sense to her, but Kate had no idea what it was.

"What if something had happened to you? What if you had gotten hurt? You scared me, Devin."

Devin's eyes darted to the water.

Kate pushed her daughter's tangled wet hair behind her ears. "Sweetheart, what are you looking for?" Kate asked more softly. "What is it? Let me help you. What do you want to find?"

Devin pinched her lips together.

"I know this has been a hard year," Kate said, "and I know it seemed like I wasn't there for you, but I was. And I am now. You've got to trust me again. You've got to talk to me. That's how we're going to get through this. Together."

Devin still didn't say anything.

"Is this about your dad? Is this about moving?"

Devin finally said, "The alligator doesn't want any more to change, either. He wants everybody to stay." Devin wiped her eyes with one hand. She wasn't wearing her glasses. "That's why he wanted me to find the box."

"What box?" Kate asked as Wes emerged from the water again.

Devin pointed to the plastic bag Wes was now pulling out of the lake. "The Alligator Box."

⚘

With his clothes sticking to his body, and inches of water pouring from his work boots, Wes made it to the trail and went to his knees beside Kate and Devin. Devin called it a box, but it didn't look like a box. It looked like there was something more sinister inside the black trash bag. He unknotted the tie and reached in . . . and drew out another black bag.

He opened it only to find another. Then two more.

Finally he pulled out an old plastic waterproof tackle box. It was sooty and burned in places, like it had been in a fire.

My God.

Wes set the box down as if it were made of glass, then sat back and stared at it. Finally, pushing his wet hair out of his face first, he slowly reached forward and unsnapped the locks. He took a deep breath as he opened the seal. Out poured a curious counterbalance of smells—musty and dank, smoky and scorched. But there was an underlying scent that was all Billy. It punched Wes in the gut. It was almost too much, all of these memories flooding back, when there were times over the past few years when he couldn't even remember what his brother looked like. The sheer tangibleness of these things, of Billy's Alligator Box, almost made him sick.

The box had been here all along.

Billy had been here all along.

And the thought that he'd almost missed it, that he never would have found it once Lost Lake was gone from him and belonged to other people, terrified him.

He reached inside, and the first thing he took out was a cardboard pencil box gone soft. He opened it and poured dozens of alligator teeth into his hand, touching them as if they were jewels, as if they flashed and sparkled. He put them back in the pencil box and set it aside. Next he brought out a small plastic alligator toy Billy used to play with at the break-fast table. Then a key chain shaped like an alligator, which Wes had given him for his sixth birthday. A cigarette lighter that had once belonged to their mother, engraved with the initials ELI. A cracked gold pocket watch Billy had hidden so their father couldn't pawn it, because it had belonged to their grandfather. And a single aquamarine cuff link Wes couldn't place.

The box was almost empty now. Wes looked inside and felt the blood rush from his face. His hand shook as he reached in and brought out a single unmailed letter, sealed in a plastic sandwich bag. He automatically looked at Kate. She saw the letter in his hand but didn't seem to recognize it.

He quickly put the things back in the box, then stood.

"That really is the Alligator Box, isn't it?" Kate asked him.

"Yes." He had to leave. That was all he could think of. He had to get away and process this. "I'm sorry, I really need to go. I'll see you tomorrow at the party." They were looking at him strangely as he clutched the box, dripping wet. He tried to smile. "No more swimming out here alone, okay?" he said to Devin.

"Thank you, Wes," Kate said.

He nodded, then walked away.

﹡

"We have to talk about this," Kate said to her curiously silent daughter after she'd taken Devin back to their cabin and washed her off. "What just happened out there? Why did you jump there, of all places, when I specifically told you it was dangerous?" This had been no accident. She'd found Devin's glasses on a stump by the trail. She'd taken them off before she'd gone into the water.

They were sitting on the couch now, Devin on her lap. Devin sighed deeply. "The alligator kept trying to give me clues to where the box was. I finally understood. I had to get it before it was too late."

"Too late for what?"

"I'm not sure."

Kate paused, changing tactics. "Did you see the box—the trash bag—through the water? Did you know what it was, or were you just guessing?"

"No, I saw your phone. I saw it the day Bulahdeen showed me the place where the knees are, but I didn't realize what it was at first. The alligator must have moved it there, to tell me exactly where to jump."

"My phone?"

Devin pointed to the coffee table, where Kate thought Devin had placed her cypress knee on their way to the bathroom. But instead of the knee, it was Kate's phone in its electric blue case, wet and covered in grime. Kate reached forward and picked up it, nonplussed.

"I didn't realize how deep the water was. I couldn't make it all the way to the bottom and stay there long enough to pull the bag out of the dirt. And there were all these roots in the way."

Just the thought of it made Kate shiver. What was going on? Devin was a dreamer, not a risk taker, so this was simply baffling. "Have you ever seen this alligator before?" Kate asked gently. "Or did this just start here?"

"He lives here."

"And he talks to you?"

"Yes."

"And he told you where the Alligator Box was?"

"That's what I keep trying to tell you!" Devin said, her skinny arms and legs trembling with frustration.

"Does he have a name?" Kate asked.

Devin suddenly stilled and looked at her curiously. "You know what his name is."

"No, I don't."

"His name is Billy."

A slight chill ran through her. It suddenly made sense, in a distant way, like remembering a decision you made long ago, one you wouldn't make now, but one that had made perfect sense back then. Putting aside her disbelief and confusion and worry for a moment—all things the adult in her felt—Kate found that the only thing left was the one true thing.

Kate had left her childhood here.

And Devin had found it.

Decades ago, Wes's father and uncle—brothers Lyle and Lazlo—jointly inherited two large plots of land on either side of the interstate. Older brother Lazlo had moved from Suley years before, gotten a job in construction in Atlanta, then met and married the daughter of the man who owned the construction company. He quickly went from a manual laborer to the man in charge, the first in a long line of ne'er-do-well, dirt-poor-but-land-rich Patterson men to do so. Lazlo convinced his younger brother Lyle to split the inheritance, giving Lazlo sole right to the acreage to the north of the interstate. Everyone thought he was being magnanimous, because Lyle and his new wife and young son Wes needed somewhere to live, and the land to the south of the interstate was beautiful and had an old hunting cabin on it. What Lazlo didn't tell his brother was that the northern land was actually prime real estate, and he had plans to develop it. The southern land, on the other hand, was basically worthless without the land that curved around it like a question mark and locked most of it in—Eby's and George's Lost Lake property.

So Lazlo developed his land, built an outlet mall and a water park, and brought a lot of money into the county. He became Suley's golden boy, while Lyle was holed away in a cabin that didn't even have electricity. Wes's younger brother, Billy, was born six years later, and their mother left them soon afterward. Wes didn't know what happened to her. Years ago, someone said they'd seen her hitchhiking just outside of Houston. Hitchhiking *west,* away from here.

One of the last times Wes had seen his uncle was after the fire, when Lazlo came in for the funeral for Wes's father and brother. When he stopped by the hospital to see Wes on his way back out of town, Wes remembered asking him when he would be going back to Atlanta with him, assuming, of course, that the only family he had left would take him in. He remembered Lazlo's vague, stammering reply, and the impact had been staggering: *Lazlo didn't want him.*

Lazlo left after the funeral, and even though he came into town almost every summer with his family, to stay for a week at the Water Park Hotel, Wes had only seen him a handful of times.

In fact, he'd seen more of Lazlo in the past few days than he had in the past ten years combined.

Sure enough, as Wes backed his van to the garage door on

the basement level of his building that afternoon, he saw Lazlo's Mercedes parked to the side. The car was running, the air conditioner undoubtedly on high.

Wes pushed the remote control to the bay door, and it rose up, exposing the cavernous concrete garage. Shelves and cubbyholes lined the walls, and the open space was divided neatly into sections labeled ELECTRIC, CARPENTRY, LAWN CARE, PLUMBING, ROOFING, MASONRY. He was meticulous about this place. "A little OCD never hurt anyone," his foster mother used to say.

There was a small glassed-in office to the side, with its own outside entrance, but no one was inside. His dispatcher, Harriet, and handyman, Buddy, were gone for the day, Fridays being half days for them. All calls were supposed to be forward to Wes's cell, which he only now realized had been in his pocket when he'd jumped into the lake to find Devin.

All he could think as he'd run to the water was, I can't lose another one. His legs still felt weak over it, his head light.

He backed the van into the garage, then got out.

"I almost gave up waiting for you," Lazlo said as he got out of his Mercedes. "Where were you?"

"I've been helping at the lake this week," Wes said. He took his cell phone out of his pocket to see if it was still working. Nothing. It was toast. He went to the phone in the small office to check for messages. Luckily, he hadn't missed any. He forwarded all calls upstairs.

"I looked for you in the restaurant first. Your cook said you were out with a girl. I thought you'd gotten lucky," Lazlo said with a "heh-heh-heh" as he entered the garage.

"I was just going up there," Wes said, walking back out of the office. Maybe it was the afternoon he'd just had, maybe it was the thought of losing Devin, or the miraculous discovery of the Alligator Box, but suddenly he felt the need to reach out to someone, someone who knew his brother. Someone who understood. "Do you want to join me? Have a beer?"

"That's nice of you to ask, son. But I don't think so. I'm just here to tell you that I'm going to Lost Lake to get Eby to sign the papers tomorrow. I thought you might want to come along, get it all squared away. Nice and neat."

"Tomorrow?" Wes asked, surprised. "Does Eby know?"

"Of course she knows," Lazlo said in a tone that suggested Wes might be daft. "She agreed to sell."

Wes shook his head. "I mean, does she know you're coming tomorrow?"

Lazlo shrugged. "I don't think so. What does it matter?"

"There's going to be a party for Eby at the lake tomorrow. Eby's great-niece is helping to organize it. A lot of people from town are coming."

Lazlo hitched his trousers up at his thighs and did a lean-sit against the carpenter's table near the staircase to the restaurant. Warm, enticing scents were floating down, basil and oregano and tomato. It made Wes long for something, something he couldn't place. A happy childhood, a home. But he'd never understood how he could miss something he'd never had.

"One last good-bye. That make sense," Lazlo said. "But I didn't know Eby had family. What's the niece's story?"

Wes shifted his weight. He shouldn't have brought up Kate. "She's widowed. She decided to take her daughter on vacation to meet Eby. Get reconnected."

"Eby's going to be coming into some money," Lazlo suggested. "Maybe she wants a piece of the pie."

"She doesn't need money," Wes said.

"All women without a husband need money."

"How would you know?"

"I've seen it happen. Not to me and Deloris, of course. She'd skewer me in a divorce. She's always looking for an excuse, so I'm always very careful about my indiscretions."

"Kate is helping Eby because Eby needs help," Wes said. "It's the reason I'm doing this, too. The entire town would help her if she would just ask."

"Hmm. That's unsettling." Lazlo got up and brushed at the back of his expensive trousers. "But this party is a good idea. A farewell party, just so there's no misunderstanding. Eby will say good-bye to everyone. I'll come. I'll even buy the meat. There's a cook there, right? She could grill it."

Wes smiled. "Lisette doesn't grill."

"Why the hell not?"

Wes blinked in surprise at his uncle's change in mood. There was a little of his father in his uncle, in that mercurial temper. "She's French."

"Oh." For whatever reason, that seemed to make sense to him. "Well, my lawyer is here. Might as well bring him tomorrow and give him a meal before we sit down with Eby. I had your and Eby's land surveyed. This should all go smoothly."

"So that was you," Wes said. "I saw the tags."

Lazlo smiled as he walked out of the garage.

Wes followed him. "Why haven't I seen Deloris or the girls yet? Don't they want to see me?" He couldn't remember the last time he'd set eyes on his aunt and cousins. He wasn't sure he'd even recognize them. He had vague memories of his aunt Deloris, rich but not beautiful, and his cousins, Lacy and Dulce, who were as sour as little green apples. They'd laughed at the way Wes and Billy were dressed the first time they met. Wes remembered thinking how safe their lives must have been to be able to laugh that way, to be able to express an opinion without fear of retribution.

"Of course they want to see you. But they're women. They like the hotel, the spa, the shopping." Lazlo stopped at his car. "Would you like to see them?"

"If I'm investing my land in this development, we're going to be working together. So surely I'll be seeing more of you, and them."

"Right, right," Lazlo said, in much the same way he'd avoided the subject when Wes had asked when he would be moving to Atlanta with him after the fire. It finally hit him with full force: It was never going to be what he wanted it to be with his uncle.

There were very few good things about his childhood. Billy. Eby. Lost Lake. Kate. Lazlo was not one of those things, and he never would be. The funny thing was, if Devin hadn't found the Alligator Box, he probably wouldn't have realized this in time. He didn't want to let them go. He couldn't.

He suddenly thought of that aquamarine cuff link in Billy's box, the one he couldn't place.

"I found something today, at the lake," Wes called after his uncle."

"Did you?" Lazlo asked with no interest, clicking the button on his key fob to unlock his car.

"It belonged to my brother," Wes said, opening the side door of the van and bringing out the Alligator Box. It was so much smaller than he remembered. But, then, Billy had been small, so even the toy fishing box had been huge in comparison. He opened the box and took the cuff link out. "Billy used to collect things, sentimental things. Things he wanted to keep secret. Things like this." He held it out to Lazlo.

"My cuff link!" In four steps, Lazlo had walked over and grabbed it like a badger. "Deloris gave me the set. I had no idea where I'd lost this. She gave me hell about it."

"You lost it at the cabin. When the water park was being built on the other side of the interstate. I remember you gave Dad a job on the site, and then you used to come by during the day, when he was at work. If Billy and I were there, you would give us a dollar and tell us to go away. You brought women out there."

"So I did, so I did." He put the cuff link in his pocket, secreting away the proof from Deloris, who was, Wes was beginning to realize, his one big fear. "What's your point?"

"The point is, you knew how bad things were. You saw how we lived. You saw what our father did to us. Why didn't you do anything?"

"Whoa, son." Lazlo held up his hands. "That was a long time ago."

Wes took a deep breath. He felt relieved now, somehow. "I'm not selling my land."

"You don't mean that," Lazlo said, unfazed.

"Yes, I do."

Lazlo laughed. "Think this through, son. That land isn't worth anything unless you sell it with Lost Lake. What do you want, some bonding time? We could do that. But Wes, this business. This isn't a family reunion."

"And I realized that just in time."

Lazlo just shrugged. "The truth is, I don't need your land. I'll develop around you. When you change your mind, let me know. No hard feelings." He opened his car door. "You're overthinking this, you know. My father beat me, and look how well I turned out. Shit happens. You step over it and keep walking."

Wes pressed the button to lower the garage door. "In case you didn't notice," Wes said, as the door closed between them, "that's exactly what I'm doing."

He stood in the darkness for several long moments before turning and walking upstairs.

12

The town of Suley was a strange and independent one. Like most small towns, the older generations were the ones who kept the secrets, to such an extent that the newer generations were growing up with no idea why they were the way they were. Like the reason they craved briny bread and choke-cherry jam. Because it was the food of the swamp. Or why they liked to run their hands over the surface of smooth dry boards of houses or fences, why it made them feel restful. Because their great-great-grandmothers had spent so much time keeping the swamp damp out of their houses that their dreams of dryness had become a fundamental part of them, something passed down like bumps on noses and crooked pinky toes.

They had no idea why the idea of someone they didn't recognize made them leery. And they didn't understand why, if they sat so long in one place that the day's shadow passed over them, that they felt like they wanted to stay hidden in that shadow forever. It was because, generations ago, their ancestors had fled into the dark safety of Okefenokee. Deserters from the Civil War and Indians run off their land—they knew what it was like to hide. It was a hard safety and a lot of work, but they knew that it was still far, far better than what they had left behind.

Okefenokee was eventually cleared of settlers, and the swamp people went their separate ways. Suley was one of the places those settlers ended up, a hundred miles west but worlds away. Lost Lake was so named because it reminded those settlers of the swamp they had lost. Not many people knew that anymore. Most people these days thought it was called Lost Lake because the lake was so hard to locate. No one ever found the road to it on the first try.

The original owner of the camp had tried to make a go of it, but he had failed for one very important reason: He hadn't included the residents. George and Eby had succeeded where he had failed because they knew that what you lost is as much a part of you as what you found. They knew that the lake was a part of Suley history, and they always welcomed the residents out.

And that was why the town had come here today, to Eby's party.

Even though most residents didn't know why they were the way they were, they all knew they were connected in some way. Losing Eby meant losing Lost Lake. And losing Lost Lake meant losing a part of themselves, a very old piece to a crumbling puzzle.

Selma heard the noise growing outside and turned up the volume on her Billie Holiday CD. There were dozens of men out there, married men. She could feel them, a prickling sensation along her skin, like goose bumps. She gave up trying to ignore them, checked her makeup, then left her cabin.

It took more effort to make an entrance these days. When she was younger, she'd been able to step into a crowd like this and conversations would stop and heads would turn. Men would be pulled to her the way a sun pulls planets into its orbit. But the older she got, the louder she had to laugh, the more attentive she had to be. Sometimes she felt relieved that she only had one charm left. There was a certain peace to knowing she was almost through. It made her picky, though, because she was, first and foremost, an avaricious woman, and her final husband would have to be rich enough to set her for life. And he needed to be old too, because then there would be a chance he would die before the charm wore off and she wouldn't have to worry about grabbing all she could. But she'd married two elderly men already, and neither time had she been lucky enough for them to die, so she couldn't count on it. It would also be nice if he didn't have children. Offspring were so difficult. All her stepchildren hated her, the daughters especially. She'd never wanted kids of her own for exactly that reason. She'd had eight charms that could force men to be with her. But she had absolutely no idea how to make anyone else do it.

When she reached the lawn, she stopped and looked around, taking stock. *Know your arena,* she always thought. There was a large vinyl sign hanging on two aluminum poles that read FAREWELL, EBY! THE TOWN OF SULEY THANKS YOU!

Lisette was sitting with a man with a huge beard who was wearing a bowling shirt with the name GRADY printed on the chest. He was reciting a recipe for chicken wings, and Lisette was writing it down, a look of complete fascination on her face—like she'd never heard of chicken wings before. Selma rolled her eyes.

Selma saw Jack and walked over to him first. He was easy and was used to her flirting, and it served the purpose of other men seeing her do it, building the anticipation a little. He was at one of the grills. Several of the town children were around him, asking him questions and generally making him uncomfortable as they waited for their food. When she approached, the children grew quiet. One boy put his thumb in his mouth.

Jack tensed when he realized she was there. Honestly, it wasn't like she'd *broken* his foot.

"Well, this turned out to be a bigger affair than I thought it would be. And there are steaks? Who popped for steaks?" she said, taking a handkerchief out of the pocket of her dress and fanning away the smoke coming at her from the grill.

"The steaks are courtesy of Lazlo Patterson, the man buying the property. He's the one responsible for the sign too. Bulahdeen hates it."

Of course she did. It didn't fit into her nice, neat dream that this was going to make a difference, when Eby had clearly made up her mind. "Where is she?"

"Last time I saw her, she was trying to untie the sign. She's managed to do it three times so far. Someone keeps putting it back up."

Selma shook her head. Crazy old woman.

She scanned the crowd for the next man to bounce to and saw Harold, the owner of the Fresh Mart. He smiled at her and eagerly beckoned her over. His daughter was with him—the girl Selma had argued with just a few days ago. Brittany. Poor girl. She was under the impression that she could stop her father from being selfish, from wanting his own pleasure. Children always think that. Sometimes Selma wished women would stop blaming her when men left them for her. She could never take a man who truly loved his wife. So, really, it wasn't her fault. They should thank her. She separated the wheat from the chaff for them.

She walked toward him, stepping through the crowd, when an arm suddenly slid around in front of her, holding out a black bottle of cold beer. "You look hot," the male voice said.

Selma took the bottle and turned. He was in his late fifties . . . too young. Disappointing. But he had money, that she could tell. And he was married. He wasn't handsome, but that didn't matter. It used to, but not anymore.

"Selma Koules," she said, holding out her hand limply in a way that made men unsure whether or not she wanted them to kiss it.

He kissed it.

She smiled to herself. He would be too easy, if she wanted him.

"Lazlo Patterson," he said.

Selma's scalp tightened at the name. *A strange reaction,* she mused. It felt almost like panic, or maybe fear, the kind of disorienting fear you feel when you're lost. "I've heard of you," she said, taking her hand away.

"And yet I know nothing about you. I don't think that's fair."

He thought he was smooth. And to anyone else, he probably was. He was good. But she was better. Huddled nearby under the shade of one of the umbrellas was a severe, unhappy soul with two unfortunate-looking young women by her side. They were shooting daggers with their eyes at Selma. Those had to be his wife and daughters. It was provocation enough to want to toy with them, but it felt so obligatory. Maybe she was just tired. She saw Bulahdeen sitting at a picnic table near the sign, chatting easily with some people from town. She was reaching behind her and untying the sign as she talked. Selma found herself hoping the old woman would wave and all but force Selma over, to include her in some way.

"I'm buying this property, you know," Lazlo said.

Without looking at him, she said, "Oh, I know."

"I'm going to do great things with it."

"I'm sure you will."

"Let me walk you around. I'll show you. It's awfully crowded here, anyway."

She turned to him and hesitated. Finally, she smiled and said, "I'm all yours."

"I should be so lucky."

As soon as he turned and led her away from the lawn, her smile dropped. She would turn it on when he faced her again, but she didn't want to leave it on in the interim. She felt like her battery was low on charge. When he led her by the dock, to the wooded trail around the lake, she slowed to a stop. He walked ahead a few steps.

On the dock was that child with the unusual sense of dress

and glasses. She was on her stomach, looking down into the water, obviously waiting for the alligator she talked so much about. Her whole world was in a bubble, shimmering around her in the sun. The light from it almost blinded Selma, but she couldn't look away.

She was getting soft.

The sooner this place sold, the better, as far as she was concerned. She had gotten too attached to it. And women like her knew the danger of attachment.

"Are you coming, beautiful?"

She was a little disgusted by him, she realized, but she sauntered over to him anyway. "The best things are worth waiting for."

*

The cake sitting on the dining room buffet table was wide and three layers tall. There was a fondant topper shaped like a branch, and from that branch draped candy strings of Spanish moss, flowing down the side of the cake like a veil. Eby kept looking over at it. Why did Lisette make it so large? They were going to be eating cake for weeks.

Eby was sitting behind the front desk in the foyer, trying to focus on the crossword in front of her. What exactly was a seven-letter word for *consequence*? And why exactly did she care? The sound of car doors being shut distracted her almost as much as the smell of chocolate cake. Bulahdeen had told her that a few people from town might show up. Eby didn't think it would happen, but the sound of voices outside had her reconsidering. It had just been so long since there'd been actual activity at the lake. She didn't want to get her hopes up. Still, she strained to make out words, to catch pieces of conversation over the ticking and hissing of the air-conditioning.

She looked back down and tried to concentrate on her puzzle. George could never stand to be inside when he knew there was a gathering out there. He'd had to be a part of everything. He'd taken credit for new friendships, summer romances, first steps, and first swims. He'd loved this place. He'd loved this town.

She heard laughter. An unfamiliar voice. She whirled her pen back and forth between her fingers. Fifty years ago, she would have opened the front door and looked out and would have seen a swarm of people, with George in the center of it all. If she opened that door now, she knew that swarm wouldn't be there. And neither would George.

Finally, she couldn't take it any more. The party wasn't officially supposed to start for another forty-five minutes, but Eby had to go out and see.

She opened the front door, and her lips parted in surprise at the size of the crowd.

The faces were all familiar ones. The past fifty years of her life were crammed into a tiny circle in front of her, nice and compact. Parked cars lined the driveway, disappearing through the trees, seemingly all the way back to the highway.

There was Billy Larkworthy and his bluegrass band, playing music under the canopy next to the dance floor. He'd been such a young man when he'd first started playing on the weekends here. He was old now. His grandson played the mandolin in the band. There were Norma and Heath Curtis, young newlyweds from town who couldn't afford a honeymoon twenty years ago, so Eby and George let them stay here for free. Ten months later, they had a baby boy, whose middle name was George. There was Grady from the pizza place, and Harold from the Fresh Mart, and Halona from the dance studio. There were dozens of young men and women Eby and George had given jobs to over the years, now grown up with families. These people had welcomed her and George into their lives, into their town, and they in turn had fallen into Eby's heart.

George would have loved this.

A flash of red hair caught her eye.

She automatically took a step forward. She saw the red hair again and hurried across the driveway and into the party. People began to recognize her, and there were pats on her back and hugs that slowed her momentum. Some people wanted to talk, and she kept saying, "Yes, of course, just give me a minute."

Another flash of red.

She followed him, lost him for a moment, then caught sight of him again near the edge of the lawn, where the bald spot of grass was. There was no noise around her any longer, just the *whoosh, whoosh* of her own blood in her ears. His back was to her as she reached her hand up to touch his shoulder.

He turned around.

It was Wes.

"Eby!" he said, bending to hug her. "Welcome to your party!"

She stuttered for a moment, unable to find her words. She hadn't realized until that moment how very much like George Wes was. "I . . . thank you. This is certainly a surprise."

"Everyone—Eby is here!" Wes called to the crowd, and there was a surge toward her. They sang "For She's a Jolly Good Fellow," and some people even gave her gifts. There was a bit of desperation to the crowd, barely noticeable behind their genuine smiles and happy memories. They weren't just saying good-bye to Eby. There was something more there. Lazlo greeted her, looking ill at ease in his dark suit in this heat. He told her that his lawyer was here and he wanted her to sign the papers today. He was going along with the party for show, but Eby could tell he just wanted to get this over with.

It took more than an hour before she was finally able to sit down. Someone put a plastic plate with a steak on it in front of her. She was a little disoriented. She kept staring at the sign.

FAREWELL, EBY.

Which meant, Farewell, George. Farewell, Suley. Farewell, Lisette. Farewell, fifty years of memories.

All this time, she'd been looking for a big sign. Just not that one. She wished she would have stayed inside.

"Quite a turnout, isn't it?" Kate said from behind her. She took a seat beside Eby and handed her a bottle of water. She was wearing a strapless celery-colored cotton dress. With her short hair and long neck, she looked stunning. She'd gotten some sun over the past few days, making her look stronger and healthier than when she arrived. Eby was glad that she'd held on to the lake this long, at least, in order to give Kate a week she really seemed to need.

Eby took the water gratefully. She unscrewed the cap and

took a long swallow. "Did you know it was going to be this big?" she asked with narrowed eyes.

Kate laughed. "We all hoped it would be. Word slipped out, and everyone wanted to come. Bulahdeen has decided to take credit for it." They watched as Bulahdeen walked up to the sign. This time the old woman balled it up and marched toward her cabin with it, and the look on her face dared anyone to stop her. "Lazlo brought the sign. She doesn't want this to be a farewell party," Kate explained.

"Truthfully, I don't want it to be a farewell party, either," Eby said on a sigh, admitting it out loud for the first time. The words felt heavy. She'd been carrying them around for too long.

Kate suddenly smiled. "Oh, Eby. I knew it! It's not too late. I think I have the solution. I want to discuss something with you."

Eby was taken aback by her ebullience. "Discuss what?"

"If you had enough money to travel without having to sell the lake, would you still sell?"

Eby put the cold bottle of water to her forehead, then to her chest. "Probably."

"Oh," Kate said, and Eby could almost see the wind blow out of her sails. "All right, then."

"Mainly because there would be no one to run it in my absence," Eby continued. "Lisette couldn't, for obvious reasons, even if she wanted to. And it would take even more money I don't have to hire employees."

Kate straightened in her seat. "What if *I* buy Lost Lake?" she asked. "Or at least buy into it? You'd have money to travel that way. Devin and I could even stay here and run the place while you're gone. That way you'd have something to come back to."

Eby laughed before she could stop herself. It was so pie-in-the-sky, like some great scheme a child would make up. "Kate . . ."

"You haven't signed anything yet," Kate quickly reminded her. "You don't have to give this place up. I have money. What if I invest in it? I love it here. So does Devin. A year. Give me a year."

Eby stared at her, beginning to understand that she was serious. Kate wasn't that child who used to spin stories any longer. Eby was seeing that now. "Can you really afford it?"

"It's the money from the sale of my house. The house *you* bought. It makes sense to invest it here. I've been thinking about this for a few days now. I could put a lot of time and energy into advertising and promotion. It's what I did with Matt's shop. I even created the logo. I'm *good* at it. I could get business up."

Eby smiled at the thought. But then she shook her head. She couldn't get her hopes up, not this late in the game. "It's too late. Lazlo and his lawyer are already here. They want the papers signed today."

"Wait," Kate said, confused. "If he has a lawyer, shouldn't you too?"

"No. I just want to get this over with."

"It's not too late, Eby."

"You should use your money on a better investment than this."

"There is no better investment than this," Kate said, turning to stare at her daughter on the dock. Three girls Devin's age had now joined her. They were laughing, their hands animated as they talked. The girls ran back up to the lawn and beckoned Devin to follow them. Devin looked behind her at the lake once, before running after them.

"You need to move on," Eby said. "We all do. Even Wes."

That got Kate's attention. "What does Wes have to do with this?"

"He's going into business with his uncle, Lazlo."

"Wait. Uncle?" Kate's entire demeanor changed. "Lazlo is Wes's *uncle*?"

"He didn't tell you?"

"No. What do you mean, he's going into business with him?"

"Once my deal with Lazlo goes through, Wes is going to give his land to his uncle as an investment in the development. That's one of the reasons I can't go back. Everything is already in motion."

It took Kate a moment to respond. "So he has a vested interest in your selling this place."

"I don't know if I would call it that," Eby said, picking up her plastic fork and knife, getting ready to tackle the overcooked steak in front of her. Her last meal as owner of this place. At least dessert was going to be good. "Wesley's relationship to this place is complicated."

They both turned when Lazlo called out over the crowd, "Can I have your attention everyone!"

Kate stood, then hesitated. "Don't sign anything. Not just yet. Promise me you'll wait just a little while today."

"All right," Eby said curiously, and watched her disappear into the crowd.

⁂

"Thank you all for coming!" Lazlo said, as if this had all been his idea. Bulahdeen, back from disposing of the sign, looked furious that he was calling attention to what she'd been trying so hard to hide. "As you know, Eby has decided to sell Lost Lake."

The crowd made noises of disappointment, and Lazlo nodded, like he understood their feelings, even shared them. Kate found Wes easily. He was taller than most, and his russet hair glinted in the sun. He was watching Lazlo dispassionately. He didn't look like someone pleased to be going into business with this man. Not that she blamed him. But still, he was.

"I know, I know," Lazlo continued. He was sweating profusely, and he dabbed at his face with a paper napkin. "But let's look at this as a step forward!"

Kate came to a stop beside Wes. He seemed aware of her presence before he even turned, like her closeness caused a change in the atmosphere surrounding him. He turned his head and smiled at her.

She stared straight ahead. "Is he really your uncle?"

His smile faded. He didn't ask how she'd found out. He turned back to watch Lazlo. "Yes."

Lazlo was saying, "Eby has been an upstanding business-woman, a community activist, and a damn fine friend to all of us over the years. But she's ready for a little fun now. I'm told she's planning to travel. I hope you'll send us all postcards, Eby!"

The crowd chuckled.

Kate's voice was low and tight as she said, "Two days ago, I said I wanted to give Eby money to save this place. You didn't say a word."

Wes shifted uncomfortably. "I didn't know what to say."

"How about, 'My uncle's buying this place and I'm investing in it.' What part of that tripped you up? I feel so foolish."

"Don't, Kate." He reached out to touch her, but she jerked away.

Lazlo continued, "Lost Lake will live on. I will make sure of it. This place will soon be a thriving community! I've decided to call it Lost Lake Commons. Lots will start at very affordable prices, with lakeside condos going at a premium. There will be a billboard with contact information on the highway soon, so I look forward to hearing from you. Tell your friends!"

"What were you doing out here all this time?" Kate asked. "You obviously don't give a damn about what happens here. You're just going to tear it all down."

"Let's lift our glasses to Eby. Have a wonderful retirement!" Lazlo said. "Maestro, music! Let's dance!"

Billy Larkworthy's Bustin' Bluegrass Band started playing again.

"Come on," Wes said, taking her hand.

She tried pulling her hand out of his, but his grip was like a Chinese finger trap. The harder you fought, the more entangled you became. The only way out of it was to relax into it. "What are you doing?" she whispered loudly as he led her onto the dance floor, where several other couples and a few enthusiastic toddlers were dancing.

"You heard the man," Wes said, putting an arm around her. "Let's dance."

He began to move. She tried stepping on his toes. It didn't work. "I don't want to dance."

"So you just want to stand here and discuss this in front of everyone?"

She set her jaw. "What's there to discuss?"

He spun her around, smiling at another couple, calling out a greeting. "You had two weeks here when you were twelve," he said in a subdued voice. "Then you come back, out of the blue, and say you're going to save everything, that you're going to make it how it used to be. Forgive me if I had my doubts. Because, even if you did manage to save the lake, you still said you were leaving, which meant leaving the rest of us to deal with the reality of living here. Just like last time."

Left them here? Is that what he thought? That she'd simply gone off and left them behind, like a glove or a toothbrush, something that was easily replaced?

"There's no reason for me to hold on to my land if Eby sells. But I only agreed to invest my land *after* Eby sold hers. Not a moment before. This has been her decision entirely." He navigated her around the dance floor easily, finding space near the edge. "I'm not blind. These past few days, I've seen what you've seen. Eby doesn't want to give up this place. And neither do I. After we found the Alligator Box yesterday, I told my uncle that our deal was off. It's one of many reasons Lazlo is ignoring me today."

She wanted to stay angry. Anger was a great motivator. She'd spent the past year feeling nothing but grief, so anger felt good. But she couldn't hang on to it. He didn't deserve it.

"I'm sorry," she finally said, not meeting his eyes.

His chest jumped as he laughed. "That sounded painful. Did it hurt?"

"Yes," she said, then added, "Will you tell Eby? Will you tell her you're not selling?"

"I'll tell her."

"Right now?"

"In a minute."

He didn't want to let go of her, she realized. He wanted to dance on this floor like he'd seen people do when he was younger. She was sure any number of women here would be more than happy to dance with him, like Brittany, the girl from the Fresh Mart, who was frowning at them from a table. But he wanted *her*. A slow awareness came over her as they moved. She wished she was still angry, because then she could concentrate on that, and not *this*. She never thought she'd feel this way again. It frightened her. She didn't want to fall for anyone. She didn't want her life to suddenly go back to the way it was when she was with Matt. She didn't think she had the strength to prop up another person for so long again.

Was that selfish? Was it different if you knew that the man you desired wanted just as much for *you* to be happy? Maybe that was the most frightening thing of all: Wes was that man. She'd known that when she was twelve, and she knew that now.

"Kate?" Wes said, when he felt her press her forehead against his chest, felt her hand squeeze his, conflicted.

It was too soon. She still dreamed of Matt sometimes. Of being on top of him, of looking down at him through a tunnel of her long hair. The smell of him sometimes met her around corners, stopping her in her tracks. But those were just needs, weren't they? Not specific to Matt, if she could feel this way again with Wes.

Oh, God. She couldn't do this again.

And yet she didn't step away. For several long, glorious moments, she just let Wes hold her, hold her up and feel her weight grow lighter. Beads of sweat trickled down her chest, between her breasts. The electric fans the band brought only managed to move the hot air around, not cool things off.

She finally looked up at him, searching his face for some answer. His eyes went to her mouth, like that day on the dock. He slowly leaned forward.

And that's when she saw the car.

As people came and left, cars had circled the lawn all day, so the blue BMW approaching didn't appear out of place to anyone except Kate.

There was nowhere to park, so the BMW simply stopped in the middle of the driveway near the main house.

And Cricket emerged.

She was wearing dark jeans and a loose white blouse, and her dark hair formed a perfect helmet around her head that the humidity could not touch. She was just so cool and measured. Nothing about being here, about stepping into this foreign situation, seemed to bother her.

Kate stepped back from Wes and immediately looked for Devin, hoping her daughter wouldn't see Cricket. She knew how she would react. If Kate had known her mother and father were planning to leave that day fifteen years ago, Kate would have cried, would have screamed, would have hidden. Anything to keep from leaving.

She found Devin sitting under a picnic table with the other girls. They were chewing on ice, secreted away in their own little fort.

"Are you all right?" Wes asked.

"Yes," she said, turning back to him. His color was high. "I'm sorry. I see someone I need to talk to. Excuse me."

She could feel his eyes on her as, every muscle in her body tense, she walked over to Cricket, who was now standing by her car. She was surveying the crowd, getting a feel for it.

Cricket took off her sunglasses and carefully put them on her head as Kate approached. "So this is what has been taking up all your time," she said calmly, so calm that she could only be angry.

"What are you doing here?" Kate demanded. She didn't belong here. Everything about Cricket being here was wrong. She brought Kate's old life with her; Kate could even feel it trying to settle over her skin, like dressing her in clothing she didn't want to wear. This must have been what Devin felt like every day of the past year.

"You forced my hand when you stopped answering your phone."

"So you drove four hours here?" Kate asked. "If you found out where it was, then you knew there was a phone number."

"But then I would have missed that charming little dance," Cricket said with a click of her tongue. "Who was that?"

Kate didn't want to tell her. This had nothing to do with her. But Kate had created this mess. She had let Cricket think that her life was hers to control. It was time to fix this. "His name is Wes."

"Is that who you really came here to see?"

Kate sighed. "No. Of course not. I told you. Devin and I found a postcard. We came here to see my great-aunt, Eby."

"So you were dancing like that with a man you just met."

Kate paused, wrestling with Cricket's control. She almost squirmed with it, but she didn't want to give Cricket the satisfaction of seeing it. "No. I met him here when I was twelve, the last time my family visited. He lives here. In Suley."

"Matt has only been gone a year," Cricket hissed.

"I know that."

"How quickly you move on," Cricket said.

"Quickly?" Kate asked, her voice rising. "I could barely function when he died. I lost all direction when I lost Matt."

"Which is why you need me. Enough of this. I came here to see what the lure of this place was, and I found it, obviously. I want you and Devin to come back with me today. We will make this new commercial and introduce you to the city. And you and Devin will be at my side when I announce I'm running for Congress. You owe me this, Kate. I've spent the past year trying to get you ready for this. It's going to happen. Where is Devin?" Cricket looked around. The little girls had left their secret hiding place and were now zigzagging through the crowd in a game of chase, invisible comet tails trailing behind them. Devin was wearing her tutu, this time with a neon green T-shirt and dozens of plastic pearl necklaces, so she was hard to miss. "My God, all that time I spent getting her out of those clothes, and you just let her wear what she wants."

"I'm letting her be a kid. This doesn't last long. It will be gone before she knows it."

"Devin! Devin!" Cricket called. She held out her arms. "Come to Grandma Cricket!"

"Cricket, don't," Kate warned.

Devin stopped in her tracks, and Kate could almost see the color drain from her face when she set eyes on her grandmother. She looked at Kate, and her expression broke Kate's heart. Kate thought Devin had been coming around, but the moment Devin saw Cricket, Kate realized that her daughter still didn't trust her. Devin still didn't trust her to make this right. Devin turned and ran away, disappearing into the crowd.

Cricket dropped her arms and turned to Kate accusingly. "Where is she going? What have you said to her about me?"

"I haven't said anything to her about you. Go home, Cricket. If you leave now, you can be back before dark," Kate said, taking a step back toward the party to go after Devin.

"Wait, is that *Lazlo Patterson*?" Cricket asked. Lazlo was standing in front of one of the fans near the dance floor, and his laughter had caught Cricket's attention.

Kate turned back to her, surprised. "You know him?"

"I'm in real estate in Atlanta," Cricket said. "Of course I know him. I've never done business with him, though. Rumor has it that he's connected. What is he doing here?"

"He wants to buy Lost Lake from my great-aunt." Kate paused. Even though she was a good six inches taller than Cricket, Kate could feel herself standing up straighter, as if steeling herself. "I want to buy it from her instead."

"You?"

"Yes, me."

"Oh, Kate," Cricket said with a shake of her head, as if she pitied Kate for even thinking such a thing. "You don't want to mess with Lazlo Patterson. You don't know anything about real estate or about running a place like this."

She honestly believed that. She had no idea that Kate ran Matt's bike shop. She didn't want to know. She didn't care. "You don't know who I am or what I can do. I know what's best for myself and my child. Go back to Atlanta, Cricket. I'm going to find Devin. If you had just given us some warning, I wouldn't have to go after her to tell her you're not here to snatch her away, like some witch in a fairy tale."

"Did you just call me a witch?" Cricket asked.

Kate walked to the lawn, searching. Cricket followed her, until Kate managed to lose her by walking directly across the dance floor in the middle of a song. Kate then walked quickly to the main house, where the scent of chocolate cake was thick and cool in the air. She checked the sitting room, the dining room, then went to the kitchen. As soon as she entered, the chair by the refrigerator shifted slightly, as if the wind from her entrance had moved it. She exited by the back of the house. No Devin. She jogged down the path to their cabin. She went inside and checked all the rooms, calling her name. Nothing. As she hurried back to the lawn, she stopped to look in the windows of the other cabins.

Now she was getting worried.

She finally found the little girls Devin had been playing with earlier, back under the picnic table, eating pilfered potato chips. She bent down and asked them, "Have you seen Devin?"

"She ran that way," one of the girls said, pointing toward the right side of the lake. "Into the woods."

"Kate?" Eby called from the next table. "What's wrong?"

Kate straightened. Lisette and Jack were now sitting with Eby. "I can't find Devin. She ran into the woods."

"What?" Eby said, standing. "Why?"

"Because my mother-in-law just showed up. And Devin probably thinks she's here to take her back to Atlanta."

Wes approached them. He'd been on the periphery for a few minutes now, watching what was going on, taking in the worry on all their faces. "What's going on?" he asked.

"Devin just ran away, into the woods," Eby told him.

"The cypress knees?" he asked Kate. He looked ready to run.

Kate shook her head. There was no taste of lake water in her mouth, no silt on her skin. Devin was dry and hot, in sunlight. Kate didn't know how she knew these things, just that this place seemed to want to let her know. "No, the other direction."

"Let's go," he said, heading for the lake. Kate followed. Eby, Lisette, and Jack brought up the rear.

"Kate? What's going on?" Cricket said, trotting up to her. "Where are you going?"

"Stay here, Cricket. Devin ran into the woods when she saw you."

"This is no place for a child. If you can't even keep an eye on her—"

"Don't." Kate stopped and spun around to face her. "Don't you dare."

Kate caught up with Wes. Cricket hesitated, then followed them anyway, because heaven forbid someone else could be right for a change.

Wes was walking fast, studying the trees along the lake path.

"Shouldn't we divide up?" Kate asked Eby. "Wouldn't that be better?"

"Of course it would be better," Cricket said. "Why are we trusting this person? Does he know where he's going?"

Eby gave Cricket a passing glance, but one that could see right through her. She almost seemed to *pity* Cricket. "Wes's ancestors are people from the swamp. They know these things. They're all like that, the people in Suley. They never get lost."

"This way," Wes said, ducking under some brush where there were a few broken limbs.

It took about ten minutes. They were all calling out Devin's name and making enough noise in the leaves and twigs that she could probably hear them coming a mile away. They were sweaty and scratched from the whip-thin limbs of new shoots, when finally Wes stopped.

"There she is," he said, pointing to an incline, where part of Devin's tattered tutu could be seen from the tree she was unsucesfully hiding behind. She was sitting on some moss, her back to the trunk. The trees were thick here, and the canopy of limbs above dappled the light around them. Kate took a moment to steady herself, to swallow the panic and anger. Devin didn't need anger. She needed someone who understood, and Kate was that person. She used to *be* Devin.

The rest stayed behind as Kate walked up to her.

Devin had her legs pulled to her chest, a sad, angry ball of tulle. "I'm not going back," she said.

Kate crouched in front of her. "You can't stay in the woods all night."

"No, I mean I'm not going back with her," Devin pushed herself up and faced the others. She pointed at Cricket.

"Devin," Kate said.

"It's wrong," Devin said to her mother. "Her house is not the right place to be. You can't just let people take things from you. You've got to fight it. Why aren't you fighting it? This is a good place. This is the *right* place. Why doesn't anyone see that? Do something!" Devin said, her voice growing louder. She looked at all of them accusingly.

They just stood there. Devin faced her mother. "You let her talk you into things you didn't want to do," she said. "Why did you do that?"

"Do something!" she shouted again.

Lisette looked away from the intensity of Devin's stare. Jack put his arm around her.

Kate shook her head, emotion thick in her throat at this wild, delicate creature, this painted child in her bright colors and glasses, in the middle of nowhere, trying to fight for something that wasn't her fight. "I was sad, sweetheart."

Devin, starting to cry, turned desperately to Cricket. "I love you, Grandma Cricket, but I don't want to live with you. Mom and I can make it on our own. Mom just thought she needed you, but she doesn't. She was just confused."

Cricket's lips pinched and she pivoted and walked away. *She hated for me to cry*, Matt once said about his mother. *Cricket*

Pheris is worse at grief than she is at love. She doesn't know how to "move on." She knows how to turn away.

"It's okay, Devin," Kate said quietly, and she lifted her crying daughter into her arms.

"We're not going back, are we?" Devin asked, her arms tightly around Kate's neck.

"No, sweetheart." Kate rocked her back and forth. "And if you had just asked me, instead of running away, I would have told you."

Cricket had started walking in one direction. But Wes headed in another. "This way," he called to her, and she reluctantly changed course. Slowly, they retraced their steps back to the lake, Kate carrying Devin the entire way.

They emerged from the trail, and the party was still in full swing, a hot mass of music and laughter and smoke from the grills. No one seemed to notice their battered group except Lazlo, who walked down to meet them, just as they reached the dock. His lawyer hurried after him, briefcase in hand.

At first, Kate had an odd impression that he was worried about them. But that notion was quickly dispelled when he said, "Eby, there you are. It's getting late. Let's go in the house where it's cool and sign these papers, shall we?" Lazlo's eyes slid to Wes. "Wes, son, have you changed your mind?"

Eby turned to him curiously.

"I told Lazlo yesterday that I wasn't going to be investing in the development, after all. I want to keep my land." Wes looked at his uncle flatly. "No, I haven't changed my mind."

Over her mother's shoulder, Devin was watching the girls on the lawn, her eyes following them like they were flashing lights. "Mom, can I go play?" Devin asked, which was code

242

for *I'm tired of trying to make you foolish adults see what's right in front of you, and I want to go be a kid now.*

Kate set her down. "Stay where I can see you."

"Bye, Grandma Cricket," Devin said, patting her arm. "We'll visit soon, okay?"

Cricket smiled slightly, and they all watched Devin run up to meet the other girls. For a moment Kate felt indescribably sad, because she couldn't go with Devin back to her child-hood. She could only stand here as an adult as the distance became greater and greater until, finally, there was an ocean between them.

Eby put her hand to her chest, her fingers worrying along the neckline of her T-shirt. "Lazlo," she said, turning back to him. "I've changed my mind, too. Lost Lake isn't for sale."

"Now, Eby," Lazlo said, condescending, impatient. "I'm afraid we had a deal."

"I haven't signed anything."

"We shook hands. We had a verbal agreement, witnessed by that mute woman." He pointed to Lisette, who sucked in her breath. "Wes might have been smart enough not to shake on it, but I'm sorry to say, you weren't. Timing is everything."

Eby stood up straighter. "I am perfectly free to change my mind."

"Do you really want to do this the hard way?" Lazlo asked. "I'll sue. We'll go to court. Legal fees will take what little money you have left, and you'll end up losing the place any-way."

Lazlo's lawyer looked uncomfortable, his eyes focused in the distance as if imagining himself somewhere cool, somewhere there was no Lazlo. Eby simply stared at him in disbelief.

Lisette was puffing angry air through her lungs. Jack looked at her in concern. Wes was shaking his head, as if this was no surprise to him.

It was Cricket who finally broke the silence by holding out her hand to Lazlo. "Cricket Pheirs, Pheris Reality in Atlanta."

Lazlo looked surprised as he shook her hand. "I know you."

Cricket laughed her business laugh. What was she doing? Was she trying to drum up business at a time like this? "We've never formally met, but, yes, I believe we've seen each other at functions."

"What are you doing here?" Lazlo asked.

"Eby is apparently my granddaughter's great-great-aunt." Cricket waved the subject away. "It's complicated."

"I don't need a real estate agent."

"I'm sure you don't. I was just going to offer some advice. And if you know me, you know my advice doesn't come cheap. There's a reason why we do these things in private," she said. "There's a crowd of people here who could complicate this process if they knew what was going on. From what I can gather, they're here in support of *her,* not you." She leaned forward and said in a confidential tone, as if speaking to the only other competent person here, "I suggest you wait for a more appropriate time. They've had a little scare. The child ran away. Emotions are high right now."

Lazlo looked Cricket up and down. Everyone who had come out of the woods had scratches or tears to their clothes or bits of debris in their hair. Everyone except Cricket. Her shirt was sticking to her chest with moisture, but her hair hadn't moved an inch and her makeup was still perfect. Her eyebrows and eyeliner were very subtle permanent

tattoos, and she had extensions on her eyelashes. Lazlo hesitated before saying, "Fine. I'll be back tomorrow. It will be
your last chance. *One* more chance, Eby. That's all I'm giving
you. Come on," he said to his lawyer, nearly knocking him
over as he shoved past him. "Christ, I hate this heat. I need
to go back to the hotel and change this suit."

As soon as he was out of earshot, Cricket turned to Eby
and said, "Get a lawyer. *Fast.*"

"What are you doing?" Kate asked, incredulous.

"Think of it as a parting gift," Cricket said as she took her
sunglasses from the top of her head and put them on. "I'll put
your things in storage when I get back."

Kate hesitated before she said, "Thank you."

"I wish you would see things my way," Cricket said,
watching Devin with the other little girls, sitting at a table
now. Devin took off a few of her necklaces and shared them.
Kate could see Cricket warring with herself. She wanted so
badly to control this, to turn Devin into something she thought
was better.

"For once in your life, Cricket, stop trying to control the
people who love you," Kate said. "Just love them as they are."

"I didn't know how to love Matt any other way," she said
softly, and it was perhaps the first true grief Kate had ever
heard in Cricket's voice. She was, for just a moment, simply
a mother who had lost her son.

"I'll never try to stop you from seeing Devin. It's up to you."

Cricket nodded, then walked over to her car and left, much
to the relief of drivers in the juggernaut of other cars that had
stopped behind hers and who were slowly trying to back out
because she was blocking the circle.

The group left behind exchanged hopeful glances. Wes and Kate's eyes met and held. Lisette lifted her notepad to write something. But Eby held up her hands. "Nothing has been settled yet. I don't want to tell anyone I've changed my mind. I don't want to get their hopes up. Especially Bulah-deen. I'll tell her later. For now, let's just enjoy the party. Wes, Jack, will you bring out the cake?"

"What's going to happen, Eby?" Kate asked, as Jack and Wes walked away. Lisette followed them, looking at Eby over her shoulder questioningly. Eby smiled at her to tell her it was all right.

"I don't know, but we'll figure it out," she said. "So that was your mother-in-law?"

Kate sighed. "That was her."

"She's an impressive woman."

"No match for Devin, apparently."

That made Eby smile. "No. I don't think any of us are."

꙰

"If Eby doesn't sell, then things will go back to normal," Jack said happily to Lisette as they walked into the main house. "Summers will be the same again." He reached over to her and took a small twig from her hair. He felt a levity come over him, the feeling he used to get when plans fell through and he didn't have to go to a dreaded function.

Lisette turned away quickly and headed for the kitchen.

"Lisette, aren't you glad?" Jack asked, following her, because it seemed to him that this was perfect. Things had been solved without anyone having to do anything.

She nodded.

"We'll see each other every year, like always. You don't have to leave."

Lisette lifted her notebook and wrote, *There are things I need to tend to in the kitchen.*

She disappeared inside, sliding the lock in place.

Wes was standing at the buffet table, his hands on one side of the large piece of wood the cake was sitting on. "Are you ready, Jack?" Wes asked.

Jack nodded absently, something the little girl said suddenly in his thoughts.

Why aren't you fighting?

*

Selma watched Lazlo gather his wife and daughters, then leave with his lawyer in his black Mercedes. She was relieved. She didn't feel like dealing with him anymore. She looked around for someone else, then sighed and sat down with her fan. She really should just go back to her cabin.

"Looking for a husband to steal?"

Selma looked up and saw the Fresh Mart girl standing there. She was wearing too much makeup, and it was melting off her face in the heat. Her hair had split ends from too many blow-dries. Youth really was wasted on the young. "Brittany. How nice to see you again."

Brittany sat down across from her. "You know, I'm beginning to think I've been too hard on you."

"Oh, really," Selma said drolly. "Do tell."

"There's something to be said about getting exactly what

you want. I want to know how you do it. I try so hard sometimes to get boys to like me. Like Wes. We had a pact, sort of. Then I saw him dance with Eby's niece. Sure, she's thin and all, but her *hair*. What's with all the crazy layers? Why won't he look at me the way he looks at her? Tell me how to be like you."

Brittany wanted it. And it would have been so easy. All Selma would have to do was blow a wish on her. But she'd never done it before. She'd always thought it was because she didn't want the competition. But deep down inside of her, she wondered if it was really fair. Young women know so little about consequences.

Selma set down her fan. "Listen, child. You wouldn't be able to get Wes even if you were like me. Because you can only steal something that wants to be stolen."

Brittany looked confused.

"For example, do you see Lisette over there with that man?" Jack and Lisette, along with Eby, Kate, and Wes, had all disappeared for a while. They were now standing on the far side of the lawn, near the dock. Obviously, they were having some little confab to which they hadn't bothered to invite Selma.

"Jack. Sure. I know who he is."

"If they got married, I would never be able to take him from Lisette. Do you know why?"

"Because Lisette would put a curse on you?" Brittany asked. They watched as Eby said something to Jack and Wes, and the two men walked across the lawn and went inside the main house. Lisette followed.

Selma sighed. "No. Because Jack loves Lisette. On the

other hand, look at your father over there with your mother. Do you see the difference?"

She did. Selma knew she did. She simply didn't want to accept it. "So you're not going to tell me how to be like you?"

"You don't want to be like me," Selma said.

"Yes, I do! I want to be happy."

"I just told you how," Selma said, angry with herself for giving away too much already. She stood and began to walk to her cabin. She had a headache.

"Selma, there you are!" Bulahdeen said, stopping her. "I haven't been able to find anybody. Where have you all been?"

Selma liked that Bulahdeen thought she had been included in the lake group's little getaway. "Here and there."

"Hasn't this been an exciting day? I got rid of the sign. But I wish that man hadn't made a speech. No one seems to like him. Eby doesn't even seem to like him. That might work in our favor. I'm glad he left. Look, they're bringing out the cake!" Jack and Wes were now exiting the house, carrying a chocolate monstrosity.

Sometimes Bulahdeen was simply exhausting. And Selma was in no mood for her right now. "Why are you trying so hard? Why is everyone trying so hard to save this place?"

"Because we love it here," Bulahdeen said.

"Speak for yourself."

Bulahdeen *tsk*ed. "Selma, if you keep acting like you don't care, pretty soon everyone is going to believe you."

"You've known me for thirty years and that is *just now* occurring to you? I'm not acting. Bulahdeen, why don't you just give up? She's selling. And, contrary to what you may believe, you can't stop it from happening. Everyone is here to say good-bye. It's what people do when they go their separate ways. They say good-bye. I've done it a lot. It goes like this."

Selma turned and walked away.

13

Bulahdeen Ramsey was born in a shanty area in upstate South Carolina that locals called the End of the World, which was just that for everyone who lived there. They knew how they were going to turn out. They knew the ending to their stories in this place, with its muddy streets, its smell of unwashed men, and grease from the kitchens that turned all the window coverings yellow. Those lucky enough to have a pig or chickens guarded them fiercely. There had been more than one lifeless body hauled away to town, shot trying to steal animals. Protein was a commodity greater than gold.

Women from the Baptist Church came once a month with charity boxes of flour and sugar and old clothes. Shoes in the winter. The men had seasonal jobs on the nearby farms. They were carted away in trucks and would stay gone for weeks at a time, coming back for sex and drink, before going back again. The women were calmer when the men were away. There was more food, less drink, no babies conceived to be born in the dead of winter, like Bulahdeen.

Doctors rarely traveled to the End of the World, because payment was never a given, not even in the form of vanilla pie or a burlap bag of walnuts. So when Bulahdeen's mother went into hard labor, no doctor was there to help her. She died giving birth. Bulahdeen's father cast her away from him and ran as far as he could. He died of drink in the river.

Bulahdeen grew up in her aunt Clara's tar-paper home. Her aunt weaned her with a cousin close to Bulahdeen in age, then set her aside, leaving Bulahdeen to figure out things on her own. Sometimes it seemed they forgot about her entirely. When the people from the county came to check on the kids, to document their health and ages, Bulahdeen was always away, staving off hunger by picking wild blackberries and chicory and fireweed in her own personal glen out near the polluted river that ran from the cannery. The school system didn't know Bulahdeen existed, so she was never made to go.

Her aunt had too many children to care for, so Bulahdeen became like a stray cat that only came close enough to be fed table scraps at night. She spent the rest of her time walking the roads and fields. In the summer she slept in the shelter made by two felled trees and a canopy of ivy. In the winter she slept on the porch, curled near the crack under the door, covered with a blanket.

When Bulahdeen was six, she was run out of her glen by some boys who had discovered it and claimed it for their own, so she was forced farther out to forage, closer to where no one at the End of the World was ever supposed to go near. The Waycross Estate. The owner of hundreds of acres of farmland lived there, the man responsible for what little wages were earned in the End of the World.

That's where she met Maudie Waycross, the boss's daughter. She was known to be pretty and generous and absolutely off limits to anyone, much like the estate itself.

She was sitting under a tree, on a quilt, picnic food in waxed paper pouches around her. She didn't seem to care about the food. She was completely engrossed in a book. She didn't even notice Bulahdeen standing there until Bulahdeen took a small step forward, thinking she could just reach over and take one of the pouches and run. When Bulahdeen stepped on a twig, the girl looked up, startled.

Bulahdeen turned to run away, but the girl called to her. "Stop!" She put the book away and smiled. "What a surprise to see you. You look like a wood nymph. You have beautiful hair."

Bulahdeen didn't say anything. She didn't know what a wood nymph was. And no one had ever told her that her hair was beautiful. It was wild and strawberry red and never fully contained with a dirty scarf and an old clip she'd found in a nearby dump site.

"I'm Maudie. What's your name?"

Several seconds passed. "Bulahdeen."

"You're from the End of the World, aren't you?"

"Yes."

"You're not supposed to be here. But I'm not supposed to be here, either. So let's not be here together. Come, sit with me. I'll share my food with you."

Bulahdeen sat on the very edge of the quilt, and Maudie handed her a sandwich. Bulahdeen ate, timidly at first, then voraciously when she realized how good it was. Maudie rested back, the book on her stomach, and looked up at the sky through the trees. She told Bulahdeen about the book she was reading, a story set in a place called England, involving a man who had a madwoman in his attic but who was in love with a young woman who taught a little girl who lived in his house. It was all very confusing to Bulahdeen.

Maudie suddenly sat up. "What's your favorite book?"

"I don't have one," Bulahdeen said, eyeing the rest of the food on the quilt.

"Don't you like to read?" Maudie asked, handing Bulahdeen an apple.

"I don't know how."

"Where do you go to school?"

"I don't go to school." Maudie just stared at her. So Bulahdeen told her about her family and her life—all of it. She hadn't meant to talk so much, but no one had ever listened the way Maudie listened. By the time she finished talking, the food was all gone—she'd eaten it all without realizing—and the sun was setting.

Maudie reached over and brushed some of Bulahdeen's hair behind her ear. "You can't change where you came from, but you can change where you go from here. Just like a book. If you don't like the ending, you make up a new one." There was yelling coming from the direction of the main house on the estate, and Maudie quickly stood. Someone was calling her name. As she gathered the quilt and the empty waxed-paper packets, she said hurriedly, "In two years, I turn eighteen. My dad thinks I'm going to marry Hamilton Beatty, because he wants me to. But I'm not. I'm leaving when I turn eighteen. I'm going to see the world! Meet me back here to-morrow, Bulahdeen."

"Why?" Bulahdeen called after her.

Maudie turned and smiled. Bulahdeen would always remember that smile, how beautiful it was, how it made Bulahdeen's stomach feel jumpy and wonderful. She'd never felt anything like it before.

Hope.

It was the first time she'd ever felt hope.

"Because we can change your ending, too," Maudie said, then ran away.

That was the day everything changed.

Maudie taught Bulahdeen to read. She got Bulahdeen enrolled in school. And nearly every day, Maudie and Bulahdeen met in the woods and ate and read to each other, and Maudie told Bulahdeen of all her plans when she would turn eighteen.

On the day of her birthday, Bulahdeen picked blackberries and made Maudie a crown of clover, and met her at their spot, only to find a wooden box sitting on the folded quilt instead. Inside the box there was a large stack of paper, envelopes, pencils, and postage stamps. There was also a small package and a note, which read:

> *I had to leave in the middle of the night. Daddy found out my*
> *plans and locked me in my room. I'm going to my aunt's*
> *house in Boston. Here is her address. Write to me there,*
> *Bulahdeen. Write to me about how you're making your own*
> *ending, and I'll tell you all about mine.*

Bulahdeen opened the package to find it was the copy of *Jane Eyre* Maudie had been reading when they'd first met.

Of course Maudie made it out. She had the means to make her own ending.

But no one got out of the End of the World.

Still, Bulahdeen wrote to Maudie. Every day at first, then every few months, when she'd collected enough events to fill a sheet of paper. Bulahdeen excelled at school, which didn't mean anything, really. She still went home to the same place and slept on the porch and waited for her life to play out.

The summer she turned fourteen, her aunt Clara made a bed for her in the corner of the kitchen because she needed the help. Several of Bulahdeen's cousins, cousins not much older than Bulahdeen, now had lap babies and hip babies and babies on the way, and all they seemed to do was eat and poop.

Bulahdeen didn't pay much attention to the men in town. If it was one thing she'd learned, it was to avoid them. But one day, when she was alone in a nearby field collecting dandelion greens to boil, out of nowhere came Big Michael, young and mean. His eyes were light blue and close set, and Bulahdeen had caught him staring at her sometimes when she would hang out a line of diapers.

He smiled at her and then picked a dandelion in full fluff from the ground. He blew on it, and tiny bits of fluff stuck to her hair like dust. He reached over to pick them out, but she backed away. Quick as a flash, he grabbed her and fell to the ground with her, face-first, the force knocking the air out of her chest. Then he was on top of her, grabbing at her skirt and pulling it up. He lifted himself slightly to pull at his own pants, and that's when she twisted herself around enough to catch him in the side of the face with her elbow. The pain was like fire in her bone, and, from the sound he made, it didn't feel too good for him either. She managed to knock him off of her, and she scrambled away on all fours before picking herself up and running faster than she'd ever run in her life.

Her aunt Clara found her in the kitchen later, cradling her arm, clothes torn, covered in dirt. The only thing she said to Bulahdeen was, "Next time, don't fight so hard. It's easier that way."

That's the moment Bulahdeen realized that she *did* fight. And she'd fought because she hadn't wanted that ending. She'd wanted something else. Not this. It had been six years since Maudie had left, and Bulahdeen hadn't received a single letter from her. Still, that night, Bulahdeen wrote to her at the address she'd given her, and told her everything that had happened. She told her she wanted things to change but she didn't know how.

She started staying longer at school, helping the teachers clean their rooms, because she wanted to stay away from the harm of home as long as possible. Then one of the teachers hired her to help bathe and feed her elderly mother in the afternoons.

One day, as Bulahdeen was leaving the home after feeding the elderly woman, hurrying because she wanted to get back to the End of the World before dark, the next-door neighbor stopped her and invited her inside. She was the local librarian and, out of the blue, she offered Bulahdeen a place to stay in the home she shared with her husband, who happened to be the police chief. They didn't have any children, and they were getting up in years, she said. She saw the way Bulahdeen tended to the old woman next door, and she said she'd give Bulahdeen room and board if she helped out with chores around the house and at the library.

Those two years with the Bartletts were the safest she'd ever known. And not a single night went by that she didn't lie in her bed and wonder at the turn her life had taken. She had no idea how she'd gotten so lucky.

Until the day before she left for college.

That's when the librarian handed her a stack of letters. They were all the letters Bulahdeen had sent to Maudie at her aunt's address in Boston.

Maudie had never made it to her aunt in Boston. No one knew where she went. No one knew what happened to her. Over the years, Bulahdeen had made up hundreds of stories about Maudie's whereabouts, none of them the truth. That was Maudie's ultimate victory. Her ending was her own. No one else could touch it.

But Maudie's aunt in Boston had read all of Bulahdeen's letters, enchanted by this depiction of the rural South. She'd begun to look forward to them. When the letter about the attack had reached her, she'd panicked. She hadn't known what to do. She'd contacted the police chief in the town where the postmark came from, and he'd told her to send the letters to him. When he'd gotten them, he'd been charmed and then alarmed, and he'd shown them to his wife. She'd recognized the name. It was the redheaded girl who'd helped tend to the elderly woman next door.

That's when Bulahdeen truly understood what Maudie had been trying to tell her all along. And she'd never once wavered in her faith that endings were never absolute.

Not until now.

She'd spent enough time in this life to know that not everything will go your way. She'd read enough books to know that they weren't all happy endings. Still, it broke her heart a little after the party when Eby finally told Bulahdeen that she had changed her mind, but that it didn't matter, because Lazlo was going to fight her.

Bulahdeen recognized people who could make their own endings, as easily as she could recognize the taste of a fine summer wine, and Lazlo was one of those people.

That meant they weren't going to win. Not because they didn't want it more, but because they didn't have the power he had to make it happen.

He was kidnapping their ending, and there was nothing more Bulahdeen could do about it.

She simply had to close the book and walk away.

After having leftover cake for breakfast because, for the first time anyone said they could recall, Lisette had slept in, Devin and Kate walked outside into the bright muggy morning. Jack was still waiting with worry in the dining room. Bulahdeen, who had been unusually quiet, was now on the dock, standing at the very end, a tiny lone figure surrounded by water. The lawn was messy, but not as messy as it had been when the party had ended last night. It looked like someone had come out and cleaned after everyone had left. Devin remembered her mother carrying her to their cabin then. She'd set her down on her bed, then she'd crawled in next to her.

"We're not going anywhere for a long while. But no matter what happens, we'll get through it together," Kate had whispered. "I'm here. I'm not going to leave."

When Devin had woken up, her mother had still been curled beside her. It had been the best feeling. She hadn't moved for nearly twenty minutes, staring at her mother's face, loving her so much that she would have done anything to preserve that moment, to stick it in a jar like a firefly and watch it forever. But then she'd finally had to get up and go to the bathroom.

As they stood there, looking at the lake, Devin was quiet, tilting her head, listening to something only she could hear through the chirping of the birds and the rustling of the trees.

"Are you all right, kiddo?" Kate asked.

"He's still anxious."

"Who?"

"The alligator. Can we go for a hike through the woods to the cabin again?" Devin asked.

"Sure. I'll get some bottles of water from the kitchen," Kate said.

"Can I go down and see Bulahdeen? I won't go anywhere. It's a Devin promise," she said when her mother hesitated.

Kate nodded, and Devin raced to the dock, feeling the fairy wings against her back and wishing she could fly. The thought of hovering above the earth, weightless in a lilac sky, appealed to her, in the same way imaginary friends appealed to her, or talking alligators. Not long ago, back in her old life, she had started to feel a restlessness, a pressure, as she outgrew all her clothes and needed the feel of her mother's hand in hers less and less, that possibilities were becoming more finite, and everything was becoming more *real.*

It didn't feel like that here. She was glad they were staying longer. It still didn't feel as permanent as she thought it would feel, but at least they weren't going back to Atlanta. She decided to be glad for that. If they went back, her mother might change again. And Devin liked her exactly as she was. Her dad was gone, but her mom was here. She was *here.*

She slowed as she reached Bulahdeen, then stopped by her side. "Hi, Bulahdeen! What are you doing out here?"

Bulahdeen brushed at her eyes under her sunglasses.

Devin instinctively reached out and took her hand. Her fingers felt like green wood. "What's the matter?"

Bulahdeen smiled and squeezed Devin's hand. "It's nothing for you to worry about, baby."

"You look sad."

"I am," Bulahdeen said. "I am sad."

"Why?"

"Because this place is special. If I can't save it, does that mean I can't save the rest of my endings? My husband Charlie's ending? The ending of the girl who saved my life when I was little? If I lose this place, I lose my sense of possibility, and that's the only thing that has kept me going."

"That's what I like about this place, too," Devin said. "Anything is possible."

"Maybe it just wasn't meant to be. They can't all be happy endings, can they?" Bulahdeen paused, then turned suddenly to see Selma standing behind them, holding a white Chinese paper parasol over her head in one hand, her high heels in another. "Selma, I didn't hear you come up," Bulahdeen said coolly.

"I took off my shoes so I wouldn't fall into this cesspool," Selma said.

"What's a cesspool?" Devin asked.

"A place beautiful women avoid," Selma told her.

"What is it, Selma?" Bulahdeen asked. "Did you want something? There are no men here, and it's not like you to come out here only to spend time with us."

"I just passed Kate, sitting over there." Selma waved in the direction of the lawn. "She wanted Devin to come up when she was ready."

"Go on, baby," Bulahdeen said, turning back to the water.

Devin and Selma walked down the dock in silence. Selma was so pretty, but sometimes, Devin thought, if she touched her, she would find that she was as sharp as wire. "Why don't you like anybody here?" Devin asked her.

Selma's mouth set into a thin line. She hesitated before she said, "Because they don't like me."

"Sure they do. They all do. I do."

"You're one in a million, kid," Selma said as they stepped off the dock and she stopped to put back on her shoes.

"That's what my mom says," Devin said, stopping with her.

There was some movement near the water.

"Oh! Look!" Devin said, excited. "Do you see him?" She crouched down near the edge, almost like she would for a small dog, to get it to come closer. She could see the alligator's eyes, just barely, over the water. He hadn't talked to her since she found the Alligator Box. Whatever was in the box hadn't made everything right. Not yet. She'd searched and she'd fought and she'd run. Devin didn't know what else to do.

Selma stood next to her, her parasol resting on her shoulder, but she wasn't looking in the water. "Who is that?" Selma asked, which Devin thought was an odd question, because clearly it was an alligator. "There was a boy there," Selma said, pointing to the trail, "walking through the woods."

Devin looked up but didn't see anyone.

And when she turned back to the water, the alligator was gone.

Eby stepped out into the sunshine and took a deep breath. She felt like she'd been away for a while. She and Lisette had slept well past breakfast, which had vexed Lisette. Even when she was sick, Lisette always went downstairs in the mornings to see Luc. Eby thought it was marvelous, the sleep, like the way you sleep when you're finally home. The dance floor and the canopy were still on the lawn, and some stray cups and plates were still scattered around, but Lisette had cleaned up the rest. Eby had heard her leave the house when everyone had gone home and the grills had finally cooled. Lisette missed nighttime.

Last night Eby had dreamed of George again, but not in Paris. He was right here. He was sitting on the lawn, and she was lying beside him in the grass with her head in his lap. He was stroking her hair, smiling down at her. There was such a feeling of peace around them, it was soft and pink and smelled of butter. She woke up to Lisette standing over her, petting her hair away from her face. Lisette had pointed to the clock on the bedside table, then left.

Eby saw Kate sitting on one of the picnic tables. She had two bottles of water in her lap.

Eby walked over to her. When her shadow fell over her, Kate turned. "I was just waiting for Devin. She wants to go for a hike."

"Like myself again."

"Is she okay today?"

"I think so. I think we're both finally okay."

Eby looked down at the lake, at Devin crouching by the water in her pink romper and fairy wings and Selma standing next to her with her white parasol. Selma pointed to something, and Eby followed her finger to the trail around the lake, where she thought she caught a fleeting glimpse of a little boy in overalls, walking away.

Eby's breath caught.

"Eby? Are you all right?" Kate asked.

Eby turned to her. "What? Oh, yes. I'm fine. I thought I saw . . . it was nothing. Just a little déjà vu." She shook her head. It was so long ago, she'd almost forgotten. "I was remembering the first picture of Lost Lake I ever saw, just after my honeymoon. It was on a postcard George showed me of some investment property. I felt like I was looking into the future. Maybe I was. Maybe I was looking at this very moment. Maybe I've come full circle."

Kate stood. "Or maybe it's just a new circle forming."

Eby smiled at her as Kate walked away to get Devin. Eby put her hand to her chest, to check for that familiar fluttering there. But it was gone now, released to the wind like a caged bird.

The only thing she could feel now was the life inside her, the beat of her heart and the filling of her lungs.

She was alive and well, with plenty of fight left in her.

She looked at the postcard scene at the lake again and shook her head.

The big sign she'd been looking for had been here all along.

PART 3

14

A short time later, already sweating as the sun rose higher in the sky, Kate and Devin broke through the woods and finally found themselves on the dirt road leading to Wes's old cabin.

They walked up the road, and as soon as the clearing came into view, so did a large white van with Wes's handyman logo on it.

Wes was leaning against the front of the van, staring at where the cabin had once stood. He was wearing shorts and a long-sleeved T-shirt, and black sunglasses hid his eyes. He was as still as a statue.

Before she could take Devin's hand to quietly lead her away, not wanting to disturb his moment with this place, Devin yelled, "Wes!" and ran toward him.

He turned quickly.

Devin reached him and hugged him, which made him smile and he put his arms gently around her fairy wings.

He watched as Kate approached him.

"We didn't know you'd be here," Kate said. "Do you want us to leave?"

"No, not at all," he said. "I had a job down the highway this morning. On my way back, I found myself turning up the old road to this place. I don't know why."

Devin ran into the clearing. Her wings were starting to droop. They'd seen better days. They'd snagged on some branches on the trail, and there was a bit of Spanish moss clinging to one of them.

Kate leaned against the van beside him. The engine was cool. He'd been here awhile. They hadn't interacted much at the party after bringing Devin back from the woods. They hadn't danced again. Kate wasn't sure where they stood.

"I talked to my uncle one last time this morning," Wes said. "I couldn't change his mind. He said he'll still be coming by late this afternoon to give Eby another chance to sign over her land. Otherwise, he said he's going to sue. I'm sorry."

She shook her head. "I'm the one who should be sorry. I'm sorry I got mad at you at the party," Kate said. "I know you'd never do anything to hurt Eby."

"What do you think she'll do? Do you think she'll fight him?"

"Oh, she'll fight him," Kate said. "But I don't know what will happen."

"What are *you* going to do?"

She pretended to think about it. "Oh, I don't know. What are the schools like around here?"

"The schools?" he asked. "They're good."

"What are their dress codes like? Do they allow tutus and fairy wings?"

He looked to Devin, then back to Kate, his brows rising from under his sunglasses. "Are you staying?"

"Fifteen years ago, I never wanted to leave in the first place," she said. "I'm just finally making my way back."

He smiled and made a *huh* sound. He paused, and she could see the tension growing in his shoulders as some sort of realization set in. "There was something of yours in the Alligator Box. If you're staying, I think I need to show it to you now."

"Something of mine?"

He pushed himself away from the van, then went to the side door and pulled it open. The Alligator Box was there, tucked in a mesh hammock. He opened the box and took out a plastic sandwich bag. Inside the bag was a letter. He handed it to her.

On wide-ruled paper, in fading gray pencil, Wes had written:

Dear Kate,

I was sad that you had to leave. You didn't even say good-bye. But that's okay. I know your parents made you go. I asked Eby for your address and I'm writing you to tell you that I'm coming to Atlanta to live! Yes, you read that right. My uncle Lazlo lives there, and he will take me and Billy and my dad in. My dad works in construction, and I'm sure Lazlo will give him a job.

Please write when you get this and tell me what school
you go to so I can go there, too, since we're in the same
grade. Won't that be great? Maybe we can get lockers
beside each other. Will they let us do that? I'll sit beside
you at lunch, if that's okay, until I meet more people.
I'm hoping Lazlo will give me an allowance if I do
chores for him and my aunt Deloris. I have two cousins
I don't like very much because I heard them once call
us embarrassing, but it will be worth it to be nearer to
you. Once I get some money, would you like to go to
the movies with me? My treat!

Listen. This is a secret. Don't tell anyone, okay? Dad
will never leave this place, and Lazlo thinks we're fine
as long as we have this land and a roof over our heads.
So I have to get rid of the cabin. I'm going to set fire to
it on Monday after Dad leaves for work. Billy and I will
be out of the house with our stuff, and we'll watch it
burn. It will take forever for the fire department to
get here. Dad got drunk once and fell down and hit his
head, and it took an hour for the ambulance to get
here. No one ever believes us when we say something's
wrong here. I don't know why.

I'm enclosing Lazlo's address in Atlanta. Write me
there, please? It's probably big in Atlanta. I hope I don't
get lost. Maybe I will finally get a bike. Is there water
there? Billy would like that.

    Sincerely yours,

    Wesley Patterson

    P.S. DON'T TELL ANYONE!

Kate's lips parted as she read it. She realized she'd been holding her breath and finally made herself exhale. It didn't help. She felt light-headed.

She looked up at Wes.

"No," he said, reading her expression. "It's not your fault."

"You set the fire. Because of me." She looked around wildly, at the bare spot where his cabin had once stood.

"No," he said again. "I did it because I wanted a new life, another life. That was true long before you showed up." He made her look him in the eye. "Kate, it's not your fault."

Kate gave him a jerky nod and handed him back the letter. He looked at it one last time before putting it back in the box. He closed the van door, and the sound echoed over the clearing.

"I didn't even know my father was at home that morning," Wes said, his hand still on the door handle. "I heard what I thought was his truck pulling away, going to work like usual. I even looked in the garage, and the truck was gone. I didn't know that he'd gotten so drunk the night before that he'd left his truck at the bar and someone had given him a ride home. The sound I heard was him being dropped off that morning. He was passed out on the floor on the far side of his bed, and I had no idea. And Billy . . . I didn't tell Billy what I was going to do. I'd packed our stuff the night before and hidden it in the woods. I doused the house with gasoline from a container my father kept to burn stumps. I picked up Billy—he was still sleeping—and I threw down a match as I reached the front door. My God, the *sound* it made. My ears popped. I ran into the woods, and Billy had woken up by this time. I remember him looking around, trying to figure out what was going on. I didn't think I had anything to worry about. He trusted me. He always trusted me. I told him what I did, and he got this worried look on his face. He started going through the things I'd taken from the house. He was looking for something."

"The Alligator Box," Kate said softly.

Wes nodded. "I'd looked everywhere for it in the house the night before. It wasn't there. I know it wasn't there. When you grow up with a father like ours, you learn to hide the things you love very well. Billy had hidey-holes all over the place. I knew where all of them were in the house, so I'd assumed he'd hidden it in one of his secret places in the woods. I can still see him taking off toward the burning house. He caught me off guard. I ran after him, but I slid in the dew and fell. I knocked one of my teeth out. I looked up to see him race into the smoke without the slightest hesitation. Completely fearless. I ran up to the porch, screaming his name. The smoke was black, and it was so hot the air singed the hair on my arms. I backed in, covering my face. I remember the explosion, and I remember the feel of the fire against my back. I remember being airborne and landing on my face again in the grass. And that's it. I woke up in the hospital. They told me that my father set the fire, and I was too shocked to correct them. I've never corrected them."

"*That's* why you asked about the letter that first day on the dock," Kate said, stunned. *"You thought I knew."*

"I hadn't thought about it in years. Not until I saw you again."

Impulsively, she drew him into her arms and held him tightly, fiercely, the way Eby would, wanting to save him from what had happened, even though it was too late. "Your secrets were always mine," Kate whispered. "I never would have said anything. Not then, not now."

Wes smiled at her with complete understanding when she stepped back. He knew the emotions she was going through. He'd been living with them for so long that it was like a second skin to him, like the scars on his back. "I know. That's why I sent it in the first place. Or thought I sent it. I don't know how it ended up in the Alligator Box." He walked back to the front of the van, and she followed. "I put the letter in the mailbox by the road. I clearly remember doing that."

Kate thought about it for a moment. "If the box was in the lake, why did Billy go back into the house?"

"I think it *was* in the house," Wes said. "You saw it. The box had been burnt. But by the time I got out of the hospital, what was left of the house had been torn down."

"So you think someone must have taken it from the rubble and put it in the lake."

"Yes. But who?" Wes shrugged helplessly. "I'll never know."

Kate thought about Devin and the alligator, and suddenly something clicked into place. Maybe Kate had grown up and lost her ability to see it, but she hadn't lost her ability to believe in it. "Devin told me something after she found the Alligator Box, and it got me thinking." She turned to him. "Do you want to hear a story?"

Wes looked at her curiously, just like he'd done when he was a boy.

She smiled though her heart felt old and heavy. "One last story, for old time's sake."

"Okay. Sure."

So she told him.

"Once upon a time there was a little boy named Billy. He loved alligators. He loved them so much that he wanted to be one. He thought about it every day. He dreamed about it every night. There was no doubt in his mind that it was going to happen. One thing Billy knew that most people don't know is that the longer you have a wish, the closer you get to it becoming true. Most people never get what they want because they *change* what they want, change it to something more practical or reachable. Billy never looked to the future and saw himself as a grown-up. He saw himself with alligator skin and alligator teeth, swimming underwater and sunning himself on some soft grass somewhere. Billy felt sorry for other people who gave up their wishes so easily.

"One morning something happened, something terrible. There was a fire, and Billy's little-boy life ended. His brother was devastated. He missed Billy. What his brother didn't realize was that Billy rose from the ashes of the fire that day. Not like a phoenix. Like an alligator. Billy got what he wished for.

"He stayed around the house for a while. He waited to see if his brother would come back. But his alligator instincts began to get the better of him, and he wanted to find water. He took his Alligator Box and he went to Lost Lake. Years and years went by, and Billy could feel the human side of himself getting smaller and smaller, until only two things remained, the two strongest, best memories of his life as a little boy. The memory of how much he loved his brother, and the memory of how safe Lost Lake made him feel. He kept to himself, stayed out of the way, because that's what alligators do. But he watched. His brother would visit the lake, and he watched him grow up to be good man. He was proud of him. He watched as the people at the lake got older and fewer people came back. Then a little girl arrived and, miraculously, she understood him. So he told her everything. He told her about the box. He said his brother felt alone in the world, and that this box would help him, because then he would know that somewhere out there Billy was safe and happy. He was sorry he took the letter from the mailbox. He just didn't want to leave."

Wes had lifted his face to the sky, listening to her with his eyes closed. He finally looked away and rubbed at his eyes under his sunglasses.

Sometimes, all you need is something to believe in.

"I'd almost forgotten how good you were at that," he finally said, and laughed a watery laugh. "Those stories were the sound track of my summer with you."

He turned and lifted himself up onto the short hood of his van, then he held out a hand to her. Smiling, she took it, and he lifted her up beside him.

They sat there for a long time in silence, their bare legs touching slightly, before Wes said softly, "Thank you for coming back."

They watched as Devin, who had been running around the clearing, stopped to kneel in front of the lone-standing chimney and look up inside it. A startled bird flew out of the top of the chimney, a black blur against the blue sky, thready with clouds that looked like pieces of string. Higher and higher it flew, until it disappeared and the only thing left was the fullness of the day in front of them.

"Thank you for waiting," she finally said.

✻

Kate knocked on Eby's bedroom door.

"Come in," Eby called.

Kate opened the door. Rays of the setting sun were sending waxy copper splashes across the far wall. Eby was sitting at her vanity in her bedroom, pulling her long silver hair into a bun at the nape of her neck. The way the shadows hit her face, she looked like she was made of veined marble.

"Am I interrupting?" Kate said, looking around. The room looked like a time capsule from the 1960s. There were two twins beds with pink quilted bedspreads and ornate headboards, dark-wood furniture, and blown-glass lamps with brown shades and pineapple finials. The wallpaper was faded pink with row after row of tiny, shiny, silver Eiffel Towers. It gave more insight into Eby's past than any photo could have.

"No." Eby patted the seat next to her on the long padded bench. "Sit here with me."

Kate slid in next to her and looked at all the postcards from Europe that Eby had tucked around the mirror.

"No Lazlo yet?" Kate asked.

"No Lazlo yet. But I called a lawyer friend of mine, just as your mother-in-law suggested. He said he'd drive into town after he gets off work today."

"That's good. Whatever happens, I want to be here, too. I want to help. And the money from the sale of my house is yours. To fight Lazlo, to go to Europe, whatever you decide."

"That means the world to me. Thank you, Kate. But that money is your nest egg, and I'm not going to let you invest in this place, in me, until I know for sure what's going to happen."

"Are these from your honeymoon?" Kate asked, indicating the postcards.

Eby stared at them. "Yes."

"Is this where you'll go back?"

"It's where I'll visit. I'll never go back, though. I mailed these to myself, from Paris and Amsterdam. I thought, when I was old, I would sit here like this and think that it was the best time in my life. I had no idea that the future held such possibilities. I think I'll keep them here now to see how far I've come."

Kate tucked her hands under her legs. "I had a similar experience today. You know that letter Wes was supposed to have sent me, the one he asked you for my address for? He found it and let me read it. He wanted to come to Atlanta, to be with me."

"He told you he set the fire," Eby said. Just like that. Like it was obvious.

"You *knew?*"

"We all knew," Eby said. "The whole town thought we'd let him down. We weren't going to let him be punished for something that we could have prevented if we'd just tried a little harder to get him out of that situation. Don't be hard on him. He's punished himself enough."

Kate nodded.

"Wesley will like having you here again," Eby said with a smile. "If you don't mind my saying."

Kate's stomach trembled with that particular anxiety that

always heralded something good. She put her hand there to stop it. She wasn't sure she trusted it. "I don't know exactly what he is to me anymore. My past? My present? My future?"

Eby squeezed her arm comfortingly. "I think Wes will be anything you want him to be."

Kate smiled at her aunt in the mirror. Kate liked having Eby near, liked her quiet and her calmness. *Whatever happens,* she seemed to say, *it's going to be all right. We'll all be all right. We're in this together.*

It had been a long, long time since Kate had felt that way.

They watched as the sun moved the light across the room, two generations of Morris women tired of curses.

And ready for a happily ever after.

Lisette was closing down the kitchen for the evening, doing her nightly ritual of counting plates and utensils, making dough for chive biscuits in the morning, then finally taking off her apron. She had wandered outside last night and had stayed up too long. She had missed breakfast, throwing off her routine. As hard as she had tried today, she still could not get it back. There was a sense of change in the air and she hated it. She had just placed the apron on the counter when Jack entered without knocking. He was wearing his traveling clothes, his polo and his blazer and his driving moccasins.

He charged in like a bull, but then he stopped, as if not knowing what came next.

"I've made a decision," he said.

She nodded. He was leaving. He had seemed so happy yesterday, when it had seemed like everything was going back to normal, when it had seemed like they were not losing Lost Lake. It had hurt more than she thought it would. He would carry on with his life, and she would continue to be such a small part of it. It had been enough for so long. She did not know why she had changed her mind.

He looked around, trying to decide what to do. He took a step toward the chair and Lisette automatically put up her hand to stop him. Luc was watching with considerable interest.

"Is that chair important to you?" Jack asked.

Lisette sighed. *Luc sits there. The boy who committed suicide because I rejected him.*

Jack read that and said, "I was beginning to suspect as much." Jack turned to the chair. It was obvious he could not see Luc, but still he said, completely seriously, "It's nice to meet you, Luc."

Luc laughed at that. Lisette censored him with just a look.

"So Luc is haunting you," Jack said, and Lisette had to wonder at how such a sensible man could so easily believe such a thing.

Lisette hesitated before she wrote, *I do not know. What I do know is that every day, I wake up and see him and I think to myself, I will not hurt another human being the way I hurt him.*

"You've never hurt me," Jack said.

Lisette shook her head sharply. Of course not. She did not let herself. And their time together was always so brief.

"I just wanted to tell you that I'm going to Richmond to close up my house for good, but I'll be back. I've always wanted to see fall at Lost Lake. And I bet Christmas here is beautiful. And if Eby loses Lost Lake, well, I think Suley would be a nice place to retire."

Her breath caught in her chest. He was staying? He was close enough that she could smell the soap he had used that morning, something rich and southern, piney and sharp. She loved that smell. She loved his coarse gray-and-white hair and the lines on his face. Luc was behind him now, and Lisette's eyes darted to the younger man. It was just now occurring to Lisette that the longer she knew Jack, the more Luc looked like him. Just recently, she had noticed a mole near his ear that she had not seen before. It was the same mole Jack had.

"I just wanted you to know that I'm not leaving you. I'm fighting for you, Lisette. Against him, if necessary." He nodded to the chair. "I've never met a person that I could be so quiet with and yet communicate so much. You have no idea what that means to someone like me. Just knowing you were in the world kept me going. And coming here every summer probably saved my life. Do you understand?" he whispered. *"You saved me."*

Lisette reached out, her hand almost reaching his hair before she stopped. Had she really? Had she saved him? Had she managed to do for him what she had not been able to do for Luc?

He smiled and took her outstretched hand. "I don't have to say it, do I? Eby called me and told me to come here and say it, as if you didn't already know. But you know, don't you?"

Lisette nodded as she watched him go, then she turned desperately to Luc with tears in her eyes. She knew Jack loved her. She had always known. It was written on his face that very first summer. And she loved him. But it felt bottled inside her chest, and she could not let it out. She did not deserve Luc's love when she was sixteen. Did she really think she deserved Jack's love now?

Luc smiled at her, then made a little shooing motion with his hand, telling her to go.

But she ran to him instead, going to her knees and burying her face in his lap. She could not see what she was gaining for all that she was losing.

She felt Luc's hand on her hair, and she looked up at him.

She did not need to write down what she wanted to tell him. He knew what she was thinking. *I do not want to lose you.*

He pointed in the direction that Jack had left.

If I go to him, will you be here when I get back?

He shook his head.

I will not go unless you promise to always be with me.

Luc reached out and touched her cheek. He mouthed the word *toujours*.

Always.

Then she watched him slowly fade away.

She opened her mouth and howled, though no sound came out. She cried and beat the chair, then beat herself, then curled into a fetal position on the floor. She hated loss. She had fought for so long to keep exactly what she had exactly the way it was, like liquid measured perfectly into a cup, because she did not ever want to feel this way again.

She did not remember much about the next few hours. She remembered coming to, opening her eyes, and the first thing she saw was a tiny spider, crawling along the floor next to the cabinets.

The last time she had felt this empty, she had gone to the

Bridge of the Untrue and jumped. She sat up. But she did not recognize that girl any longer. The past fifty years had changed her. Eby had made her a different person—her goodness, her vitality, her fearlessness. She had watched Eby go through that most horrible time in her life, when George died, and she had seen her recover. She had seen her face losing Lost Lake, and she did not cease to function. She continued on.

Because of Eby, she knew something now that she did not know then.

Lisette took a deep breath and stood up.

When your cup is empty, you do not mourn what is gone.

Because if you do, you will miss the opportunity to fill it again.

15

*S*elma *walked into the* lobby of the Water Park Hotel. She rolled her eyes as she looked around. A hotel this nice nearby, and yet she'd chosen to spend every summer for the past thirty years at Lost Lake. The hotel was located next to the water park—an amusement park whose biggest attraction seemed to be waterslides and some great pool that made waves children could surf on. The park was for the children, but the hotel was for the adults. Smart move, she thought. Lazlo was not an idiot. At least there was that.

The chandeliers sprinkled multicolored lights onto the marble floors. The entire far wall was a water feature, a thin sheet of water flowing down two stories of rocks, looking as if you could walk right through it into another world. There were signs pointing to the spa, several gift shops, two restaurants—one family-friendly, one more elegant—and a bar.

This might not be so bad, Selma kept telling herself. She could probably get a new car and a condo out of this. Some jewelry she could pawn later. But this wasn't how she'd planned to use her last charm. The last one was supposed to be used to finally get everything she wanted.

She walked up to the reception desk. The clerk was a young man, but his eyes did what all male eyes did when she wore this particular dress: They dropped to her outrageously exposed cleavage and lingered helplessly.

"Would you please ring Mr. Lazlo Patterson and tell him his four-o'clock appointment is here," Selma said, giving him a slow smile.

"Certainly, ma'am," the boy said, tearing his eyes away from her. She was old enough to be his grandmother. She wondered if he realized that. Probably not. No one sees your age if you're bold enough. He murmured a few words into the phone, then paused and said to Selma, "Ma'am, he says he doesn't have a four-o'clock appointment."

"How silly of him to forget," Selma said. "Tell him it's Selma, from Lost Lake."

The boy relayed her message, then hung up the phone. "He said he'll be right down."

Selma turned and walked across the lobby to the bar, giving the boy a show. She took a seat and ordered a Scotch, neat.

She sighed and shook her head in disbelief that she was actually doing this. She'd seduced a lot of men in her life, but never one that she *actively* disliked.

She reached into her small red purse. She found the charm inside by its warmth. Her fingers closed around it gently, and she felt it tremble like a caught butterfly. For a moment she felt sadness. She didn't want to let it go. This was the last of who she was, of what she'd spent a lifetime being.

"You could have gotten me into a lot of trouble. I was

with my wife," Lazlo said, appearing by her side. He was as distasteful as she remembered—hair dyed that ridiculous black, a bad face-lift that raised his brows to an unnatural angle. His eyes went right to her cleavage. He didn't even look away to order his drink "That was a nice touch, saying we have an appointment."

"You sound surprised," Selma said seductively. "I'm very good at what I do."

"Of that I have no doubt. But we have to be discreet. My wife . . ."

Selma leaned in and whispered, "You don't need her. You have me."

She could see he was amused by that. He'd probably been faced with clingy women before. He wanted a good tickle, but then he would send her on her way. She had a sudden vision of her life if she'd never had her charms. How desperate and how sad it would have been, meeting men like this in bars for only a few hours of attention. A whole night, at best.

She'd gotten what she wanted out of life. And she didn't regret it.

She didn't regret a thing.

And with that, she opened her palm and watched her last charm disappear.

*

The next morning, at the lake, Selma was nowhere to be seen.

"Where is Selma?" Bulahdeen asked when she walked into the main house for breakfast. She was glad they weren't having cake again. Sugar was nice, but her childhood would always have her believing that protien was the best treat. "She wasn't here for dinner last night on the lawn, and now she's not here for breakfast. Her car is gone. Did she check out?" For a moment, Bulahdeen wondered if Selma had made good on her promise to leave her here.

"No," Eby said, as Bulahdeen's eyes followed the plate of bacon Eby set on the buffet table. There was a tension in the air that no one was acknowledging. Lazlo hadn't shown up yesterday, like he was toying with them. Hateful man. "She's still booked."

"When was the last time anyone saw her?" Bulahdeen asked.

"I saw her yesterday," Devin said. "She went back to her cabin and got *really* dressed up, then left."

"Has anyone checked her cabin?" Everyone shook their heads. They didn't seem terribly concerned. "Eby, could I take the spare key and check?"

Eby smiled and went to the front desk. She handed Bulahdeen the key and said, "It's on your head if she finds out someone went into her cabin without her permission."

Bulahdeen took the key and walked to Selma's cabin. She'd been sharp with Selma yesterday on the dock, and she regretted it. She'd been mad at her for saying good-bye at the party. But being mad at someone for acting exactly the way you assume they'll act is no one's fault but your own.

When Bulahdeen entered, Selma's perfume greeted her like a wet dog, getting all over her. That woman loved her perfume.

Bulahdeen stood in the middle of the cabin and looked around, frowning. Nothing looked out of place. Well, *everything* was out of place, but that was how Selma liked it. The couch was littered with reading materials carelessly scattered around. The bathroom was full of her pots and potions and scented lotions. She could see from here that the bed was covered in candy wrappers and hadn't been slept in. Where did she go? Bulahdeen worried about Selma. She was always pushing people away. That's why Bulahdeen always pushed back. For nearly thirty years, ever since meeting her here at the lake, she had called Selma on the first Thursday of every month, and if Selma didn't feel like talking, well, then, Bulahdeen did all the talking, filling her in on everything going on in her life. The one month Bulahdeen forgot to call, when Charlie was first moved into the nursing home and Bulahdeen was tired and frazzled and spending all her time getting him settled, Selma showed up, having driven all night from Mississippi, because she couldn't get in touch with Bulahdeen. She'd been mad that Bulahdeen wasn't dead, for all the trouble she'd caused, and she'd refused to take Bulahdeen's calls for months afterward. But she'd come around.

Bulahdeen's eyes landed on the mantle, where Selma had placed the photos of her husbands. She displayed them in much the same way a hunter displays a moose head. She'd hunted them down. It had taken work. And she was proud of her trophies. Bulahdeen had always been fascinated by Selma's power over men. She was utterly in control. Always. That seemed to defeat the point of being with a man, but to each his own. Selma too made her own endings.

That's when it occurred to her.

Bulahdeen saw the box on the mantle and picked it up. She slowly lifted the lid.

When she looked inside, she thought, *I'll be damned.*

Sometimes, the best endings are the ones that surprise you.

Sometimes, the best are the ones that have everything happening exactly how you want it to happen. But the absolute *perfect* endings are when you get a little of both.

She put the box back, then she locked the door behind her and went back to the main house.

"Any clues?" Kate asked.

"One or two," Bulahdeen said, handing the key back to Eby. "She'll be back. She never goes anywhere without her husbands."

The phone rang and Eby went to answer it.

Bulahdeen went to the buffet table to fill up her plate. Being nosy was hard work. She stopped when she saw a chair in the corner. "Isn't that the chair Lisette always keeps in the kitchen?"

"Yes," Jack said from his table by the door. He was supposed to have left yesterday. When Bulahdeen saw Lisette sneaking out of his cabin early this morning, she knew why he hadn't.

"What's it doing out here?"

"She doesn't need it anymore."

She turned to him curiously. "And how do you know that?"

Jack kept his eyes on his plate, but he began to blush. Bulahdeen laughed and turned back to the buffet. She paused when she saw the bowl of mixed fruit. For the first time ever, they were cut into all sorts of shapes. The pineapples were stars. The strawberries were mice faces. What the . . . ? This was happy food. Lisette was making *happy* food.

Eby got off the phone. She walked to the archway leading to the dining room and said, "I don't know what to think of this." She put her long hands to her cheeks. Bulahdeen always thought Eby had beautiful hands. She was trembling.

"What's wrong, Eby?" Kate asked.

"That was Lazlo Patterson."

"Is he coming by?" Kate asked. "Do you have time to get your lawyer out here?"

"He's not coming by. He said he's having a family situation. He told his wife he was divorcing her this morning. Between that and Wes not selling his land . . ." She laughed. "He's decided to *drop the project*."

Everyone got to their feet and surged toward Eby in the foyer with a flurry of questions.

"What game is he playing now?" Kate asked.

"I don't think he's playing," Eby said in amazement. "I told him to give it to me in writing, and he agreed. And he sent his lawyer home."

"So you're not selling Lost Lake?" Bulahdeen asked. "Hot diggity!"

"Apparently not. Not to Lazlo, anyway," Eby said. "Kate, are you still looking for that investment?"

"I am," she said, taking Eby's hand. "I am *so* ready."

"Yes," Devin said as she ran to the window as if looking for something outside, some immediate reaction to what was happening. "Wes is getting out of his van," she said. "And Selma is driving up, too."

Kate went quickly to the door and opened it. "Hi, neighbor," Kate said to Wes.

"Lazlo is letting Eby keep the property," Wes told her, excitement all over his face. "I saw his lawyer in town, picking up coffee before he left to go back to Atlanta. I wanted to be the first to tell you."

"We just heard," Kate said, laughing. "What happened?"

Wes shrugged, smiling back at her. "I don't know."

Eby walked to the doorway, beside Kate. "Wes, have you had breakfast?"

"No."

"Then come in. We've got some business to discuss. Kate is going to take over the place while I travel, and she's going to need a good handyman."

Kate nodded and extended her hand to Wes. He held her eyes as he approached her and took it.

And with that, Wes walked inside, and finally came home.

Bulahdeen pushed past where everyone was now talking excitedly in the doorway.

"There you are," Bulahdeen called to Selma, who had just gotten out of her car. No one was welcoming her back, though if they knew what she'd done, they would have. "You've been gone a while."

Selma was wearing a stunningly low-cut red dress, and her hair was disheveled. She put her hand on her neck, to hide the love bite there. "Have you seen the hotel by the water park?" she said to Bulahdeen from the driveway. "It's divine. What are we all doing *here*?"

"What, indeed," Bulahdeen said. "Come in for breakfast. We've just had some wonderful news."

"I've already eaten," Selma said, closing her car door and walking toward the cabins.

"Then come to my cabin later," Bulahdeen said, walking out of the house and following her. "We'll have tea and some nice pinwheel cookies."

"Why?" Selma asked suspiciously.

"Because that's what friends do."

"You're not my friend, Bulahdeen," she said, hopping from foot to foot as she walked away, taking off her heels. "I don't have friends."

"You are my friend." Bulahdeen huffed after her. "You're my best friend. And you know it. Why else would you have used your last charm on a man you're disgusted by, in order to save a place you don't even like? You did it for me. You did it for all of us. You do great endings. I like your style."

"You're a crazy old woman," Selma said as she reached her cabin and walked up the steps of her stoop. She took her key out of her purse, but then turned. "How did you know I'd used my last charm?"

Bulahdeen leaned against the railing of the steps, out of breath. "I looked."

"You went into my cabin without my permission?" Selma asked, indignant.

"I thought you'd been kidnapped by Bigfoot."

"I would have had a better time," Selma murmured, turning back and slipping the key into the lock.

"If you put ice on that hickey, it'll go away faster," Bulahdeen said, climbing the steps and waiting for Selma to open the door.

Selma put her hand on her neck. "Ice on my neck? That's freezing!"

"That's why they call it ice."

"Are you really coming in?" Selma asked.

"Of course."

"I'm never getting rid of you, am I?"

"Nope."

Selma walked in and held the door to her cabin open, shaking her head impatiently as Bulahdeen walked inside.

And just before Selma closed the door, she smiled.

※

From the lake, the alligator watched the house. He watched Wes arrive and walk inside with that girl he had always loved. He watched the beautiful woman walk away with the old woman, and they disappeared down the pathway toward the cabins. The little girl with the glasses was standing at the dining room window. She held her hand up, pressing it against the glass. She was smiling at him.

He floated there with ease, submerged except for his eyes. He was remembering something from long ago, a feeling he used to know, in his life before this. He used to know the name for it, that moment when you know everything is going to be okay. Now it was barely there, on the fringe of his primordial memory.

He wondered if it would ever go away entirely, this sense of two worlds. One day, as he floated here, would he see this place and these people and not recognize them anymore?

One day, maybe.

But not today.

He took one last look at the little girl, then he submerged himself fully into the water and swam away.

Acknowledgments

In early 2011, I was surprised by a diagnosis of advanced-stage breast cancer. I couldn't see it then, but that year of horrible change brought me to an amazing place in my life. But I didn't get there alone.

Thank you to the outstanding doctors and nurses at Hope Cancer Center and Mission Cancer Center. My mom, Louise, and my dad, Zack; Michelle Pittman; Heidi Carmack; Kelby and Hanna; Billy Swilling; Jenn McKinlay and all the Loopy Duetters, Meg Waite Clayton, Kelly Harms Wimmer, Susan McBride, Menna Van Praag, and Lynnie Thieme for the tunes; Tracy Rathbone; Helene Saucedo; Nancy and Sandy Hensley; Debbie Wellmon; Beth Elliott; Stephanie Coleman Chan; Alexandra Saperstein for the Curly-Wurlys; Erin Campbell; the Jarretts; the Hortons; the Gibbs; Dix Creek Chapel; Carolyn Mays and Francesca Best at Hodder; Pat Hoopengarner; Penny Carrell; and all my family, friends, and colleagues who supported me. Jennifer Enderlin and everyone at St. Martin's Press, for being there when I leapt, because after the year I'd had, I didn't want to be afraid to do it. It's been a phenomenal experience. My agent, Andrea Cirillo, and everyone at JRA, for your caring and confidence and all-around awesomeness. Shuana Summers and everyone at Random House. It was a wild, wonderful publishing ride with you. Lastly, my readers, most of whom I have never met, but who were there for me when I was diagnosed in a way I never expected. Your good thoughts, your prayers, your notes, your cards, your gifts came to me at a time when I needed them the most. The fullness of my heart is beyond measure.

I just celebrated my second year in remission.